While England Sleeps

While England Sleeps

A Novel

∞

DAVID LEAVITT

B L O O M S B U R Y

NEW YORK • LONDON • NEW DELHI • SYDNEY

Published by Bloomsbury USA, New York

Bloomsbury is a trademark of Bloomsbury Publishing Plc

All papers used by Bloomsbury USA are natural, recyclable products made
from wood grown in well-managed forests. The manufacturing processes
conform to the environmental regulations of the country of origin.

LIBRARY OF CONGRESS CATALOGING-IN-PUBLICATION DATA HAS BEEN APPLIED FOR.

ISBN: 978-1-62040-708-0

First published by Houghton Mifflin in 1993
This U.S. edition published by Bloomsbury USA in 2014

1 3 5 7 9 10 8 6 4 2

Typeset by Hewer Text UK Ltd, Edinburgh
Printed and bound in the U.S.A. by Thomson-Shore Inc., Dexter, Michigan

Bloomsbury books may be purchased for business or promotional use. For
information on bulk purchases please contact Macmillan Corporate and
Premium Sales Department at specialmarkets@macmillan.com.

Acknowledgments

Gratitude and appreciation to Kathryn Barrett, Judith Flanders, Bridget Love, Dawn Seferian, Andrew Wylie, and most especially to Mark Mitchell.

. . . and then the huge peaceful wilderness of outer London, the barges on the miry river, the familiar streets, the posters telling of cricket matches and Royal weddings, the men in bowler hats, the pigeons in Trafalgar Square, the red busses, the blue policemen—all sleeping the deep, deep sleep of England, from which I sometimes fear that we shall never wake till we are jerked out of it by the roar of bombs.

—George Orwell, Homage to Catalonia

PROLOGUE: 1978

$\sim$

In the early 1950s, history and politics conspired to create a circumstance in which it was impossible for me to ply my chosen trade—namely, writing. Because I had briefly been a Communist in 1937, the film studios on which I depended to earn my living now dared not hire me, the American publishers that had brought out my earlier novels let them lapse out of print. So I decided to take advantage of the situation by writing the one story I could never publish in my lifetime. When, after all, would such an opportunity arise again?

It was, coincidentally, the story of why I became a Communist in 1937. The answer—in brief—was love.

I have not always been a screenwriter, just as I have not always been an American. Once, in fact, in what seems now a very distant part of my life, I was English and a novelist, well respected, though in histories of the period I will probably be better remembered for the friends I made than I will be for what I wrote. Then one spring afternoon shortly after V-E Day I followed a young man into the public

1

lavatory at the Tottenham Court Road tube station. Together we went into a stall, whereupon, before I could touch his cock—it was, I am pleased to report, prominently erect—this young man handcuffed me and announced that he was an officer of His Majesty's police. Well-positioned friends managed to suppress the coverage of my arrest in the tabloids; nonetheless the incident left me ill disposed toward the country of my birth, with the result that three weeks after being found not guilty of immorality for lack of sufficient evidence, I boarded a ship bound for America, vowing that I should never return to England as long as I lived.

After a few aimless months in New York, I went to Los Angeles, where people invited me to a lot of parties. In those days being English had some cachet in Hollywood, as did being a novelist. Still, the ambition of intellectual dilettantes on the West Coast of America—as opposed to their brethren on the East—has never been so much to pedestal serious artists as to corrupt them. Vast sums of money were offered to me if I should do a screenplay; of course I accepted, and discovered, to my surprise, that I had a talent for "screwball comedies." I wrote a total of twenty-two over a ten-year period, nineteen of which were produced. These days they are little appreciated, though a few—*Casino* and *Living It Up*, in particular—periodically feature on those programs that intercut old films with competitions in which viewers call in the answers to movie trivia questions and win toasters, vacuum cleaners and the like. Each time one airs I receive a small residual payment, a payment that once, by identifying what animal Paulette Goddard was likened to in the credit sequence of Cukor's *The Women*, I managed to supplement with a La-Z-Boy rocker and a year's supply of Lemon Pledge. "And so today's winner on *Dialing for Dollars* is Mr. B. W. Botsford of West Hollywood. Congratulations! And now back to *The Prescotts Divorce*, starring Gloria Gallahue, Dick Maynard and Jinx Morgan."

And written by—I hesitate to add—Mr. B. W. Botsford of West Hollywood.

The Prescotts Divorce. I watched that film the other night and it embarrassed me. So dated, so coy, so evasively homosexual only a fellow homosexual might recognize the subtext. As for the actors I made into stars, they are the sort who nowadays feature in that peculiar series of little paperback books called *Whatever Happened to . . .*, books in which you learn that Gloria Gallahue waits tables at a Denny's in Tempe, Arizona, that Jinx Morgan, after fifty face-lifts, landed the role of Magenta Porterfield on *Secret Sturm und Drang*, that Dick Maynard became a washing machine salesman and disappeared into the suburban San Fernando Valley, the cultivation of which, along with the blacklisting of many good men and women, is what the nefarious decade of the fifties, at least in America, will chiefly be remembered for.

"Mr. Botsford, is it true that in 1937 you were a card-carrying member of the Communist Party?"

"I never carry cards. One is so likely to lose them."

Suddenly the commissions ceased. Film stars, fearful of being blacklisted themselves, stopped inviting me to their parties (though privately, in anguished, guilty voices, they begged that I "understand"). I never ratted on anyone, but then again, I never stood up to McCarthy and his cronies, either. One exposure tends to lead to another. Being branded a Communist in Los Angeles in 1955 was bad enough; being branded a homosexual Communist in Los Angeles in 1955 would have been more than my English upbringing could have survived.

No one can say I spent those years unprofitably, however. Their profit was simply a secret, not to be shared.

Because, in that blackest spring of 1955, I wrote a novel I never published, a novel that, for the twenty years since, has sat moldering among candy wrappers and cat toys in my kitchen. Well, now I am an old man, poor and invisible, unappreciated except by a single eely-skinned film studies graduate student from the University of Rochester, so I am going to hide the manuscript behind the cuckoo clock in my living room. Yes, the cuckoo clock with the big bugged-out eyes that I always used to joke were the eyes of God. No one but God is going to be allowed to read the manuscript while I'm alive, though after I've passed on, some archaeologist of the obscure may unearth it and think it worth bringing to the attention of the public. Or not. Or perhaps the discoverer will be a maid or mover, who will take one look at the yellowed pages and throw them in the trash.

Supposing, however, that the manuscript survives, and that in some unimaginable future you, reader, have sat down to peruse it, I ask only that you be gentler with my memory than history has been. Because my incumbency in the halls of fame was brief, do not, like the editors of *Whatever Happened to . . .*, remember me merely for the long downward spiral it precipitated. I was a young man once, who smoked cigarettes on the Quai d'Orsay, who fell in love with a boy named Edward in a basement near the Earl's Court tube.

Under no circumstances should the narrator of this story be construed as "reliable," particularly where history is concerned; the politics of those times confuse me now as they confused me then; I was a social, rather than an ideological, Communist. More important, as a writer I have always valued the personal over the global, for who, after all, populate our globe but beings who are both ridiculous and beautiful? Memory may be an unreliable guide, but it is also the only guide I have. Be sure of this, though: I never altered anything to make myself look better.

Finally, if you perceive, in this frank admission of moral failure, some small belated modicum of courage, its author's efforts will not have been in vain. We do what we can, even if usually we do it too late.

The Underground Bird

Chapter One

It began like this: a bird flying through the chambers of the underground, like a fly caught in a nautilus. No one noticed but me. First the wind blew—that smoky, petrol-smelling wind that presages the arrival of the train—and then the twin lights pierced the darkness, and then there it was, gray and white, a dove, I think, chased by the train's smoking terror. It fluttered and hovered above my head for a moment, as if trying to figure out where the sky was, then sailed up the exit stairs and was gone.

The train pulled in. I got on. It was June 28th, 1936—my mother's birthday. (But she had died six months earlier.) In Germany, flocks of *Hitlerjugend* bullied the customers at Jewish stores; in Spain, the infant republic battled the Fascist threat; in England, women in shops argued over the price of leeks. Worst of all, I could not write. A neatly typed copy of the novel I'd started the year before was sitting in a bureau drawer at my parents' house in Richmond. I couldn't even bear to look at it.

I was on my way to lunch with Aunt Constance, and as usual, I was late. Aunt Constance was a widow, and a novelist in her own right—much more famous than I could ever hope to be. Each April and November, with gratifying punctuality, she produced a tome, which unhappy women all over England flocked to buy. This was because her works, unlike mine, eschewed sex and scenes of high dudgeon in favor of the chronicling of small domestic transports.

She supported me in those days between the wars, though capriciously, sending checks that arrived according to no particular schedule and that were written for such wildly disparate amounts that my brother, Channing, and I had privately started referring to her as "Aunt Inconstance." In return I was expected to meet her for a monthly meal at the Hotel Lancaster, a dreary establishment just off the Edgware Road, where she installed herself on the occasions of her visits to London. All the inmates at this institution were women, and most were permanent: widows without means, retired secretaries—in short, her readership. I remember it as a languorous, stupefied place, its lounge insulated from sunlight by heavy curtains, its lamps so dim you could barely read by them. The Lancaster's pace was slower than mine, with the result that when I rushed in, I inevitably knocked over an ancient denizen on her way to the dining room, or startled the porter, who spent most of his day in a stupor bordering on catatonia. In the lounge, various soft, heavy figures sat or reclined in various soft, heavy chairs. An arrhythmic snore spiraled upward into a whistle before sinking back down to earth.

This afternoon Aunt Constance was dozing on a chintz sofa. Her eyelids fluttered when I leaned over her.

"Oh, Brian. Hello, dear. You certainly are prompt. I was listening to the wireless."

"Hello, Aunt Constance."

She sat up. "Let me look at you. Yes, you are too thin. Hasn't your sister been feeding you?"

Hoisting herself out of her seat, she escorted me into the dining room. She looked splendid, as usual: florid and floral, her silky abundant hair pinned atop her head in the shape of a brioche. While we fiddled with our menus she inquired after my sister, Caroline, my brother, Channing, most especially after our poor besieged childhood nanny, whom we had dragged out of peaceful retirement to keep house in the wake of Mother's death. Nanny had been the model for the heroines of no fewer than six of Aunt Constance's novels.

Channing and Caroline were quarreling, I told her, because Caroline had reorganized the kitchen. Caroline believed in order and the future, while Channing felt that to move as much as a single spoon from the place Mother had appointed for it was to desecrate her memory.

"I have seen peculiar symptoms of grief before," Aunt Constance observed. "My treasured housekeeper, Mrs. Potter, when her husband went, took to sleepwalking, while the Shepard girl became immoral. The strangest case, however, was Maudie Ryan. Do you remember Maudie Ryan? She was with your mother at school. Her fiancé was exploded in France during the war, after which she cooked and cooked. Cakes, puddings, hideous spicy stews." She shook her head in disapproval at the mention of the stews. "You must be patient with your siblings, dear. They don't feel as literally as you do."

An elderly hostess took our order. Given the delicately constituted natures of most of its clientele, the Hotel Lancaster could be relied upon to serve eminently bland meals, which pleased Aunt Constance, who was slave to an insolent stomach.

"I am having some trouble writing," I said when the hostess had gone. "Each time I sit down to work at my novel I become obsessed with some tiny chore that needs to be done, or my eye fixates on a spot of dirt on the wall, or the page itself starts to break up into an abstraction."

"And are you thinking I might advise you?" Aunt Constance asked.

"Well—yes. Rather."

"Oh, dear." She put down her water glass. "You see, I don't suppose I ever *have* had any problems in that particular area, except—yes, once, as I recall, years ago, I had written two novels and I simply couldn't think of an idea for another one. This didn't trouble me at the time. As I remember, I simply said to myself, 'Constance, you've written your novels, now you must settle down and be an ordinary woman and do what ordinary women do.' So I went out to the garden and started making a bouquet of roses, and somehow I thought of a girl named Rose, and a yew tree, and a soldier, and I dropped the roses, went inside and wrote *Kilkenny Spring*. Now, dear, before I forget, here is a copy of my latest for you. It is the story of a char with nine children and a fondness for Bovril." Chuckling, she handed me *Betty Brennan*, inscribed, like all her other books, "to my dear great-nephew Brian, with hope for his future novelistic career."

"Thanks very much, Aunt Constance," I said. "I shall begin it on the train."

"Yes, well, if you like. Not my best, I fear, but it will have to suffice. A pity. My readers do have such expectations of me." She fished her spectacles out of her purse and peered at me diagnostically. "Now, dear, how are you getting along? Have you met a girl yet? Would you like to be introduced to Edith Archibald's niece Philippa? According to Edith she is an extremely pleasant girl, though shy, probably due to the harelip—oh, of course it's been surgically repaired. An avid reader, Edith says—"

"Aunt Constance, you know I don't have time for girls. My *work*."

"Brian, how old are you now?"

"Almost twenty-three."

"Twenty-three! When I was twenty-three, Freddie and I had been married five years already! You must start thinking about the future, my dear. The fact is I haven't much hope for Channing, he is lost in books, and as for Caroline—well, I don't mean to be cruel, but she's nearly twenty-five. It really is most probably too late." With her shoulder she indicated her fellow residents at the Hotel Lancaster, all eating alone. "Trust me," she said. "It is terrible to be old and alone. Oh, not for me—I have decades of memories to draw on. But never to have known love, never to have felt the strength of an arm draped over one's shoulder, the warmth of his lips pressing against—" Stopping short, she coughed and desisted. Little did she know that the warmth of his lips pressing was *exactly* what I longed for.

"Now, here's what I propose: a small dinner, with Philippa and Edith. I shall arrange a private room. How does that sound?"

It sounded beastly.

"You know your poor mother would have wanted it. It was her fondest wish to see at least one of her children—"

"All right, Aunt Constance. Yes. I'll come."

"You won't regret it. From what Edith's told me, Philippa Archibald sounds like a most *stable* young woman. And now, dear, let me give you some more money. That jacket you're wearing is positively threadbare."

At least there was no pretense with Aunt Inconstance. Doing as she pleased brought one immediate rewards.

It was gray every day that year, no sun for so long it became a thing of memory, all London a perpetual sneeze and nose-blow. Mediterraneans would have gone mad, Americans would have called lawyers and threatened to sue, but we English accept bad weather with the same glum equanimity with which we accept semidetached houses and Wall's sausages. In their vaguely depressed way, people got on with things, which meant waiting in endless rainy queues.

Queues everywhere: if you put a sign on a wall that said, "Queue here," they would have lined up in front of it.

I was at an odd moment in my life. For the past two years I'd been living in Germany, ostensibly writing. In fact I'd spent most of my afternoons smoking cigarettes in cafés and most of my evenings smoking cigarettes in a leather-curtained bar. There were beers, there were boys. Mostly there were cigarettes.

Then Mother died, and I had to come home. I didn't have the money to get back to Germany after that, and Aunt Constance—having concluded, apparently, that Germany was not good for me—elected not to give me any more. I had nowhere to go, so I lingered in Richmond, parentless, sorting through the detritus of Mother's and Father's lives, while my siblings bickered and poor old Nanny, who had been dragged back from Eastbourne to take care of us all again, tried to keep the peace. Finally I could bear it no more; I accepted a long-standing invitation from Rupert Halliwell, a Cambridge chum who was rich and had recently acquired grandiose digs in Cadogan Square.

Rupert and I had not known each other well at Cambridge: still, something in his passion for antique crystal had spoken to something in my passion for Digby Grafton, who rowed. Rupert was a short, plump, pale fellow, rather resembling one of those blanc-manges or mousses Aunt Constance always referred to as a "shape." He had fat wrists, fussy tastes, doleful eyes.

I arrived at four on a Wednesday. A cowering little maid led me into the drawing room, where soon enough Rupert joined me, looking droopy and sad as ever in his smoking jacket. "Awfully kind of you to put me up, Rupert," I said to him as we shook hands. "Oh, nonsense," he replied dismissively. "The pleasure is mine entirely. In any case, it sounds as if you were roasting alive in that household."

"It *is* good to be out of there."

We sat down to tea, which the maid brought in along with a set of lovely blue-and-gold enamel cups—"Eighteenth century," Rupert informed me. "They belonged to Queen Beatrix and are the only set of their kind still in existence." Next I complimented him on the sofa. "Yes, it is lovely, isn't it? But it's covered in a very rare type of Indian handwoven silk that, if it's ever stained, is impossible to clean." "Oh, really," I said, endeavoring to hold my cup at a distance. Then he showed me his collection of antique crystal vases. "Three are chipped," he pointed out, "the result of clumsiness on the part of domestic servants." No wonder the poor maid's hands shook as she picked up the tea tray!

We finished off our tea and Rupert showed me up to my room. "I think you'll find you have everything you need," he said.

"Yes," I said, "I'm sure I will."

I started to unpack, but instead of leaving he sat down on the edge of the bed. Needless to say I felt rather self-conscious, his sad eyes fastened on me as I put away my clothes.

"How's your mother?" I asked him.

"The same. Pain is her companion, her daily tormentor. She can hardly get out of bed now, but I visit every day, which is a great pleasure for her. Really, she's too good for the earth."

In fact the woman was a beast, and not nearly as sick as she pretended. When she bought Rupert the house in Cadogan Square I had hoped it might mean a final severing of the umbilical cord. Instead he simply replicated her fondness for objects that were both impossibly delicate and irreplaceable. (Why is it that the rich, who have been spared material worry, feel obligated to create, all around themselves, the potential for disaster?) Rupert was, at twenty, a decidedly unformed young creature who had chosen to emulate the habits of the extremely aged. And yet somehow they didn't quite stick to him; you couldn't help wondering how long the "stage" would last.

I finished unpacking and was eager to write in my journal, so I told Rupert I wanted to have a nap before dinner. Regretfully he stood. "Are you sure there's nothing else I can do for you?" he asked, his eyes wide and wet as ever. "No, I'm fine, really," I said. "All right," he said, then, with extreme slowness, shut the door behind himself.

I flung myself onto the bed. Poor Rupert! Most of my friends had no patience for him; for them, he was merely an example of the deadening self-indulgence into which the bourgeoisie was irrevocably descending. Rupert and his kind, according to my friends, were dead branches on a living tree that must be pruned for the sake of the tree.

I understood this point of view. Still, there was something so sad and ineffectual about Rupert, locked up in his palace with all his precious objects to protect and no occupation and that beastly mother summoning him to her sickbed every half minute, that I couldn't help but feel a kind of pity for him. I doubted he had ever had sex with anyone, male or female. He loved to hear my recitations of erotic philandering and yet would never himself have dared venture even to the pubs I sometimes frequented, with their cargo of friendly police and guardsmen. Instead, ludicrously, he seemed to have attached all his erotic feelings to me, lingering at my door or staring longingly into my averted eyes, hoping against hope, I supposed, that I would invite him in for seduction. What a laughable thought—I, who had no aptitude for seduction! He would be a cold and anguished lover, I suspected. I could not imagine him naked; he dressed and held himself in such a way as to discourage contemplation of his body, even, perhaps, to deny the existence of a body at all. And yet, somewhere under there, there had to be nakedness.

We ate a quiet, congenial dinner that night, during which most of the conversation focused on Digby Grafton's wedding, to which Rupert—but not I—had been invited. Afterwards, pleading fatigue, I excused myself and took to my room.

At half past twelve—I was already in bed—the door creaked open. "Brian, I'm dreadfully sorry to wake you, but I've just had the most frightful row with Mother. Might I sit down?"

"Of course, Rupert," I said.

He tiptoed in, perched on the edge of the bed, then began his tearful litany of regrets—how Mother was always chastising him and telling him what a failure he was; her agony and pain, which justified everything; his loneliness and need for love. I knew what he wanted, yet somehow could not bring myself to give it to him—I drew back from his white, fleshy forearms, the soft black hairs on his wrists. So I consoled him as best I could, explaining that certainly Mother didn't mean it, that she loved him desperately and it was only the pain speaking, and eventually, feeling ashamed and realizing he could get no more from me, he apologized for the interruption and bade me good night.

It was difficult for me to go back to sleep after that. Digby haunted my thoughts: his beautiful dark skin and wheat-colored hair. Digby naked by the lake, shaking water from his body, the drops hanging like beads of glass from the hair on his chest and legs and around his long, disinterested cock, which of course was normal and rose only for girls. My obsession with that cock, my longing to draw back its helmet of foreskin and lick the treacly fluid dripping from the head, kept me thrashing, so much so that I had to wank off four times before I was finally able to get to sleep.

The next morning I woke late, cross and with a sore throat. Rupert was in the sitting room, endlessly turning an irreplaceable silver spoon in an irreplaceable china cup presumably filled with the rarest and most perishable of teas. He informed me in curt tones that he had invited a guest to dinner, a "charming lady" who took great pleasure in meeting "artistic young people" and in whose good graces it was imperative that he should establish himself. "And it would probably be a good idea *not* to bring up politics, Brian. Lady Abernathy is—well, rather unmodern in her ideas. We wouldn't want to shock her."

I stared out the window. Rain thudded against the glass, so much rain that I wondered for a moment if perhaps that was Rupert's problem, if like so many Englishmen he had simply got soggy in the head. I wished I could concoct an excuse to get out of the house that evening; unfortunately none came to mind. As Rupert's guest, I appeared to be his slave.

The phone rang. To my amazement, it was for me.

"Brian, it's Rose Dent. Nigel's mother. I hope you don't mind me ringing you here; your sister gave me the number. I've called to tell you Nigel's in London."

I was shocked. Nigel hadn't given me any indication he intended to visit London.

"How long is he going to be here?" I asked hopefully.

"Oh, but that's just it. He's leaving tomorrow. He's been here a fortnight already."

"A fortnight?"

"Very busy, I'm afraid. But he did wish to see you. Tell me, could you pop round for tea today—say, around four? But I must warn you that Nigel has a cold and might not be in the best of spirits."

I said of course I would come. She rang off, and I sat down to ponder why on earth Nigel might have come to London for a fortnight and not called me. This wasn't like him.

Nigel and I had been inseparable since public school, where I fagged for him—shined his shoes, made his bed, and so forth. You could say our relationship hadn't progressed much since then. Even now the bark of his disapproval reduced me to a quaking first former, desperate to please this older, bigger, deep-voiced master, and in the end always flubbing the simplest task. I "followed" him to Cambridge, then to Stuttgart, where he went to study piano with the renowned Clara Lemper, and from where he wrote the first of his "Letters from Abroad"—essays on musical and political themes that would later make him more famous even than his recordings of Ravel and Liszt. In Stuttgart we practically lived together, and, though I now had a deeper voice than his, I continued to shine his shoes and make his bed. I was, as far as I knew, his closest ally: we shared early drafts, confidences, even lovers. Oh, certainly, our friendship had a fractious edge. He tormented me regularly, the way an older brother will torment a younger. Still, I loved him and had no doubt that he loved me. For him to have spent two weeks in London without ringing me—well, something would have had to be gravely wrong.

I passed the afternoon in a state of restless anxiety, then at three headed off to the Dents' house in St. John's Wood. The rain was pissing down and I had left my umbrella on the underground and so asked Rupert if I might borrow one. Drearily he rummaged in a cupboard before locating the necessary implement.

The tube ride to St. John's Wood took almost forty minutes, presumably because of the weather. Happily the rain had cleared up by the time I got there. I walked through a puddled and intermittently sunny atmosphere to the Dent house. I was sent up to his room—Mrs. Dent's room, rather, claimed by Nigel for the duration of his stay. There he was, in bed, very red in the nose, surrounded by papers and books. The place reeked of cigarettes. On the floor were stacked stained teacups, which Mrs. Dent hastily gathered.

"Hello, Brian. How nice to see you," said Mrs. Dent.

"I haven't shit for three days," Nigel announced. "Just wanted you to know."

Mrs. Dent left hurriedly.

It was obvious that he was indeed not in the best of spirits—in fact he was in a bloody beastly frame of mind, cruel and teasing, as if testing how much I would take from him before I lashed back. Still, I was determined not to give in.

"So what's brought you to London, Nigel?" I asked, trying to sound as if I really didn't care.

"Negotiating a contract with Heinemann. They want to collect my 'Letters from Abroad.' I'm not sure, though. Heinemann is not exactly *avant-garde*."

Pride and envy coursed through my blood in equal measure at this information. Also bewilderment; the Nigel I knew, upon receiving such monumentally good news, would have called me instantly.

"Nigel, that's wonderful," I said. "Congratulations."

"Yes, well. Now I've got something to say to you, Brian, and it isn't going to be pleasant. I'm sure you're wondering why I haven't rung you up when I've been in London close to a fortnight. Well, that's why I wanted you to come by today, to explain to you that I've had it with you. You annoy me thoroughly. You're sniveling and loud and alto-gether too much of a presence. You parrot my views. You dress embarrassingly. And as for that story you sent me—dreadfully bad. Unspeakably bad. I thought you had potential once, Brian, I really did, but you've quite extinguished what little hope I had for you with this"—he held the offending sheets out in front of him, as if they positively reeked—"this loose stool."

My mouth opened in instinctive protest. "It's only a first draft—" I began.

"A first draft! A first draft!" He gave one of his whooping laughs. "You really are such a big girl's blouse, Brian, the biggest blouse any girl ever wore. I attack your story, which, by the way, I honestly consider to be shit, and what do you do? Do you defend it, or yourself? No! You try to sneak away from it, you try to disclaim it."

"But really, I think you're right, it does need work—"

"But that's just my point! First draft my arse—you thought it was brilliant until this minute! If you really aspire to be a literary man, you must learn to hold your own, and not just gobble like a turkey and agree with what everyone else says just to please them. And you must get out of the habit of changing your views so that they match mine. If you say, 'I think S. is a good poet,' and I say, 'I think he's shit,' the next minute you're kicking dirt back like a cat to cover it up. Which brings me to my final point. Tonight, as you may have heard, Anne Cheney is having a dinner in my honor. I don't know if you're invited, but if you are, I should prefer you not attend. And if you do attend, I shall leave."

The bluntness of this demand stunned me. "Well, all right, Nigel," I said. "If that's how you feel, I think I shall leave right now."

"Don't be ridiculous, you've just arrived. Have some tea."

I glared at him.

"Oh, you're pathetic. Just because I've said what I've said, you act as if we're no longer friends. All right, go then, if that's how you feel."

I walked out of the room, upsetting, along the way, a cup of cold tea his mother had somehow neglected to clear away. Nigel took no notice and, getting out of bed, followed me into the hall. "A new piece I've written," he announced, thrusting an envelope into my hand. "It's about left-handed pianism. It is to be the leadoff for the new volume."

"Thank you," I said. We shook hands grimly, and I departed.

On the tube ride back I read Nigel's essay—it seemed brilliant to me, which made me even more miserable—and arrived back at Rupert's around six. Almost as soon as I'd stepped through the door

I had the ghostly sensation that I was not holding something I should have been holding. Of course—it was Rupert's umbrella! So before going into the sitting room, where Rupert was waiting with tea, I asked the maid if I might use the telephone. Nigel's mother answered: no, she was sorry, I hadn't left any umbrella; indeed, as far as she was aware, when I arrived I hadn't been carrying an umbrella at all. I thanked her and rang off, feeling annoyed at the money I would have to waste replacing not only Rupert's umbrella but my own. Two in two days was a record, even for me!

Rupert was in his smoking jacket, pouring tea. He seemed to be in considerably higher spirits. "Hello! Do sit down. I've just had a fresh pot brewed. How was Nigel?"

"Rupert," I said, "I'm afraid I've lost that umbrella you loaned me. Awfully sorry. I'm such an oaf when it comes to umbrellas."

His smile disappeared.

"What?" he said.

"I said I'm afraid I've lost that umbrella you loaned me."

"Where?"

"On the underground. Rupert, I—"

"Then it's hopeless. We'll never get it back."

He stood, turning away from me, his face ashen. Really, I was thinking, all this fuss over an umbrella!

"Of course I'll replace it," I offered.

"Replace it! Good God, don't you have eyes? Didn't you see the silver on the base? The ivory handle? The monogram?"

"Well, as I said—"

"That was no ordinary umbrella you lost, Brian! My God, it was antique! From before the war! Worth a hundred pounds, at least!"

"A hundred pounds," I repeated faintly. "Oh, God." I sat down, aghast—a hundred pounds for an umbrella! Then I stood up again. "I'll call the lost property office at Baker Street," I said. "Maybe someone—"

"Don't even bother. Any idiot could tell how much that umbrella was worth. Probably it's being dismantled as we speak, the silver melted down to sell, the ivory—" A tear snaked out of his left eye. He fell back into the cushions in an attitude of despair, and I turned away, overcome by contradictory emotions: horror and guilt at having lost something of such value, and at the same time amazement that Rupert would have loaned me the umbrella in the first place. Certainly had I been aware that it was not just an ordinary umbrella, I never would have taken it.

"Rupert," I said finally, "I don't care if it cost a *thousand* pounds; I'll replace it"—wondering where on earth I'd come up with that sort of money. But Rupert gulped and heaved, and with what seemed Herculean effort recovered his good breeding.

"Don't give it another thought; it's in the nature of umbrellas to be lost. I've simply overreacted because of its sentimental value, for which I apologize heartily. Now have some tea."

He poured out the tea, which by now was bitter and black, and with great wrenching and ripping hauled the conversation away from that fatal object with which we had both become—and would remain for some time—horribly and unalterably obsessed. "Did I tell you about Daisy Parker's wedding? What a nightmare *that* was! Her old flame showed up, drunk, just as I was giving my toast!" I hardly listened. Instead my mind was crawling backward, trying to recollect the exact moment the umbrella had been misplaced.

After tea I went upstairs to rest but could not stop thinking about the wretched umbrella, which in truth I had hardly looked at. Was I a fool not to have appreciated its value? No, it had simply never occurred to me that there could be such a thing in the world as a hundred-pound brolly!

Around seven-thirty the doorbell rang. Dutifully I dragged myself downstairs. Across the living room sofa from Rupert, a jowly old woman was peering through an old-fashioned *pince-nez* at the antique crystal collection. I recognized her face, though I wasn't sure where from.

"Brian, may I introduce Lady Abernathy? Lady Abernathy, Mr. Botsford."

"How do you do."

Her hand barely grazed my own, and she returned to examining the crystal. I sat next to Rupert. A mask of politesse barely covered the stricken look that had taken his face like a palsy.

"Brian is a writer," Rupert said to Lady Abernathy, as we sat down to table. "He's just about to finish his first novel."

"Ah," Lady Abernathy said. "And am I correct in presuming that it will be a modern novel?"

"I suppose you could say so. Yes."

"Then I'm afraid I shall never read it. The other day, I attempted to read a novel by Mrs. Woolf that dear Rupert had recommended. Quite horrifying. After fifty pages I was obliged to reach for my Bible."

"So you value traditional works, Lady Abernathy," Rupert said.

"There is only one novel I consider worth reading anymore—*Jane Eyre*. I read it every Christmas."

"Ah, the Brontës," Rupert said. "So quintessentially English."

"Rupert," Lady Abernathy said, "I have brought a letter I wrote. I wondered if you might read it and give me your opinion before I post it."

"Of course," Rupert said. "And to whom is the letter to be sent?"

"To Mr. Hitler."

Rupert went white. "Mr. Hitler?"

"Indeed. I felt he might appreciate knowing that in spite of what the press may claim, there are many of us here in England who recognize his capacities and understand that he alone can save his country."

"Of course I'll be happy to read it for you, Lady Abernathy," Rupert stammered. "Do you wish me to make substantive criticism or simply check the grammar?"

"I am more concerned that the style be . . . flowing, shall we say? And you were always such a talented writer, Rupert. *He* should write novels," she added to me.

"How impressive it is, Lady Abernathy," Rupert said, "that you consider it worth your valuable time to engage with the politics of the day."

"Thank you. However, in doing so I am merely carrying on in the tradition of the late Lord Abernathy. He was, as you know, an inveterate letter writer, and never one to shrink from an opinion because it was unpopular."

An awful silence ensued. The maid brought in the soup.

"I suppose the war in Spain can only become worse," I said.

"I was just recalling, Lady Abernathy," Rupert said, "the great pleasure I took at Lady Manley's tea last week upon hearing your charming recollections of Deauville."

"Rupert, dear, your friend has no interest in tedious anecdotes of my youth." She turned to me. "I have been keeping abreast of the situation in Spain and can only say my hopes are with the rebels. Why, just the other night at dinner I was discussing the matter with Herr—oh, I am so bad with names—the German ambassador, and we quite agreed, the rebels are the only hope for Spain."

"I'm afraid I'm of the opposite opinion," I said. "The Republican government is an elected body."

"I haven't had the pleasure of meeting the German ambassador," Rupert interjected, "although Mummy dined with his wife when she was in Dresden last year. She brought back the loveliest china—"

"Mr. Botsford, you are young," Lady Abernathy said, "and, if I might be so bold, susceptible to the worst sort of influences."

"I appreciate your frankness, Lady Abernathy," I said. "If I may be so frank myself—"

"By all means."

"The German ambassador is Hitler's hack. I have lived in Germany, I have seen the blood that flows when the National Socialists—"

"I have always felt politics to be beneath artists," Rupert thrust in. "Artists must look beyond petty mortal conflict. It is what I so admire about Brian's work—at least those snippets I was privileged to read during our years at Cambridge. There is a serenity of vision that seems to rise above the din of the contemporary."

"The German ambassador," Lady Abernathy said, "is a gentleman in every way. Ah, I fear his government has been quite misrepresented in the popular press, which is not surprising, given the fact that the popular press is now almost entirely under Jewish control. It's no wonder that young people see such a distorted picture. The Jews as a race, if I might quote Lord Abernathy—"

My chair made screeching noises as I pushed it out from the table.

"Excuse me, but under the circumstances, I must retire."

"Pardon me, Brian?"

"Are you not feeling well?" Lady Abernathy asked.

"I can only say that under the circumstances, I must retire."

"Brian—"

I turned and walked up the stairs and into my bedroom, where I immediately started packing. Even though I felt calm, my pulse was racing. What would Nigel have counseled me to do? Storm away? Upend the table? "Lady Abernathy, if your hatred of foreigners is as boundless as that of your hero Mr. Hitler, then I am afraid, being half Polish myself, my continued presence at the table will upset your appetite, something I would never dream of doing." Oh, but one never thought up such clever retorts until one had already left the table. *L'esprit de l'escalier*, the French call it. And how I wished I had walked away indignantly rather than fearfully!

I had gathered together my clothes and books and was about to leave the room when I remembered the umbrella. Putting my things down for a moment, I wrote Rupert a check for a hundred pounds (Aunt Constance's gift had been forty), left it on the edge of the bed where he had perched, then fled downstairs and out the servants' door.

It was drizzling out. I caught a taxi to the underground, then the District Line to Richmond. I had twenty-two pounds to my name.

In the morning I told Nanny the story of the umbrella. "What I don't understand," I concluded, "is why someone would loan out a hundred-pound umbrella in the first place."

"It seems obvious to me," Nanny said. "He was trying to impress you."

"Impress me? I don't care about umbrellas! For me, umbrellas only exist when it rains!"

"Apparently they mean more than that to him," Nanny said.

"Apparently so," I said, and thought of Forster, *Howards End*, literature's cache of fatal umbrellas.

"Well, it doesn't matter," I concluded. "It's lost. The umbrella's lost. Just another object in a history of lost objects. I shall never speak of it again."

But I was wrong.

That afternoon I went out to look for cheap rooms, and by the next morning had installed myself in a bed-sitter in Earl's Court that had for the past twenty-seven years been the domain of one Muriel White, a stenographer. It had a coin-operated gas fire and a lavatory the flushes of which sounded like the coughing fits of a dying emphysemic. And here I settled—jobless, rent paid to the end of the month—and tried to decide what to do next.

Every day I listened to the wireless. The situation in Germany grew worse every day; every day, it seemed, Hitler made more advances, the noose tightened around the necks of the Jews. Meanwhile the European nations had signed a nonintervention treaty in regard to Spain, which the Germans and Russians appeared to be blatantly defying. Curse Eden! Curse England for her cowardice!

I made halfhearted attempts to work on my novel, but in light of present events—in light of hideous Lady Abernathy's opinions—it seemed a useless endeavor. Once, it had been enough to explore the delicate shadings of a conversation, the etiquette according to which an old woman poured out tea, the thoughts of a young boy as he descended in a lift toward the underground platforms. Now, however, history was pressing down from all sides, and sensibility seemed more than insufficient: it seemed criminal. Soldiers, not writers, determined the fate of the world.

An envelope arrived one afternoon in the post, forwarded from Richmond. It contained the check I'd written to Rupert, uncashed. No note. Rupert, I was beginning to suspect, wasn't nearly so fragile as his teacups. So now I had one hundred and seventeen pounds to my name. Enough for a few months, at most.

Nigel's essay on left-handed pianism was published in *The Gramophone* and hailed as a masterpiece.

Around that time rumors started circulating among my friends in London and Cambridge about a fellow called Desmond Leacock, the heir apparent to the publishing firm of Leacock and Strauss. He had taken a double first at Oxford and wore on his face a look of tortured regret, which only added to his attractiveness. Leacock had always had an air about him of heroic predestination, so it was no surprise to any of us when one day he decamped to Spain and joined up with the Republican forces. Conflicting reports about his progress through Catalonia and Aragon came through the mail and the telephone: Monday he was dead, Tuesday he had lost a leg, Wednesday he had led his troops to victory, Thursday he had deserted. What finally evaporated these rumors was his physical return to London, bruised and half starved but with all his limbs intact. He was to give a talk about his experiences in the war in a basement in Chelsea.

Political speeches, like sermons, can be a call to arms if one is there to hear them. In novels they have the effect of glue poured directly onto the page. Therefore I am going to ask you to take it on faith that Desmond Leacock's speech that evening stirred the heart of my generation and that we left it convinced that only by shoring up Spain against the Fascist threat might we prevent Hitler from taking power in Germany.

In short, knowing nothing about battle, knowing only that I could not afford to keep paying rent on my rooms for much longer, that the prospect of returning to Richmond was unbearable and that Nigel, my closest friend, had turned against me, I decided to go to war.

My first step was to attend an Aid to Spain meeting in another basement, this time in Earl's Court.

My life changed irrevocably that night, though not in any of the ways I expected.

Chapter Two

I come from an unusually mixed-up family. My father was a doctor, scion of several generations of doctors who ran the local surgery in a village called Elmsford, near Rye. Very E. F. Benson, his childhood, filled with sandwich cake and antiques, summer people and oddball year-round residents who were forever showing up at the surgery with imaginary liver ailments. He studied medicine in London, where Mother was born. *Her* mother came from Belgrave Square but defied the wishes of her family by marrying a Pole named Tadeusz Bortciewicz. My great-grandparents summarily disowned her. Grandfather died only a few years later, and Grandmother—now penniless—had to go begging to her relations in order to survive, with the result that Mother and Constance grew up dependent on officious aunts before whom they were expected to perform acts of obeisance. She and Father married for love, which was rare in those days. Of course Father would have preferred to move back to Elmsford and take over the family surgery, but Mother would have gone mad in Elmsford. So they settled in Richmond, which was

London, really, but had a villagey air. They were good parents. The worst thing they ever did to us was die.

Various orators, at their funerals, praised my parents' tolerance and gentility. But though they cared about the fate of the world, they were by no means radicals. Indeed, if there *is* Communism in my blood, it is probably attributable to Grandfather Bortciewicz, who was a talented oboist. I doubt I got it from Elmsford, where the word "Communist" had to be whispered. I certainly didn't get it from Belgrave Square.

Those years between the wars were full of meetings that took place in basements. The rooms blur in my memory; all of them had mildewed walls and a few bare bulbs hanging from the ceiling, which gave them a dim, ecclesiastical glow. Chairs had been set up, but no one was sitting in them. Instead schools of young men and women flocked and gathered. Most of them had tiny standard-order Oxbridge glasses perched on their noses, and some of them were friends of mine: Anne Cheney, Emma Leland and her fiancé, Tim Sprigg, whom I knew to be a fruit. Then there were the genuine workers, their faces grimy from factories. Among their number I often recognized the driver of a bus I used to take regularly with my mother from Richmond into the West End. Once I smiled and raised a hand in what I hoped would be a comradely and affectionate gesture, but he turned away, embarrassed; even in this Communist haven, an irrevocable gulf of class separated us.

That night in Earl's Court, a heavyset young man with bright blond hair took to the podium and called the meeting to order. He looked familiar to me, though at first I couldn't place him. Of course! He was John Northrop, with whom I'd gone to school. We had even wanked together once! (As I recalled, his cock was enormous.) Having identified himself as the chairman of the local Communist cell, he gave us first an update on the situation in Aragon, then a history of the long and fractious relationship between the Castilians, in Madrid, and the Catalans, in Barcelona. Apparently there existed between these two groups an intense, deeply buried animosity. Language was at its core; Spain as a country, it seemed, existed only as the result of wars, its borders a testament to battles lost or won, depending on whom you asked. Within its technical frontiers, in the meantime, discrete localities, clinging fiercely to their own tongues and cultures, continued to play out these antique resentments, in the process creating a current of antagonism that undercut the Republican front in ways too baroque for non-Mediterraneans to understand. This idea fascinated me. In my own imagination Spain existed so vividly as an idea—fan dances, castanets—that I had trouble accepting the fact of its national arbitrariness. In truth, however, *most* countries come into being solely as the result of war. Island nations such as my own are the exception.

In the Pyrenees, Northrop told us, was a tiny bubble of Spain preserved whole a few miles inside the body of France. This cartographical aberration had come about as the result of a treaty written sometime in the fifteenth century. And it had lasted.

With a piece of chalk, Northrop mapped the war's complex political geography. I had trouble keeping track of all the acronyms but was able to grasp that blankets were needed most desperately; also, ambulance drivers, medics, medical supplies; above all, soldiers, men willing to risk their lives defending the Spanish workers against the brutalities of the Fascists and Falangists. He called for volunteers. Emma Leland announced cheerfully that she would drive down in her little roadster and do whatever she could, an offer Northrop greeted with a benign smile and thanked her for, which was really the only way to deal with Emma. If I am to trust histories of the period more than my own memory, the rousing calls to action made at that meeting must have moved us to tears. What lingers, however, is the hollowed-out voice of Emma Leland offering to "pop down" to Barcelona as if Barcelona were the local farmers' market.

The meeting broke up. The would-be soldiers gathered in a corner to find out what to do next. Meanwhile a group of Oxbridge types mulled, drinking tea out of paper cups and discussing various rumors from the Continent. Someone said Franco had been shot, someone else insisted that this was unsubstantiated rot. A vulgar joke was made about the Foreign Secretary.

I noticed an attractive boy of nineteen or so standing alone at a slight distance from the chatting crowd. He was wearing a cap, a worn sweater and a jacket with patches on the elbows, and had propped against his leg a ravaged leather satchel, which looked as if it had been carrying his books since childhood. In his hands he held a paper cup of tea, which he periodically tasted, found too hot and blew on. His hair was dark blond, shaggy and haphazardly cut, and he had a bracingly clean face and green eyes, which according to Mediterraneans are supposed to connote treachery. Near him the crowd buzzed, a young woman threw back her head and laughed, Emma Leland started telling the same story about Daisy Parker's wedding that Rupert had told to relieve the tension of the lost umbrella. Everyone had gone to school with someone's brother or known each other up at Cambridge. These were serious young leftist intellectuals, many of them Communists devoted to the idea of a classless society, but they were also upper class and English and so almost unconsciously sought out others of their kind and mixed with them, while the working-class youth stood alone just outside the perimeter of this charmed circle, listening hungrily, coming as close as he dared, barred from entry by an invisible boundary of accent.

White teeth shone, witticisms flew amid the dark mutterings of war. I was gazing at the young man, thinking about the leanness of his legs, when he accidentally caught my stare. Our eyes met, and then, furiously, he turned away from me and took too large a swallow of his tea, scalding his tongue so that the tea ran down his chin and splashed onto his fingers. With his fist he wiped his chin. Then he brushed his wet fingers against his trousers, leaving a smear. I felt that rare shock of mutual desire and got an erection, and I could tell from the way he was rearranging his legs that he had got one too.

I wandered over to near where he was standing. I felt him sensing my presence and stiffening in response to it, even though he did not look at me. Soon we were more or less side by side against the wall, both looking straight ahead. I swung my leg out, and our pants brushed. He pulled away as if he'd got a shock. Then he let his leg slide back to where it had been, so that it rubbed slightly against mine. When I turned he was staring at the crowd, his face flushed.

"Not the best tea, is it?" I said.

"I've had better."

He kept his eyes nervously averted and did not look at me.

"My name is Brian," I said. "Brian Botsford."

"Edward," he said, then—as an afterthought—added his last name. "Phelan."

His hands were large and callused, his handshake rough.

"Do you live in Earl's Court?"

"No, I live with my mum and dad near Upney. I work over at Earl's Court station, though. The underground station."

"Really," I said. "Are you a driver?"

"Ticket collector."

"That's very interesting. You see, I'm a writer, and I'm writing a novel—"

"I like to read novels. I like to read what's that fellow's name who wrote the novels about the center of the earth."

"Jules Verne."

"That's him."

"Well, by coincidence my novel's got a character who's quite keen on the London underground."

"Has it now? I tell you, you do see it all, in the station. You see every walk of life and type of person. I could tell you stories."

"I'm sure you could."

We had sat down. His leg was shaking uncontrollably, like a dog's when you scratch its stomach. "Do you live nearby?" he asked.

"Not too far."

"Alone?"

"Yes." (And how delicious it was to live alone!)

In a single swallow he finished his tea before thrusting the empty cup onto a table. Then he turned and for the first time looked me square in the eye.

"Would you like to have a walk?" he asked. "It's a warm evening."

"That would be lovely," I said. "I'll just say goodbye to my friends."

Emma embraced me. "Brian, you old rotter, you've hardly said hello and already you're leaving."

"I'm afraid I've got to," I said. "I'm late for dinner."

" 'E 's a busy little bee, in't he?" Emma said.

"Yes, I suppose I am. Well, goodbye." And I beat a hasty retreat.

Edward stood waiting by the door. He looked nervous, as if he was afraid of losing me to the crowd or, worse, being seen leaving with me, thus provoking a scandal.

We stepped into the street. It was a humid night. Lamplight reflected in oil puddles on the murky pavement. Edward's loping gait, as we walked toward my bed-sitter—our unspoken but obvious destination—thrilled me inordinately. As it turned out, he possessed a wealth of technical information about the underground, and so we talked about the design for the escalators in the new Southgate station on the Piccadilly Line and the process by which the arrival of

Wimbledon and Ealing Broadway trains into Earl's Court station is, and occasionally is not, successfully orchestrated. It seemed to make him more comfortable to know he had some expertise in an area I found of interest. Still, I adjusted my vocabulary in order not to use words he might not understand.

We arrived at my bed-sitter and were barely inside the door when he reached his hands around my neck, pulled my face toward his and kissed me. He tasted of honey and cigarettes. There was something compelling, almost needful about his kiss. Then he pulled away. I switched on the light. He pushed me across the room, onto the bed. The old springs squeaked; he pried open my mouth and once again thrust his tongue down my throat. I groped the front of his trousers. What I felt there was a hot trembling, and he cried out, and I pulled my hand away. I hadn't even unbuttoned him.

He lay back, heaving. "I nearly burst," he said.

"Get undressed," I said.

He looked at me intently. Then he stood, threw off his jacket, tugged his sweater and shirt simultaneously over his head, roughly undid his belt and pulled down his trousers. His body was pale, mostly hairless, lean and tightly strung. A zealous erection tented his white drawers, a wet gray stain spreading from the tip. He pulled the drawers down, and his penis swung out and snapped back, hitting his abdomen with an audible slap. Then he tried to step toward the bed, but he had neglected to take off his shoes, and since his trousers and drawers were still tangled around his ankles, he stumbled and with a bewildered cry fell next to me, his legs held fast by a complication of leather and cloth.

"Here," I said, laughing a little, "relax." Delicately I unlaced his shoes and pulled them off, along with the trousers and drawers. His socks were narrow and black and left grooves in the skin of his calves when I peeled them away. I opened the drawer of the bedside table and took out a bottle of mineral oil. He stared at the thick oil as if he wanted to drink it. "Lie on your back," I said. He did. I brushed a finger against his testicles, which had formed a single walnut-sized globe, drum-tight and cleaved in the middle, and he let out a moan so loud I had to put my hand over his mouth, fearful he might wake my neighbors. "Now relax," I repeated, opening the bottle, pouring the oil and rubbing my hands together, to warm it.

Then I touched my slick palm to his penis, and he opened his mouth as if to scream, but held his breath. Three steady strokes and he came, the semen spurting out in thick streaks, some of it landing in his hair and his mouth. His abdomen rocked like a stormy ocean as the orgasm subsided. He heaved. I was afraid he might choke.

"It's all right," I said, brushing back his hair, which was slick with sweat. "It's over now."

His breathing grew quieter. He sat up. I lay on the bed, my hands behind my head, still fully dressed, even my shoes still on, my erection visibly outlined in my pants.

"I'm sorry—I didn't mean to—"

He looked embarrassed, so I took his hand.

"Don't apologize. It was enough, watching you."

"I'm not usually that quick, it's just—it's been a while."

Then he bent over me and groped my crotch in a friendly way. I let out an unintended cry.

"Got quite a big one, you have," he said.

"Like to see it?"

"Wouldn't mind. But I've got to go now. My mum's expecting me for supper."

He stood, pulled on his drawers and trousers and buckled his belt, then sat down on a chair to put on his socks.

"I live in a bigger room than this," he said.

"Most people do. But I'm without a job right now, you see, and this was all I could afford."

For a moment he was silent, as if trying to unpuzzle the mysterious relation (or lack thereof) between my seeming rich and being poor.

He stood again and wandered over to the bookshelf, which was buckling and spilling.

"I don't think I've ever seen so many books in one room except at the library."

"Do you like to read?"

"Oh, I love to read. I believe in improving myself, even though I'm not highly educated. I go every week to a concert or a recital. I very much enjoy music. And every Sunday I go to the National Gallery and try to copy a painting, though I'm not very good at it. And I try to read three books a week. How many books a week do you read?"

"It depends. Sometimes none."

"I could read a lot more than three except as I have to get up so early for work and sometimes my mum needs me to do work in the house. She's got her hands full these days. Who's your favorite author?"

I pondered. "Shakespeare," I said finally.

"I've read Shakespeare," Edward said. " 'When in disgrace with fortune and men's eyes / I all alone beweep my outcast state / And trouble deaf heaven with my bootless cries.' I've memorized six of the sonnets."

"That's very good. And who's *your* favorite author?"

"First, Charles Dickens. Second, Jules Verne. Third, I would have to say, is either Jane Austen or that American fellow Hemingway. I do like his books. But I couldn't decide for third. I never can make up my mind. If my mum says, 'Edward, which of these materials do you prefer for a tablecloth, the gingham or the lace,' I say, 'Mum, I like them both equal.' "

"I can never make up my mind either," I said, and smiled. He looked across the room at me, as if the tenderness in my voice surprised him, but he did not turn away from it or change the subject. I supposed he was suddenly realizing that I could be falling in love with him and not just wanting to use his body, and was finding, to his surprise, that this knowledge pleased him.

A needle of light from the narrow window pierced his eyes, which were suddenly moist. Then he turned away, toward the books, and ran his hand through his hair. He still had his shirt off. Spots rose on the upper cords of his back.

"I could visit you again, maybe," he said. "After work. We could talk more about books. This week I'm reading *Twenty Thousand Leagues under the Sea, The Murder of Roger Ackroyd* and *Central Line Tube Stock: An Illustrated History*. The last one's different, though. That's for work."

I stepped toward him and handed him a card on which I'd scribbled my address. He took it. Our lips grazed.

"And how will you get back tonight?" I asked.

"The underground."

"It's a long way." Reaching into my wallet, I removed a pound note and handed it to him. "Why not take a cab?"

"I don't want your money," he said, stepping back from me.

"I'm sorry, I just thought—"

"You think I just did this for money? I'm not like that."

Hurriedly he pulled on his shirt and buttoned it, gathered his jacket and satchel.

"I'm sorry, Edward," I said. "I only wanted to give you the money so you could take a cab—"

"The tube'll be just fine, thank you."

"You know, if it's ever late and you're too tired to go home, you're welcome to stay here."

"No, no, that would never do," he answered swiftly. "My mum would miss me."

"Well, then, I do hope you'll come again." I didn't know what else to say.

He looked at me, though guardedly.

"You have very green eyes," I said. "Very beautiful."

"So are yours," he said.

"Really?"

"Beautiful. Not green. I think you're very handsome, but then everyone must tell you that."

"No, no, they don't do. I'm glad you think so."

We both blushed. I kissed him. His Adam's apple bobbed, and he looked at me, and I guided his hand to my erection, which he squeezed.

Then he pulled his hand away.

"What brought you to that meeting?" he asked.

I thought about it for a moment. "I suppose," I said finally, "it's because I lived in Germany for two years. I've seen what the Nazis can do. And I don't feel I can stand by, the way most people in this country seem prepared to do, while Hitler takes over Europe. But if the forces of democracy *could* win in Spain—well, don't you think it would make things a lot tougher for the Nazis? That's why I went to the meeting."

Edward frowned. "I see what you're saying," he said. "I see how you could look at it that way. Myself, I never thought about it in connection with Germany. In my case, what it was was my brother Frank. He died in a factory accident last year—he was with the union and got mangled up in a big printing machine. Suspicious-type accident. And since then I've been thinking, what did he die for that

I shouldn't fight in Spain? That's a *real* workers' revolution over there."

"So you're a Communist, I take it."

"Well, I haven't joined the Party, if that's what you're asking. But in my heart of hearts, yes, I suppose." He looked up at me cautiously. "And you?"

I had a prepared answer to this question. "Though I'm in sympathy with the goals of the Party in specific instances," I said, "no, philosophically I do not consider myself a Communist. That doesn't mean I wouldn't fight alongside Communists, however. To achieve a common goal."

"All that keeps me from signing up is my mum," Edward said. "It would kill her to lose her second son."

"Is that what stopped you tonight?"

"I suppose. What stopped you?"

I considered for a moment. "I think," I said finally, "it was meeting you."

He looked into my eyes intently, as if searching for a clue that might help him interpret this remark.

Then he turned brusquely away.

"Well, I must be off. See you again, I hope."

"I hope so too."

"Goodbye."

"Goodbye."

And he was gone.

I closed the door behind him. What a strange encounter! I thought. And yet I wasn't surprised. There had been something so mysterious, so almost spectral about the swiftness of our meeting, that it seemed appropriate he should disappear as suddenly as he had first come into my range of vision.

I sat down on the sofa and lit a cigarette. I was thinking back to those nights when Nigel and I had sat and drunk and imagined for each other the ideal "friend" each of us hoped someday to meet. Was Edward that friend, I wondered now, that Nigel conjured for me on cold Cambridge nights? In a physical sense, certainly. And there was something extraordinarily tender about his naive aspirations to better himself. He made me want to guide him, to take him to places that amaze and silence: that church in Rome with its Caravaggios; Notre-Dame. Suddenly I was lost in fantasy, spinning a life out of our one night, envisioning us, Edward and me, living together, traveling together. Nights in sagging beds in pensions in Corsica, looking at the stars from a houseboat in Amsterdam. What bliss that would be! And how mad of me to imagine!

He was on his way back to Upney, I supposed. If indeed he lived in Upney, if he wasn't lying, if indeed he really worked for the underground and was who he said he was. Upney: so far from Richmond, from everything I knew! That he was of the working class, I had to admit, thrilled me inordinately. No public school boy would have been capable of such raw sexual display. Yet Edward was not embarrassed. His need was unsuppressed and unsuppressible; it had not been detoured into collections of rare eighteenth-century teacups or encyclopedic research projects or money counting in the City. And that was why I wanted to find him again: I longed for that rawness that had been bred out of me. Nigel could insist until he was blue in the face that homosexuals should constitute a classless society; the fact remained that for both of us there was no place more exciting than the servant's hall.

I stood from the sofa. I took the towel with which Edward had wiped himself. With one hand I held it to my mouth, the smell still strong, bleachy and metallic, and with my other hand undid my trousers and in a matter of seconds brought myself off.

Needless to say, I did not go to war until later.

Chapter Three

‿

It continued, unremittingly, to rain. Then one morning, for just a few moments, the sun came out. In the street old women looked into the sky with amazement, deflated their umbrellas, then shook them out like wet dogs. For ten minutes or so the sun shone smugly in the slate-blue sky, as if to mock their hesitation, their lack of faith—and then a drop of water fell, and another, and another, and in what seemed a matter of seconds the sky had clouded over, rain was sheeting down as the disumbrellaed populace, victims of a heavenly prank, rushed madly for shelter.

I woke early. I always woke early in those days—dragged from sleep by a panicked need to switch on the wireless and hear whether the war had started yet. In the post box was a letter from Nigel. He had fallen in love with a nineteen-year-old Bavarian boy called Fritz and with him had fled Berlin for Paris.

The last week things got so bad I started fearing for our lives. Each night I could hear screams coming from the street, and in the morning I would step outside to find fresh blood spilled on the pavement. Nearby the *Nazijugend* practiced their absurd little calisthenic drills, almost like a taunt. What bothered me, however, was not the sight of the blood but the smell of it. Faintly metallic and salty, like semen. By the way, the Nazis do not like homosexuals primarily, according to everyone, because a number of the Party's original high officials were homosexuals themselves and believed they could combat the threat of exposure by practicing excessive brutality. Few of them survived the purge. And do you remember the little florist's shop where we used to buy those glorious roses? The couple who ran it? Both handsome, rugged fellows, their arms corded with muscles, their hair thick and blond and blazing. They walked to work each morning holding hands, and told Horst that their love for each other was as unwavering as their faith in the great Aryan nation. Together they joined the Nazi Party. Horst begged them not to do it, but they insisted that the party objected only to decadent homosexuals, whereas they themselves were not decadent homosexuals at all, they were Aryan brethren, united, their love an exalted flame. A few weeks later they disappeared. The flower shop was sacked, the windows smashed, the roses torn and ravaged. No one has heard from them since.

The station, by the time we left, was a Gomorrah, a hell. Who was a Jew, who was traveling on false passports, who would and would not be allowed to leave the country? I saw a family: an elegant-looking man wearing a *pince-nez* and a smooth black suit, his wife carefully buttoned into a sable coat, rocking a baby whose nose was running, while their other child, a miserable-looking little girl in a green pea coat, sat stone still on a curb. Nervously they guarded boxes and trunks and suitcases piled haphazardly like an Italian hill town. There was a smudge on the man's cheek, a stain on his shirt. On closer inspection I saw that one of his eyes had been blackened. Clearly they needed quite desperately to get out of the country. And would they? In such a situation you can only think of yourself.

Fritz and I boarded the train. I was treated cordially—the Führer does so love the English—though I worried for Fritz, who had hinted his papers might not be entirely in order. Whatever problems there were, however, the inspector either failed to notice or chose to ignore. He had a more important priority, that being the hunting out of those attempting to flee on false passports.

Across the platform from our train was one bound for Amsterdam. As it left, smoke puffed up in billows. I caught a last glance of the man with the *pince-nez*. He was arguing with an inspector, while his elegant wife and sick baby and stoic little girl stared at the departing train. They got smaller and smaller until they disappeared into the smoke. Thus we left Germany.

Paris is a relief, by comparison. We have rooms in an old pension near Saint-Sulpice. No plumbing and an elderly neighbor who appears to be a leper, but at least here we have escaped the smell of blood—forever, I hope, though I doubt it. We make love obsessively, madly. Our energy is undepletable. Last night I had seven orgasms.

This is not natural. This is the end of the world.

I folded the letter inside the envelope. I needed to walk, even though I had no umbrella, even though the rain was pouring down now with a force that made me wonder if that brief spasm of sunlight had been a dream. On the street, in spite of the downpour, a boy was picking his girl some flowers that the council had planted along the pavement. An old woman approached them, shaking her umbrella. "You don't do that!" she shouted. "Maybe in Germany, yes, but this is England! You don't pick flowers in England!"

The rain was coming down so powerfully I had to keep my head bent in order to see where I was going; rainwater sheeted the lenses of my spectacles. I was thinking of Rupert's terrorized maid, heedlessly shattering some irreplaceable piece of china. What would Rupert do? Shout at her? Fire her? Doubtlessly. So Rupert fires the maid, the maid must move back with her mother, the two of them, together, hate Rupert and his precious china. Rupert, in the meanwhile, buys another piece of china, hires another maid, watches the maid break the china, fires her and hires another maid and fires this maid as well. Soon all the maids hate Rupert, while Rupert hates his mother and his schoolmasters and me, though he dares not say so. Hitler, Nigel told me, wanted once to be a painter but failed to gain admission to an art academy. If Hitler had been admitted to art school, might he now be a contented watercolorist, and Europe at peace?

I was no innocent. I was cruel to Rupert, those evenings when he came to me, longing to be loved. I enjoyed rejecting him. Rejecting him excited me. Losing his umbrella, perhaps, excited me.

It shouldn't have surprised me that at the darkest moments of history, the libido, rather than do the decent thing and make itself scarce, rears its figurative head more unrelentingly than ever. I was young enough, however, to believe my supposedly aimless ramble had only by coincidence brought me into the vicinity of the Earl's Court underground station. To shelter from the rain there, I reasoned, would be the most natural thing in the world.

So I hurried in. It was an old station, damp and drafty. The tiles on the walls of the ticket hall were sweating, a degraded-looking char was listlessly nudging a body of mop water around the floor, at the ticket office an elderly woman was arguing with the ticket clerk over change. And at the gate to the platforms, just where I expected him to be, taller than I remembered and looking quite dashing in his dark uniform, his shiny dark cap, stood Edward. A train had just pulled in; a crowd of newly arrived passengers surged through the gate. His brow furrowed with concentration, he eased them by, took their tickets, tore the green cheap day returns and gave the second halves back with hardly a blink. No would-be fare beater could get past *his* gimlet green eye. Then everyone had got through except for an old woman who stood on the other side of the gate from Edward, furiously emptying her purse, seeking out amid the refuse that had collected there the little stub that might free her. "I know I have it somewhere," she muttered.

"It's all right, Mum, you can go through, I trust you," Edward said.

"Well, that's kind of you," the old woman said, "though I should hope you'd know me by now. I've only been coming through this station twice a day five days a week for the last thirty-six years." She waddled past. He laughed and leaned back, his left leg shaking the way it had at the meeting. Then he saw me.

"Well, hello," he said. "What are you doing here?"

"Sheltering from the rain."

"It's pissing buckets, isn't it? What luck, though. I've been meaning to ring you up, only the night after the last time I saw you Mum went down with the influenza and Dad went and broke his leg and now he's in hospital. So I've been having to do a lot around the house, I can tell you. And we don't have a phone; to call I have to go down to the pub, where everyone can hear—"

"Of course," I said.

There was a quivering roar as another train entered the station. "That'll be the Hounslow," he said. "I'll have to get busy again in a second. But I wanted to tell you what I'd read this week. I read *The Well of Loneliness* by Miss Radclyffe Hall—"

"*The Well of Loneliness*! But it was banned."

"My sister Lucy got a copy. It opened up my eyes, let me tell you."

A screech sounded, brake sparking against track. "Uh-oh, here come the elephants. Listen, I'd love to talk to you some more—"

"Why not drop by?" I ventured. "After you finish work?"

He gulped, as if literally digesting the offer, then said, "All right, yes. I finish at five. Would that be all right?"

"Perfect. See you later, then."

"Yes. Later."

The crowd engulfed him.

The rain had stopped by the time I got outside again. Water spots stained my spectacles. With my shirttail I wiped them clear.

On the way home I bought sandwiches and cream cakes. The flat was already scrupulously clean—a symptom of my current enthusiasm for all activities that did not involve arranging words on a sheet of paper—so I had a bath, shaved, scrubbed my face and teeth vigorously, then sat down to wait.

The bell rang promptly at quarter past five. "Sorry I'm late. I got held up," Edward said.

"Don't worry," I said. "Come in."

We shook hands. He was still carrying the same worn satchel, though this time he had on a tie.

He wiped his feet on the mat. Nervously we took our places on the sofa, having made sure first that a respectable distance separated us.

"Would you like some tea?" I asked. "It's just made."

"Oh, that would be lovely, yes."

I poured the tea and sat next to him again on the sofa. Stiffly he sipped, did not look at me. The silence stretched out. Even though earlier in the afternoon I had drawn up a mental list of conversation topics—the underground, Upney, Spain—I now found myself unable to think of a single thing to say. It was as if, having gone to bed together on the occasion of our first meeting, Edward and I could not quite reconcile ourselves to the fact that our bodies knew each other so much more intimately than our minds did.

"I was sorry to hear about your dad," I said finally. "Is he all right?"

"Hah!" Edward said. "He fell in the gutter outside the pub, that's how he busted his leg. He was pissed to the gills. Mum says he's got what's coming to him; she won't have us showing him any sympathy. And to make matters worse, she's flat on her back with the flu, poor old girl. And to top *that* off, Nellie's gone and run off to Glasgow to take care of her old grandma—or so she *says*—leaving the two brats with us to take care of, so the place is a bit crowded right now. Nellie's my sister-in-law. Except as she and Frank were never married legally. Oh, they were going to do, only then Frank got killed in that accident I was telling you about. He left behind Nellie and little Headley and another one on the way—that's Pearlene. Always fond of strange names, Nellie is. Anyway, she's not been living with us, just on us—she and the kids were in Walthamstow, in furnished rooms— and then the same day Dad breaks his leg and Mum's down with the flu, suddenly Nellie announces old Grandma's sick in Glasgow and can we take the kids. But it's all right. Lucy hates it, of course, but Sarah's good with children. Sarah's my other sister. She's quite simple."

Anxiety, which left me at a loss for words, clearly had the opposite effect on Edward.

"My goodness, your family life certainly is complicated," I said.

"Well, like I was telling you, that's why I couldn't come to see you. I'd finish with work and have to race home to help out before Lucy went off for one of her evenings. God knows where she goes, really. She's got her own life, though she's only eighteen."

"By the way, Edward, how old are you?"

"Twenty in three months and fourteen days. Where's your toilet? When I drink tea I'm a sieve, I tell you."

I pointed him toward the lavatory. He did not close the door. I could hear the loud spray of his pissing, then the familiar wheezing crash as the lavatory flushed and water came down in torrents.

He was still buttoning his fly as he returned to the sofa. "I do talk a bit," he said, sitting down. "You'll have to excuse me. Mum says sometimes I'm like a tap that won't shut off; not that she's any better, mind you."

"Don't apologize. Your family sounds fascinating."

"Well, we aren't the average."

"More tea?"

"Yes, thank you."

I poured it out. Edward turned; we smiled at each other. Tentatively I put my hand on his head and pulled it toward mine. We kissed; with our tongues we opened each other's mouths. Then we were standing, guiding each other to the bed.

My fear that, like the first time, Edward would simply lie back and expect me to relieve him proved to be ungrounded. Instead he scrupulously undressed me, examining, with an almost clinical curiosity, each part of my body as he uncovered it: my toes, my feet, my calves and thighs and stomach. Would he approve of what he found? How pale my body appeared to me at that moment—pale and soft and *English!* His, by comparison, had a high color and a hardness that I found enviable as well as exciting. Then his hand found my cock.

It was dark when we came, simultaneously, our mouths pressed together to stifle each other's cries.

Afterwards we lay still, not touching, silent, both of us slightly taken aback by the extent to which we had abandoned all pretense of decorum. In what seemed like another life (but it had been minutes ago!), I recalled Edward on his knees, his bum pointed in the air, wanting me to bugger him. I recalled the jangling crash as his belt fell from the bed onto the floor.

I got up and made more tea and brought it to the bed, along with the cakes and sandwiches I'd bought. We were both ravenous. We lay naked in bed, stuffing cream cakes into our faces. Edward's cock—so big and angry when it was hard—had shrunk to almost nothing. "A grower, not a shower," Nigel would have said, but Nigel was nowhere near now. Nigel was away.

Edward told me more about his family. His "dad," it turned out, was not his father, just his mother's most recent husband. *Her* name was Lil, and she had been a music hall dancer. The bunch of them—Lil, "Dad" (his lack of a surname seemed to signify his interchangeability with past and future versions), Edward, Lucy, Sarah, and now the incongruously named Headley and Pearlene—shared a crowded little two-bedroomed house. Because Edward had been given the dining room, Lucy and Sarah were forced to share a bedroom, much to Lucy's consternation.

"And you say it was Lucy who gave you *The Well of Loneliness*?"

"Some people march to a different drummer," Edward said. "Lucy marches to a different orchestra."

"*The Well of Loneliness*," I said. "Extraordinary, for a girl of her—"

"Hey, excuse me, but just because we didn't go to public school doesn't mean we're know-nothings. We're quite up on what's going on in the world of high culture, my sister and me, thank you very much."

"I'm sorry—I didn't mean to imply—it's just—*The Well of Loneliness*—and when I think of my own sister—though perhaps *that's* been Caroline's problem all along—"

Edward laughed.

"And you think Lucy's—well, like Miss Hall?"

"She certainly doesn't dress in men's clothes, if that's what you're asking. At least in front of us."

He finished the last of the sandwiches, then announced he had to be going. My heart sank, I so badly wanted him to stay.

He stood before me, dressing—a spectacle I found nearly as arousing as the spectacle of his undressing. Then, when he had finished, he sat down on the edge of the bed.

"Brian," he said, "remember the last time we spoke—you said if I ever needed to, I might stay the night here?"

"Yes, I remember."

"I was just asking because—well, with Headley and Pearlene, things are getting rather cramped at home. I don't even have my own room no more, I have to share it with *them*, and I'm not sleeping much as a result, I can tell you. And yesterday Mum said—well, she said, 'Edward, it would make everything lots easier if you found somewhere else to stay for a while, once I'm over this influenza—just a month or so, mind you, until Nellie's back'—and I was thinking . . . perhaps I might stay here, if you'd have me. Of course I'd pay my share; we'd split everything down the middle—"

"I should think that would be wonderful," I said.

Edward seemed surprised at how readily I had assented. "Well, lovely, then," he said. "That will be lovely. Probably I'll move in beginning of next month—if that's all right."

"Whenever you like. Sooner if you like—tomorrow—tonight!"

He laughed. "Mum's got to get over her flu, remember. Until then she needs me around the house."

"I know. I suppose I'm just eager, that's all."

"Me too."

"Are you?"

With astonishing gentleness, he cupped my face in his hands.

"You really do have the most beautiful eyes," he said.

Chapter Four

As I mentioned earlier, I was working, back then, on a novel. A good part of it took place on the trains and in the stations of the underground, which was one reason I considered my encounter with Edward mystically significant. Since early childhood, after all, I had nurtured a passion for the underground that Nigel thought ridiculous and that, when queried, I found myself hard-pressed to explain. (Most true passions are difficult to explain.) What can I say, except that I loved everything about the underground? I loved the deep tunnels, the smoky trains, the intricate interlocking of the lines, each of which had its own particularities, its identity, if you will. I used to loiter at Richmond Station just so I could gaze at the red circle speared with blue; watch the trains coming and going; mostly, study the map, its vaguely insectoid shape, its tangle of colored yarn that, on closer inspection, revealed itself to be something more sensible: a simulacrum of connectedness; a game of choices. I'd stand for hours asking myself questions such as, if I needed to go from Chancery Lane to Rickmansworth, which would be the shortest route? Which would be the longest? Which would allow me to ride on the most colored lines? To take the quick route seemed obvious to me then, even crude, the alternative of the unimaginative mind. I preferred—I believed in—the long way round.

The red circle, speared with blue, contained the name of the station. It promised other stations: Richmond promised Kew Gardens, which promised Gunnersbury, which promised Turnham Green and Stamford Brook and Hammersmith and London. London! The deep lines, the Piccadilly and the Northern and the Bakerloo! The escalators that tipped down what seemed like miles, the endless tubular corridors with their warm odor of exhaust, the wind of the trains, the mysterious, subterranean wind of the trains. To the north, more stations. To the east, to the west, more stations. Stations spawning like islands, all waiting to be visited, and the name of each one contained, identically, within that red circle, that blue spear!

Not much of this ended up finding its way into the novel, which had aspirations to literary seriousness. Regretfully, I only went so far as to let my passion fly for a few short paragraphs, during which I described the underground as "another London, subterranean and sinister and Gothic." The novel had for a hero a neophyte writer (of course), one Nicholas Holden, who watches with fascination the expansion of the Piccadilly Line out to the distant suburb of Cockfosters, where his friend Avery James, the brilliant young painter, lives. Like Nigel, Avery is aggressively antibourgeois, and so the dreaded suburbs come to embody for him exactly the opposite of what they embody for most people; genius lingers in the semide-tached houses, and the moment when the train emerges out of the tube and into the light is a moment of revelation:

> All at once the blackness lifted, and we were thrust into cold sun and dust. For a few seconds I had to shield my eyes against the

massive brightness, the backs of houses bearing down on me through the train's windows. Oh, how I longed to descend once again into that dark vein, where I could see as Avery saw—with the Inward Eye!

Nicholas craves "the end of the line," which is both death and a safe haven, "that elusive center, the center that *will* hold." And yet he does not quite believe that the distant suburbs to which the Piccadilly Line takes him actually exist: "How *could* one believe in Arnos Grove, in Enfield West, in Southgate, when one was standing in a crowded cavern deep beneath the earth, and a hat was flying down the platform, blown by the hot, bitter, smoky wind? Hyde Park Corner is reality, but Cockfosters, shimmering Cockfosters, is an ideal!" In fact Cockfosters was nowhere—a station near a cemetery off a suburban road—but I didn't care about that. I loved the name. I loved all underground stations with peculiar names—Headstone Lane, Old Street, Burnt Oak, Elephant & Castle. Also, I loved that Cockfosters was both the end of the line and somewhere no one I knew had ever had reason to visit. Not a community or town, exactly. Rather, a place invented by the underground. A terminus. The end of the map, the edge of the flat earth the map imagines. Beyond Cockfosters you could not go. You had to turn back. The tracks themselves stopped. The miles of tracks simply, mysteriously stopped.

"Imagine Cockfosters," Avery is always saying to Nicholas in the novel. But Nicholas's problem is that he *cannot* imagine Cockfosters. That was my problem as well. Nor did I ever, in all my years in London, dare to go there. Oh, I nearly did. I got as far as Southgate once, where the escalators have gleaming gold handrails. Then I got scared. I turned back. You see, I was afraid that if I actually *went* to Cockfosters, I would discover it was just a place, like any other place. Shops and houses. Women carting groceries. And that reality, for some reason, my youthful imagination could not bear to contemplate.

That was the novel that, in the fall of 1936, I had written half of; the novel that, to my chagrin, I did not seem to have it in myself to complete and that I knew I would never complete until I, like Nicholas, "imagined Cockfosters," something at the moment I could not find it in myself to do.

Since I seemed to be incapable of doing any work on my novel, therefore, and since not writing was driving me mad in much the same way that writing had driven me mad back when I wrote, I decided to return to journal writing. Simply to put things down, to get sentences onto paper, was my goal. I had no ambitions beyond the restoration of sanity. Toward that end, I bought a notebook with a mottled black-and-white cover that suggested ink spills and exuded a comforting, musty aroma, the aroma of stationers' shops on rainy days. I also bought a natty blue Waterman's fountain pen and several bottles of ink.

Here is how the journal begins:

Autumn 1936. I must write. Something, anything.

I was thinking, the other day, about the names of the underground stations and what they suggest. Here is what I came up with:

Old Street: the pavement is erupting. Cobwebs gird the entrance to Miss Havisham's dress shop. A grocer specializes in a brand of custard powder not available since 1894.

Elephant & Castle: The elephant is Indian and has an emerald on her forehead. The castle is Briana's castle from *The Faerie Queene*: Briana, whose lover (an ogre) demanded that she sew for him a shroud of human hair. Knights and damsels arrive by

train, are lured within and shorn of their locks and beards. For
the rest of their lives they will wander in madness through the
forest of the station, tearing at what was once their hair.

Burnt Oak: Burnt during a war. When you touch the leaves, ash
rubs off on your fingers. If you cut into the charred bark, a resin
runs out that is black as pitch and carries the smell of death.

"We will probably have left Paris by the time you receive this," Nigel
wrote that week.

This is what happened. A few nights ago Fritz and I were drinking wine in a cheap bistro, when suddenly, uncontrollably, he
started weeping. I asked him what was the matter, and he said
that he felt very sorry because he had not been truthful with me.
Oh, he had not *lied* to me, never that—nonetheless he had somewhat rearranged the facts of his background. It turns out that his
father is not, as he told me previously, a carpenter from
Dusseldorf. His father is ——, an army general and well-known
Nazi! Apparently one afternoon last year Frau —— happened
upon Fritz and one of his cousins *in flagrante delicto*, after which
there was hell to pay. Fritz was ordered immediately into the
army, at which point he fled to Stuttgart, where he ended up
eking out a living as a thief and male prostitute, every moment
on the watch in case his father's "spies" had caught up with him.
Needless to say the story thrilled me, adding as it did to the sense
of illicitness that underscored our love affair. But: "There is
more, Nigel—oh, Nigel, I hardly know how to tell you—" It turns
out that a few years earlier a friend of his had coerced him into
signing several petitions being circulated by the Communist
Party. There was every likelihood the police had got his name
from one of those petitions, and therefore every likelihood,

when we left Germany, that he would be held back at the border—
he got through on sheer luck, in the end, and had not told me in
advance of our departure because he feared my anxiety would
give him away. "So you see? I have deceived you. I wouldn't
blame you if you never forgave me."

I admit I was a bit shaken to learn we had run such a risk without my knowing it. Nonetheless I said that he was probably wise
not to tell me—I am notoriously bad at keeping a straight face—
and that there was no reason for him to feel remorseful. He
thanked me for being so generous, then said that the real problem was what would happen should he be forced to return to
Germany—no doubt his father had the Gestapo on his trail even
now, in addition to which his passport would run out in just
under a year. To reassure him I promised that I would do everything in my power to help him emigrate to South America. This
seemed to put him at ease. *I* felt oddly uneasy, however.

Two days later I returned from shopping to find Fritz miser-
ably ensconced on a bench in the courtyard of our pension,
handcuffed, while a policeman argued with a rather seedy-look-
ing middle-aged man and a leprous old woman shrieking accu-
sations in the background. It seemed that the old woman, the
owner of the pension, had summoned the police, claiming that
Fritz was a male prostitute and that he was bringing clients back
to our room when I was out! The policeman had found Fritz in
the room with this man, though even he had to admit that they
had been doing nothing untoward; indeed, Fritz insisted he had
invited the fellow back for a game of cards. The matter was then
dropped. Nonetheless, the policeman told Fritz he would be wise
to get out of France. Before leaving he took down Fritz's name
and passport number. So it seems likely that any day now we will
be asked to leave. The question is where to go.

For the moment we are just staying put, taking things as they come, which is easier said than done. Both of us have been plagued by nightmares, as well as acute paranoia. The other day we were walking near St. Germain, when I became convinced we were being trailed. I dragged Fritz down curving streets and narrow alleys and out again onto the boulevards, sure that the Gestapo were chasing us. Were they? Who can know? Undoubtedly Fritz's father has provided them with his photo. We stay at home most days (a different pension this time!), waiting for the inevitable knock.

I don't think the police can force Fritz to return to Germany, I think they can only force him to leave France, so I have been investigating countries that might accept us: Sweden is a possibility. Horst's brother lives in Stockholm and would take us in. But how many months would it be before the Gestapo tracked him down as well, or France and Sweden exchanged lists of undesirables? The best answer, it seems to me, would be to acquire for Fritz an immigrant visa to South America then get the two of us safely onto a boat as quickly as possible. According to Horst such things can be bought, though the price is dear. I have got in contact with a solicitor in London who apparently specializes in matters of this sort.

In the meantime my love for Fritz only deepens. It is true that our days are full of bickering and anxiety; by night, however, we go on prolonged excursions into a different country, a country that exists only between lovers. How wonderful to explore its corners and intricacies, this place I have until now known only fleetingly! When we make love, Fritz's blue eyes seem almost to bore into my own; he stares at me plaintively. I can read the intensity of his pleasure like lines of text. To kiss Fritz is to put your lips against the thin, delicate rim of a china teacup and then discover that the teacup, rather than porcelain-rigid, is instead possessed of its own fine musculature. Kissing him opens the door to that other country to which I wish we could emigrate forever, but of course you cannot buy passports to places like that. So I dream up a house with a few small rooms and warped, painted floors, perched on a cliff high over the crashing sea, in a city of tilting houses, a city that is safe and distant from war. At least that is how I imagine the place.

But wait! you are probably thinking. What kind of idealist *is* this fellow who would so casually conceive and then abandon the idea of fighting for the Republican cause in Spain? No kind of idealist at all, in fact. To the charge of moral fluxion I must plead guilty and can offer by way of excuse only the observation that such ideological promiscuity as I exhibited in those days comes naturally to the young. Life at that age is a banquet at which many dishes are served: we choose what tastes best, oblivious to nutrition, not to mention the starving hordes outside the door.

In any case, since I was not going to Spain—since, indeed, I now had good reason to keep my rooms in Earl's Court—it occurred to me that I should have to start earning some money. While it was true that Edward's imminent tenantship would cut my rent by half, half the rent I paid was still more than I could count on receiving from Aunt Inconstance, who, in recent weeks, had become more determined than ever to fix me up with Edith Archibald's hare-lipped niece. Her tenacity surprised me, since each previous attempt she'd made to marry me off she'd eventually had to give up on, my pronounced lack of enthusiasm being, she said, "most dispiriting."

Not this time. Now, thrice weekly, Aunt Constance sent anxious letters, never accompanied by checks and featuring her signature overdependence on underlining, as well as graphic descriptions of whatever gastrointestinal sufferings she was concurrently enduring. "My vexatious stomach will be the *end* of me," she wrote in one particularly memorable missive.

> It is as unpredictable as a girl of *twelve*. In addition, I am plagued by an indescribable *sensation*—a sort of *thickened* feeling just behind my diaphragm. My doctor insists it is nothing—he is *less* than *useless*—Harley Street not being what it was. Suppositories *do* help, though.
>
> Are you writing? I am nearly through with *Humbly Beats the Heart* and—were it not for this *misbehaving stomach*—would have already sent it off. By the by, Edith Archibald tells me Philippa has now returned to London and has taken a job with a publishing concern. (Not my *own*, I hesitate to add!!) Apparently she knew Caroline at school and met *you* once when the two of you were *children!!* She is now *most eager* to reestablish the acquaintance.
>
> Now, take a deep breath, for Aunt Constance is going to scold her nephew: you are being quite *tiresome*, dear boy, trying to wriggle out of committing yourself to a meeting with Philippa Archibald. Naughty, naughty! Know, however, that Aunt Constance is aware of your evasive tactics and that she has your *best interest* at heart, as well as the memory of your poor mother, God rest her soul. Once you meet Philippa, I *assure* you, a *change* will come over you, a *world of love* will open. Alone, you will have only poverty and misfortune to look forward to . . .

In other words, I had two choices: either go through with her little *soirée* or receive no financial support to speak of. Aunt Constance drove a hard bargain.

I wrote her back and told her to pick the evening, and the next morning found in my post a check for twenty pounds.

In those days before he moved into my flat, Edward came by most evenings after work anyway, full of irate passenger stories and Upney gossip. Lil, for instance, seemed finally to be recovering from her bout of influenza, though "Dad" was still in hospital. The family's financial situation, moreover, was becoming rather strained. Because of her illness, Lil had been unable to take in sewing (her usual source of income), while "Dad," in or out of hospital, was from what Edward told me a hopeless drunk and not to be counted on for anything. Lucy appeared to contribute nothing to the family's finances and to get away with it unchallenged, which meant that the only income at the moment was Edward's salary from the under-ground, supplemented by the paltry sums Sarah brought in doing sewing of her own. Add to that the extra stress of two small children, and the Phelans were in dire straits.

Though I was ready to hand over to Edward a good chunk of Aunt Constance's most recent bribe, I hesitated to broach the subject, given his reaction when I had tried to pay his cab fare that first night. I suspected he might not take kindly to this far more substantial offer. Then one evening he arrived for tea, and it was obvious from the ravenous way he ate the cakes I'd laid out that he hadn't had a proper meal in some time. I could stand it no longer. Very delicately, I suggested that perhaps a small loan could be arranged, to be repaid in a few months. And to my surprise, he meekly thanked me and said that yes, a very *small* loan *would* be appreciated, just until Lil was back on her feet and the children off their hands, and on the condi-tion that a contract for its repayment be written from the start. In addition, I must come to supper in Upney—he had told his family about me, and they were curious to make my acquaintance.

A dinner was arranged for the following Tuesday evening. By coincidence, that same afternoon a deliveryman arrived with a package from Harrods: a selection of French cheeses mercurially sent by Aunt Constance and accompanied by the following note:

Was shopping the other afternoon and suddenly became concerned that you might not have anything to serve at your *drinks parties*. So I have arranged to have this assemblage of *delicious* cheeses delivered to you in the hopes that it will *drastically improve* the quality of your *soirées. Bon appétit!*

By the way, Philippa Archibald has had to take leave of London for several months; it seems her elderly grandmother is quite *ill.* (She is that sort of young lady—*responsible*.) Sadly, we shall have to postpone our evening.

A reprieve, it seemed; and yet how little Aunt Constance knew of my life! (Drinks parties?) Now I only feared lest the cheeses were intended as substitute for—rather than complement to—next month's check.

News of Continental disaster was raining down on us daily, like chunks of plaster from a ceiling of questionable integrity. In Andalusia, the Falangists continued their programmatic terror, herding prisoners from their cells by night and shooting them between the eyes. In Madrid, Largo Caballero formed an uneasy alliance with the Anarchists, who had decided to abolish marriage as well as money. In Burgos, Franco was declared generalissimo. Meanwhile the European countries, under the shameful leadership of Anthony Eden, continued to stick by the nonaggression pact, which Germany and Russia were blatantly defying. For me, the saddest figure of all was poor old Unamuno, the rector at the

University of Salamanca and a nationalist sympathizer, who found himself sharing a platform one day with the one-eyed chief of the Spanish foreign legion. When the legionnaire's supporters started shouting "Long live death!" the scholarly old humanist found he could stand it no more. Grabbing the microphone from the nonplussed general, he condemned the slogan, pleading that in order to win, the Fascists would have to convince as well as conquer. "Death to intelligence!" was the crowd's answer. That was the end of Unamuno; he had lost his privileged position within the new order. A few months later, broken and obscure, he died.

Poor Unamuno. Was it coincidence that from within the labyrinth of his peculiar name the word "human" struggled to free itself?

Tuesday came. I met Edward at the station at dusk, and together we boarded an Upminster train. He wore a shirt with a stiff collar and a tie, had had his hair cut and neck shaved. (It was furiously nicked.) At first we barely spoke. Edward was eyeing the Harrods bag with some suspicion. (Understandably—Aunt Constance's cheeses gave off exactly the same odor as a baby with unchanged nappies, with the result that the other passengers, rather than making faces at me, made them at an infant in a pram whose mother was seated next to us; the young woman was as perplexed by the stares as she was by the smell, and on several occasions turned the baby over just to make sure it had not soiled itself; it had not, and she could only shrug in embarrassed bewilderment, while the offended passengers held their noses and looked on.) To put Edward at his ease, I asked him whether further expansion of the underground was planned for the near future, and he visibly brightened as he described to me his own idea for such expansion: a new branch of the Piccadilly into Hackney and then Walthamstow, where previously Nellie had lived with her children.

The train had emerged aboveground; outside the windows, yardfuls of untrimmed grasses quivered slightly in the chill dusk light.

Warehouses passed us, then the stodgy upright brick backs of stodgy upright brick East London houses, then more warehouses. A wounded blue dark was descending. Lights flickered on in windows like fireflies; wilted trees and dingy backyards separated the suburban stations that were now bleeding into each other with trancelike regularity. Soon Edward tapped me; we stood; it seemed we were arriving somewhere.

We disembarked at Upney Station. For about twenty minutes Edward led me along a circuitous sequence of nearly identical streets, all of them dreary. Both the landscape and the architecture in this neighborhood were conspicuously drained of bright color: ashen trees, brown brick houses, closed windows only occasionally enlivened by some halfhearted flounce of curtain, or a child's face suctioned against the glass. It was like walking in a film.

The Phelans' house, when we reached it, was indistinguishable from the ones around it, so much so that I wondered if I might ever be able to find it again without Edward to guide me. He hit the brass knocker a few times, turned his key. The door creaked open. I followed him into a stuffy, humid corridor redolent of wet dog and boiled cabbage. A calico cat sitting on the sill stared at us and licked itself.

We hung up our coats. Quite suddenly a child of about four came barreling out of another room into the hall, braked furiously, then stood stock-still at our feet. I smiled down at the child. Its face contorted. "Now, Headley, don't you start that," Edward said, and of course that did it: Headley burst into a fit of hoarse, enraged weeping. "Headley, you be a nice boy," Edward said. "This is my friend Mr. Botsford." I reached a hand toward the child, who shrieked in horror and ran out a swinging door. "You'll have to excuse Headley," Edward said, then nudged me through the same swinging door into the kitchen, which was small but cheerful, brightly lit, and the scene of some pandemonium. Conflicting noises: the high-pitched bird song of a florid woman in a pink kimono (Lil, I presumed) as she strove to console Headley with baby talk; an irregular thudding as a young girl with a rigid oval face and hair the color of dirty water (Sarah?) chopped carrots; the barking of the aforementioned unseen dog; the shrieking of the aforementioned, very recently seen Headley. And what smells! Cabbage and beef, child's vomit, the echo smell of a fart that had apparently happened several minutes earlier. Indeed, the only person in the room not emitting some fearsome noise or odor was the baby, the unfortunately named Pearlene, who sat very still in her high chair, her not uncurious huge gray eyes staring out at me as mucus dripped unheeded from her nose.

Edward introduced me to Lil, who without getting up warmly shook my hand with one of hers while with the other she patted Headley's back. Headley had his face tightly buried in her kimono. A dark wet stain seeped out from where he had planted his screaming and vampiric mouth. Edward had talked of Lil so often that she'd taken on an independent life in my mind. For some reason I'd envisioned her as fat, and bloated from drink, and *old,* when in fact she was—or at least looked—*young,* with flushed cheeks, freckles, eyes green as Edward's, and stiff blond high-piled hair, and bright teeth. Though Headley's head consumed, for the moment, the entirety of her ample bosom, the shortness of her kimono gave a good view of her legs, which were elegant and slender, very much the legs of a music hall dancer. I felt ashamed—was it only because of her class that I assumed Lil would be hideous? Yet I also missed the Lil I'd invented, and vowed to preserve in my journal a description of her; what we imagine buckles and crumbles so easily, after all, under the sheer massive weight of the real.

Sarah, on the other hand, was exactly as I expected her to be, shy and plain, furiously concentrating on her carrots so as to avoid at all costs the ordeal of contact or conversation with a stranger.

"Now, Sarah," Lil said, "don't be shy. Say hello to Mr. Botsford."

"Pleased to meet you," Sarah said, almost inaudibly.

"Do sit down," Lil said, clearing a chair of old newspapers. "I'm afraid my kitchen's no Buckingham Palace, but it's home, and I try to keep it cheerful and comfortable-like. As I'm sure Edward's told you, I've been down with the influenza. A killer, that influenza; it's just a blessing the children never got it. Now, Headley, enough, darling, get off." But removing Headley was like removing a barnacle from the side of a boat.

It was from Lil, I was learning, that Edward had acquired his garrulousness. She talked almost without cease; I had the suspicion that we could have all left the room for half an hour, gone on a walk, come back, and found her still chattering amiably to air. "Headley's a bit sensitive," she was saying, "since his *m-u-m* went up to *G-l-a-s-g*—Edward, how do you spell Glasgow? Oops!" The mention of that northern city set Headley off again. "Sarah," Lil said, "get Mr. Botsford a cup of tea. I can't do it myself, what with this crying child on my lap."

"Please call me Brian, Mrs. Phelan."

"Mrs. Phelan!" (Her laugh earsplittingly shrill.) "Lovey, I haven't been Mrs. Phelan since 1924. So just call me Lil, thank you very much; everyone else does that doesn't call me Mum. Unless you prefer to call me Mum." She smiled winningly, as if this were a real invitation. "Your own mum's passed on, hasn't she?"

"Yes," I said. (What else had Edward told her?)

"Well, lovey, I'm perfectly happy to be substitute mum to you. God knows with all these, one more wouldn't make much difference." She looked with some irritation toward Sarah, who had abandoned her carrots and was gazing at me in awe. "Sarah!" she shouted, and slapped her hand against the table so that Sarah jumped. "Now what did I tell you?"

"I—I—"

"I told you to get Mr. Botsford—Brian—his tea!"

Sarah lurched up, poured hot water into a small teapot and set it in front of me.

"Thank you," I said. Our eyes met briefly—hers were full of terror and hunger.

"You're welcome," she said, very fast and very softly.

"Cup!" Lil barked.

Again Sarah jumped, rushed to supply the necessary utensil, then returned to her carrots.

Lil was sniffing. "What a smell! Lord, Pearlene, what have we been feeding you?"

From her high chair the baby gazed at Lil beatifically. No one had bothered to wipe away the mucus, which was now dribbling precariously off the edge of her chin.

"Oh, the smell's not the baby," I said. "It's these cheeses." I opened the bag. "I thought you might enjoy them. Only they've gotten a bit *ripe*. French cheeses. Very high quality."

"Well, that was thoughtful of you," Lil said, eyeing the bag dubiously.

"Baby-shit cheese!" Edward laughed. "And they say France is so sophisticated!"

"Edward, that's no way to talk," Lil said. "I think it's very thoughtful of Brian to bring us the cheese. We'll have it after dinner, just like at a real elegant party, like in the cinema. Sarah, put it in the larder."

Holding the bag at arm's length, Sarah lugged it off.

"Headley, love, you've had your cry now," Lil said. "It's time to get off. Come on, that's a good boy."

Reluctantly Headley allowed himself to be removed from Lil's soggy bosom.

"Supper's nearly ready," announced the returning Sarah in a hushed, anxious voice.

"Very good," Lil said. She stood and stretched her legs. "Shall we repair to the dining room?"—her voice suddenly that of an actress aping nobility in a cheap theatrical.

"Yes," I said, and followed her in.

Dinner consisted of beef, potatoes and cabbage—the carrots were either abandoned or had been intended for another meal altogether. But though the Phelans acted as if this were an ordinary meal to which I, having "just dropped by," had been invited on the spur of the moment, it was clear that quite a bit of effort and expense had gone into it: not only had the dining room been resurrected; we were eating off good china (or what passed for good china in Upney). The beef, moreover, was tender, and I couldn't help but worry lest it had cost so much that it would mean no meat at all for the rest of the week. "Care for some more?" Lil asked when I had cleared my plate. "Give him some more, Sarah." Food was being heaped in front of me before I had a chance to say a word. No one else, I noticed, got offered seconds, though Edward eyed the pot hungrily.

For the first half of the meal, conversation centered on the decision of one Cousin Beryl to open a teashop in Dorking.

Edward was for; Lil against. I was asked if I had ever been to Dorking, and I had to admit I hadn't—a confession that provoked from Lil a rather pitying gaze that seemed to say, Poor untraveled waif, you *have* led a sheltered life. Then Lil started asking me questions: where my family lived, why I had left home, who cooked in Richmond and whether my sister Caroline had a "young man" and how my brother Channing was getting on with his examinations. She seemed to be intensely interested in these details, as if she derived from accounts of other people's domestic arrangements the same sort of pleasure more educated people derived from novels, and I answered her queries as best I could. Mostly I wanted to look at her, to watch her talk and laugh and smile her fine smile. There was something so *fresh* about Lil! No doubt she had been a beautiful girl, and would be a beautiful old woman as well. And like Edward—like Pearlene, for that matter—she had such *extraordinary* eyes.

"I can't tell you, Brian, how grateful I am to you for taking my boy in," Lil was saying. "It'll be such a relief for him, living in Earl's Court— he'll be able to sleep a full hour later each morning and not have to make that long, long trip home! And it does a mother's heart good to know he'll be in such capable hands. Why, you're just the sort of friend a mother would hope her boy might find—a gentleman. I hope you'll always be my boy's friend; he needs a friend like you, I must say."

"It's a pleasure for me," I said. (Was I mad, or was there something ambiguous—almost suggestive—about Lil's use of the word "friend"?)

"And I hope you'll always feel you've a home here, Brian. Though goodness knows it ain't much of one, I've done my best to make it happy for my little ones. My sister Ellen always says, 'Lil, you're mad to have had so many kids,' but she's just jealous, having only one herself and a bad lot at that. 'Ellen,' I tell her, 'my only regret is I didn't have ten more.' And it's true." Tears misted her eyes. "I'm sorry," she said. "I *am* a good one at working myself up."

"Now, Mum," Edward said, "it's all right; don't let's get all weepy."

"You're right, Edward. I just think of your brother and I—" She dabbed her eyes with a napkin. "Sarah, why not bring in the cheese now, love?"

Obediently Sarah stood and went into the kitchen, returning a few moments later with the cheeses on a tray. One was a grainy orange cylinder dotted with mold, the second a slobbering wedge, the third a dented square pillow the color of sheets that have not been washed for some time.

Everyone regarded the cheese suspiciously.

"I'm afraid we haven't got any cream crackers," Edward said.

"That's all right. No need for cream crackers. We can just eat it as is." Nervously I sank my knife into the wedge and took an odorous sliver onto my plate.

The jangling of keys sounded, then the barking of the invisible dog.

"That'd be Lucy," Edward said. "Late as usual."

The dining room door opened, and a young girl walked in. She had bobbed blond hair and wore on her pretty face the alert expression of a young terrier.

"Sorry I'm late," she said. "God, what's that smell?"

"We're just having cheese," Edward said.

"Cheese!" Lucy said. "Since when?"

"Cheese Mr. Botsford brought," Edward said. "Remember? I told you I was bringing my friend Mr. Botsford to supper, and you promised not to be late?"

"Sorry, Edward, I got held up." She sat down in the empty seat next to mine. "Hello, I'm Lucy."

"Brian," I said. "How do you do?"

"Likewise, I'm sure. Excuse me, my feet are absolutely killing me." She took off her shoes and threw them casually toward the kitchen door.

"Lucy, please!" Lil impotently remarked.

"Is that a *livarot*?" Lucy asked, eyeing the cheese.

"Why, yes," I said. "You know *livarot*?"

Ignoring my question, she sliced into the wedge with her knife and took a taste. "It is *livarot*," she said. "And this one—is that a *vacherin*?"

"You certainly do know your cheeses."

"She's got a French friend," Sarah said, almost inaudibly.

"Shut up, you idiot," Lucy snapped.

"Say what?" Edward asked. "What did you say, Sarah?"

"She's got a French friend," Sarah said again, her eyes opening wider now, her mouth bursting into a smile.

"All right, and see if I keep any of your pathetic little secrets from now on," Lucy said. "See how you feel when I announce to the whole world you're in love with Mr. Snapes at the post office."

Sarah's face went white, her mouth opened.

"Sarah," Lil said. "Mr. Snapes! With the crossed eyes!"

"And he's got no hair!" Edward added. They both started laughing. Mortified, Sarah pushed out her chair and fled the room.

"Sarah," Edward called after her, "don't be so sensitive, we were only teasing! Poor dear, no one ever takes her seriously."

Distantly a door slammed. The unseen dog started up its barking. Headley gave a little shriek like a warning signal.

"You didn't say anything about a French friend," Edward remarked leeringly.

"Don't see why I should report every detail of my personal life to you," Lucy said, cutting once again into the *vacherin*. "Have you got a fag, Mr. Botsford?"

"Certainly." I took the cigarette case from my pocket.

"My, a cigarette case," Lil said. "You *are* a gentleman."

"Of sorts," I said, lighting Lucy's cigarette. Lil laughed, then started coughing. "Lucy, take that outside. You know I can't stomach smoke since this influenza."

"All right," Lucy said, standing and sauntering to the door. "Mr. Botsford, would you care to join me for a cigarette?"

"Yes—of course," I said. And followed her out. The door was made of splintery wood and opened onto a dreary garden in which a few ragged lettuce heads lounged among the weeds. Beyond the fence another garden, a mirror image of the Phelans', led up to a mirror house.

I lit my own cigarette. Lucy was leaning against the railing, gazing dreamily at the wretched expanse that passed for a view.

"So is my brother buggering you?" she asked quite casually.

For a split second I was taken aback.

"No," I answered. "As a matter of fact, I'm buggering him."

"How interesting," Lucy said. "I always assumed it would be the other way round. I suppose I don't know my brother as well as I thought I did."

"Of course it's quite possible we'll try it that way too."

"Men *are* wonderfully capable."

"Aren't we."

Lucy blew smoke rings. "I *do* have a French friend, you know. And my friend's going to take me to live in Paris, and I shall never ever ever return to bloody cold horrible dreary London as long as I live."

"How nice for you."

"You think I'm making it up, but I'm not. We're leaving next month, my friend and I, to live in this absolutely wonderful flat on the Boulevard Saint-Germain, and I shall spend all day reading in cafés and drinking gallons of very black French coffee."

Friend! How fond this family was of that maddening and elusive word!

"You remind me of a girl I used to know," I said. "She had several French friends as well. But wouldn't you know it, every one of them just happened to disappear with all her money the day before the two of them were supposed to elope."

"My friend would never do that. My friend has all the money in the world."

"I hope so, for your sake."

A scream issued from inside the house. I turned to see what had provoked it, but only caught a glimpse of Edward hastily backing off from frosted glass. "Oh, Headley!" Lucy said. "I hate, hate, hate, hate, hate children, and once I arrive in Paris I shall be glad never to see another one again."

"I don't know how to break this to you," I said, "but there *are* children in Paris."

"Not on the Boulevard Saint-Germain."

"Perhaps not." We were silent for a moment. "So I suppose you don't want children of your own?"

"Oh, no. They would only get in the way. I intend to spend my life painting pictures and writing books and performing in plays. That's the difference between us, you see: my brother wants to improve himself, but I want to change the world."

"You may change your *mind* when you're older. About children, I mean."

"Shall not."

The door swung open; Edward sauntered out like a peacock. "And what are you two gossiping about?" he asked.

"I was just asking Mr. Botsford if you buggered him, and he told me he buggered you," Lucy said. "Is that true, Edward? What does it feel like? Was it the first time? Was it bliss?"

Edward's brilliant tail feathers instantly fell. "Mother's got coffee and cake," he stammered. "If you want some, come into the dining room."

We followed him back inside. Conversation returned almost immediately to the apparently indefatigable topic of Cousin Beryl's teashop in Dorking. Sarah did not reemerge from internal exile.

Eventually I stood, expressed my heartfelt thanks to the family and said I must be going.

"But it's nearly eleven!" Lil said. "The trains'll stop running soon, and in any case it'll take you hours to get to Earl's Court. Why not stay here tonight and catch the train back in the morning with Edward?"

"Yes, why not?" Lucy echoed.

I hesitated. "Really, that's kind of you, but there can't possibly be room."

"You can share Edward's bed," Lil said.

"Somehow I'm sure he wouldn't mind that," Lucy said.

Edward glared at his sister, but said, "No, no, that would be fine."

My cheeks flushed, the idea so excited me—it would, after all, be the first time Edward and I had actually spent the night together. Still, I felt obliged to hesitate.

"Well, if you're sure it won't be too much trouble," I said, "then thank you."

"Now, if you boys would just set up the beds, I'll get Sarah to help calm the children," Lil said, then retreated to the kitchen, while Edward and I pushed the table to the corner and set up a pair of narrow beds that had been dismantled and stowed in a closet, as well as a rather rickety-looking crib. The children, who had already fallen asleep, were carried back in and carefully laid in their places. Pearlene made not a sound, while from his cot Headley wheezed asthmatically.

"Good night, lovey," Lil whispered, so as not to wake the children. "Very happy to have met you. Edward knows where the towels are." She gave me a wet kiss on the cheek, a kiss that lasted, I thought, a bit too long, then departed, closing the door behind her and leaving in her wake a pronounced milky smell.

And finally Edward and I were alone—alone, that is, except for the sleeping children. We stripped to our drawers—embarrassed, somehow, to be doing so—then climbed together into his narrow bed. It was cold; I felt Edward's nipples, hardened from the chill, rake against my chest. Reaching down, I pulled off his drawers; he did the same to mine, so that the two pairs bunched together at the foot of the bed. His erection silky and stone hard against my own.

For a long time we lay together, rubbing and shifting and trying to relax ourselves, even though our bodies were continuously pressing each other into states of arousal. Only our fear of waking the children kept us chaste. I don't know how we slept, and I certainly wasn't conscious of falling asleep, but at some point I opened my eyes, and heard a cock crowing, and saw that the room had filled with smoky dawn light. No time at all seemed to have passed.

Pearlene had woken. From her crib, she gazed at me, her gray eyes wide as planets, while across the room her brother exhaled ragged ribbons of breath. Edward had his arm draped over my chest. I could feel little bursts of warmth on my back as he breathed against me. I could hear the knock and whistle of the water pipes, the purr of the calico cat. And at that moment a happiness filled me that was pure and perfect and yet it was bled with despair—as if I had been handed a cup of ambrosial nectar to drink from and knew that once I finished drinking, the cup would be withdrawn forever, and nothing to come would ever taste as good.

Chapter Five

I t seems to me that some explanation is required now of my attitude toward homosexuality back in the fall of 1936.

To start with, at that time I'd gone to bed with probably three
dozen boys, all of them either German or English; never with a
woman. Nonetheless—and incredible though it may seem—I still
assumed that a day would come when I would fall in love with some
lovely, intelligent girl, whom I would marry and who would bear
me children. And what of my attraction to men? To tell the truth, I
didn't worry much about it. I pretended my homosexuality was a
function of my youth, that when I "grew up" it would fall away, like
baby teeth, to be replaced by something more mature and permanent. I, after all, was no pansy; the boy in Croydon who hanged
himself after his father caught him in makeup and garters, he was
a pansy, as was Oscar Wilde, my first-form Latin tutor, Channing's
friend Peter Lovesey's brother. Pansies farted differently, and went
to pubs where the barstools didn't have seats, and had very little in
common with my crowd, by which I meant Nigel and Horst and our

other homosexual friends, all of whom were aggressively, unreservedly masculine, reveled in things male, and held no truck with sissies and fairies, the overrefined Rupert Halliwells of the world. To the untrained eye nothing distinguished *us* from "normal" men—though I must confess that by 1936 the majority of my friends had stopped deluding themselves into believing their homosexuality was merely a phase. They claimed, rather, to have sworn off women, by choice. For them, homosexuality was an act of rebellion, a way of flouting the rigid mores of Edwardian England, but they were also fundamentally misogynists who would have much preferred living in a world devoid of things feminine, where men bred parthenogenically. Women, according to these friends, were the "class enemy" in a sexual revolution. Infuriated by our indifference to them (and to the natural order), they schemed to trap and convert us, thus foiling the challenge we presented to the invincible heterosexual bond.

Such thinking excited me—anything smacking of rebellion did—but it also frightened me. It seemed to me then that my friends' misogyny blinded them to the fact that heterosexual men, not women, had been up until now, and would probably always be, their most relentless enemies. My friends didn't like women, however, and therefore couldn't acknowledge that women might be truer comrades to us than the John Northrops whose approval we so desperately craved. So I refused to make the same choice they did, although, crucially, I still believed it *was* a choice.

There was another reason I didn't swear off women, the way Nigel and the others did, and that, put simply, was fear. What would it be like, I worried, growing middle-aged and old as a homosexual? Old queens, I knew, lingered in public lavatories, perpetually ignored or scorned or asked arrogantly for money. How desperately I didn't want to end up like them! And how much more pleasant a prospect it was to envision myself, at seventy, in a house in the country with a warm hearth, and all around me the voices of children and dogs.

As I said earlier, I was in those days an aficionado of the London underground and would sometimes spend hours poring over an underground map, enraptured by the elegant bright colors and odd station names. This map offers only the roughest simulacrum of reality. It shrinks the vast journey to the suburbs, it magnifies the clogged network of veins that underlies the City, it smooths out every unsightly curve and angle. The result is an illusion of order and coherence, discrete and colorful lines seamlessly linking one destination to another. Yet riding on the underground, one *believes* that map, one feels oneself traveling not under the panicked confusion of urban life but rather through the map itself, pulsing smoothly along a red line to the point of intersection with a brown line that in turn will take one to the point of intersection with a green line. Aboveground the world continues in its disorderly way; below-ground everything connects.

So it was with the girl I imagined I'd someday marry: she was the end of the line that was my hypothetical youth.

I remember, in the early thirties, watching with great interest the expansion of the Piccadilly Line out to Arnos Grove, Southgate, Cockfosters—remote suburban stations that for me were hypothetical, for who would ever have occasion to visit them? The same with adulthood: though I knew it existed, it remained as abstract a destination for me as the suburbs the underground was rapidly inventing.

Yet I did end up going there, before the year was out.

From Nigel:

I write from Paris, but will have left before you receive this. Fritz can stay no longer. As we feared, the Gestapo are onto him. Last night in a restaurant two men at the next table tried to approach us. Horst, who was with us, insisted they were just German businessmen, but Fritz says he recognizes agents when he sees them, and I am inclined to believe he knows from whence he speaks. The police are also watching him, so I thought it best we get out of France. We go to Utrecht tomorrow, presumably en route to Stockholm. No address in Utrecht as yet; we shall have to look for a hotel. I have got in touch with the solicitor I mentioned in my last letter, one S. Greene; he has assured me he can obtain for Fritz both a visa and passage to Ecuador, but his fee is £750! So far I have borrowed a hundred from Mother, on the basis of which Greene has begun the negotiations—my only fear is that it will be too late for Fritz. Poor Fritz—he is only twenty! For the first time he looks haggard and genuinely fearful. All last week he never went out, just sat in our room, staring at the door, dreading the knock. I try to keep him cheerful, but it's difficult—and God knows where I shall find the necessary £650!

Once we are settled in Utrecht I shall come over to London briefly to speak with Greene. I don't dare bring F. with me; Greene has checked—his name is already on the English list, no doubt thanks to his father. Will wire you new address in Utrecht once we have one; meantime you can send letters *poste restante*. Must rush to catch train. N.

Edward arrived in my flat the first Sunday in October. "Hello," he said cheerfully. "Hello," I said cheerfully.

We kissed. His cheeks were red and cold, and he was huffing slightly.

He set down his three battered, bursting cases and went to wash his hands. "Tea?" I asked. "Yes, thank you," he answered, then proceeded to unpack with amazing rapidity and concentration, hanging his suits in the wardrobe, stacking his socks and shirts in the drawers I'd emptied for him, propping his books on the shelf I'd designated as his. As he put each item away, he crossed it off a list he'd brought, just to make sure nothing had been lost or forgotten. (In that same bruised black notebook, I learned later, he kept logs that tracked the hours he slept each night, the clothes he purchased, his bowel movements, weight, even the amplitude and intensity of his orgasms, not to mention the books he read, every one of which was meticulously registered by title, author, publisher and both date and place of purchase or borrowing. Of course he kept his books alphabetized—such a contrast to my own, which were a chaotic jumble!)

His clothes securely put away, Edward next went into the bathroom and set out his tooth powder, brush, comb, razor and shaving mug. Lil had sent a fruitcake with him, and this we ate with tea, after which he got up, took the tea things to the kitchen and thoroughly rinsed them, as if to demonstrate his responsibility, the extent to which, having moved in, he now took a proprietary pride in the place.

I had fetched an old gramophone from Richmond a few days earlier. Now I put on a record. To my amazement, Edward took me in his arms, and we started dancing, two awkward, ungainly men, neither having the slightest idea how not to lead. It was dusk, sweater weather, the first gusty autumn drafts seeping in under the doorframes and window frames. Even so we stripped off our clothes, our bodies flushed with heat, our erections swatting each other, silky leg hairs softly slipping, while the voice on the gramophone bleated and Edward's voice matched it, note for note.

Edward kissed me. The record stopped. I bent onto my knees, I started kissing his chest, his stomach, going further down . . . What I wanted to do I knew was depraved. I should have been thinking, It will shock Edward, he'll run screaming away . . . but his indrawn breaths, as I kissed his body, encouraged me, and then there was his cock, hard and springy as a mushroom, the tip pearled with glistening dew, just inches from my lips. God knows I felt ashamed—really, I thought, I should go and hand myself over to the sexologists right away—and so I started making my way back up his stomach, toward his mouth, but he pushed my head down again, and said, "Do it," his voice raspy.

"Edward, do you know—"

"Do it." There was need and anger in his voice. He pulled my head toward him; the tip of his cock skidded my teeth. I took it in. His cock ballooned, Edward jolted and shuddered and came without warning, suddenly flooding my mouth with his semen, warm and slightly thickened and tasting a bit like a sauce of milk and flour that has had too much salt added to it. Then he pulled back, he dropped to his knees, his chest shivering, his eyes huge and hungry, and ran his fingers through my hair and, kissing me, sucked his own sperm from my mouth, licked the spillage off my face, so that I knew there was no limit, no distance we could not go with each other.

I ran into John Northrop one afternoon at the grocer's. To my amazement, he recognized me, though whether from school or from the meeting he'd presided over, I couldn't be sure.

Northrop, as I recalled, was from Shropshire, and physically he was a proper Shropshire lad, right out of Housman: big, blond, hale, though the muscle that braced his huge chest and abdomen was running to fat, no doubt the result of one too many beers. Irretrievably heterosexual, too. And yet there was something both sexy and reassuring about his bearishness. You felt you could trust him to do something absolutely filthy to you without causing permanent damage.

He suggested a pint, and I accepted. "I've been following your career since school," he told me, once we were settled at the pub with our beers. "Oh, I know, you're thinking, That Northrop, he's probably illiterate, but the fact is I do read a novel here and there, or a short story in a magazine. And God knows your friend Nigel Dent's become famous enough lately, not only with his piano-playing, but also those letters he writes for the newspaper. Where is he now?"

"Utrecht."

"Fellows like you, with a talent for the word, I don't have to tell you, you're just what the Brigade needs. Those pamphlets we're always publishing, for example. I always say they really could be something, if only those leftist hacks knew the first bloody thing about putting one word after another. I'm no exception. Oh, yes, stand me in front of a podium and I can whip a room into a frenzy. But ask me to write a pamphlet? I'm a wreck. I tear my hair. I throw the typewriter out the window." He laughed, shook his head, took a sip of his beer. "Now, if we had fellows like you and Dent writing, that could make a difference."

"I'd have to think about it," I said.

"Of course," Northrop said. "By the way, are you still planning on going over to Spain? Things are getting pretty hot over there, let me tell you. The stakes get higher every day." He lowered his voice. "I did notice you didn't sign up at the end, at that meeting. You left with that other fellow instead. Young fellow."

"Yes?"

"Friend of yours?"

"He shares my digs."

"What's his job?"

"Works at the tube station. He's a ticket taker."

Northrop smiled broadly. "You see? You're a Communist already! By asking that young fellow to share your rooms, you challenged bourgeois complacency." He raised his glass in a toast. "Balls to the class system, I say! Workers of the world, unite!"

"Cheers," I said.

Northrop coughed.

"So why didn't you sign up, in the end?" he asked next.

"I suppose I got cold feet," I admitted. "I mean, really, men like you and me—what do we know about battle? All the fighting we've ever done was on cricket fields."

"They say once a gun's in your hand you're a soldier," Northrop said.

"I suppose you'll be going over."

"Oh, yes. And I'll tell you why. Because someday, when all of this is over, among those of us who are lucky enough to survive, there's going to be a reckoning. We're going to look each other over and say, Where were you when the chips were down? What did you do? And when that day comes, I want to be able to answer, I fought. I risked my life and fought, and I'm proud to have done it, no matter if I'm legless or eyeless or like that fellow in the novel by Hemingway." His teeth gleamed. "Sometime in the next two years someone's going to change the world. Someone's got to. What's at stake is whether it's going to be us."

Grimly I stared into the dregs of my beer.

"Spain's our chance. I intend to be there even if I have to die there."

"And if we lose?"

He looked away.

"We won't lose," he said.

"How do you know?"

"We can't afford to," Northrop said. "*They* can afford to. They can always afford to."

I looked at the clock. "Gosh, Northrop," I said, "it's been wonderful chatting with you, but I've got to run. The market'll be closing in half an hour."

I thrust some coins at him. He didn't refuse them.

"Think about what I said," Northrop called to me as I headed out the door.

"Oh, I will," I said. "You can count on that."

"And mention it to Dent as well, if you see him! I'd love to have the chance to chat with him next time he's in London; did you see that piece of his in *The Gramophone*? Quite extraordinary."

"I'll pass on your regards," I muttered grimly, wondering why I hadn't realized all along it was Nigel he was really after.

Aunt Constance got me a job, tutoring a cretinous fat child with bulbous lips and just the faintest trace of a mustache. The child was stupid and had an obnoxious habit of parroting its parents' views—"It's the opinion of my father that only the lazy and useless are unemployed," etc. Still, that same father paid well, and as the child had as little interest in learning as I had in teaching, our afternoons together, while always dull, were never strenuous.

The child—I forget its name—left at four. Then, around five-thirty, Edward came home, bearing groceries. We drank our tea, he washed up, we made love. We almost always made love in the afternoon, Edward and I. Rarely at night, when shadows claimed the furniture, and a mysterious softness enveloped the bleach-cleaned atmosphere of the flat. Never in the morning, even though, as is usual with young men, we woke with erections. Either the sun was too merciless; or we had overslept and Edward was late for work; or we were hesitant to kiss until we'd brushed our teeth, at which point we found ourselves awake, our minds on other things.

No, the tea hour was our time: the hour, in England, for starched collars and crumpets. How thrilling and dirty it was to strip off at five in the afternoon, to stand naked and hard in the immodest light, while upstairs our lady neighbors spread their toast with Marmite and spoke of the Royal Family! I liked to fuck Edward against a particular wall where the sun came down in louvered columns. Bars of light bisected his rump while he leaned there, hands in the air, his mouth against the wallpaper. As cooking smells wandered in from neighboring flats, I'd take him like that, bugger him relentlessly, until he came in a wet patch against the wall. It was always dark by then. Half naked, I'd rush to the kitchen for a cloth to wipe up the stain. Then we'd clean ourselves off, turn on the wireless and cook supper.

It is curious to me, in retrospect, that though I fucked him routinely, Edward showed little interest in doing the same to me. I wondered about this. I never had been buggered, although once I'd experimented with a carrot from the larder—the sensation I recalled most vividly, from that attempt, was numbing cold. And certainly I hadn't experienced anything like the paroxysms of pleasure that claimed Edward, those afternoons against the wall— paroxysms so intense I couldn't help but wonder what I might be missing. A carrot, after all, is not a cock—at least, judging from the way Edward carried on.

One afternoon we were horsing around on the bed. I lifted my arse in the air and just stayed like that. At first Edward seemed taken aback. He did nothing. Then he wrestled me around onto my stomach.

Another time, when he came home from work, I arranged myself against the wall where I fucked him, in much the same position he usually assumed. "Doing stretching exercises?" he asked as he headed into the kitchen to pour himself some tea. "Stretching exercises, yes," I said. If indeed Edward understood what I was trying to tell him, it appeared he was not going to let on. Indeed, I couldn't help but wonder if, having discovered in me a dependable source of pleasure, he feared lest I should become so addicted to the joys of taking it up the bum that I'd lose my interest in "being the man" for him.

In those days I enjoyed an active social life. There seems to be so much to do when one is young! Dinner parties, salons, *soirées* . . . A wealthy dowager who enjoyed the company of clever homosexuals invited me regularly to her Thursday afternoons, and I usually went, if for nothing else then for the food, which was good and plentiful. Then there were those little suppers concocted by my Cambridge chums—clumsy, drunken evenings where one ate spaghetti off mismatched plates, standing up in the kitchen, and argued politics. And I had other friends, wealthy friends like Rupert, who hosted balls at country estates where the lawns glistened wetly and hundred-year-old carp swam in the ponds. These activities I relished—I think all writers do, trapped as we are most of the day in the solitary confinement of our brains. Indeed, until he came to live at my flat, it never occurred to me that Edward's arrival might curtail them. Now, however, with each invitation I received, I found myself obliged to make a choice: should I bring Edward along (and in so doing offer our relationship up for public scrutiny)? Should I continue going out alone (and risk hurting him)? Or should I simply stop going out altogether?

I confess that for the first few weeks I opted for the third, and easiest, alternative. It hardly felt like a sacrifice; my relationship with Edward was still so new that even the most alluring proposal paled in comparison to the prospect of a night alone with him. The bloom, however, must eventually fade from every love affair, even the most durable, and ours was no exception. I remember waking one morning feeling just the slightest tinge of boredom, like a child who balks at having to eat the same thing day after day for breakfast; a satiation, if you will; the tiniest, most tentative bud of wanderlust . . . Then I knew it would be only a matter of time before the invitation arrived that was just too tempting to pass up.

It came soon enough. One afternoon, out of the blue, Louise Haines, with whom I had been friends in Germany, rang up. I was delighted and surprised, not having seen or heard from her in almost two years.

"Darling, how *are* you?" she exclaimed in her signature raspy contralto. "I've just arrived a week ago. I've been dying to call you, of course, but you know how things are—so much to do. Yes, I'm here with friends from Paris, and there's been just all of London to show them, and then on Saturday, of course, I had to go to Ruislip to visit Mother—too trying! Can you ever forgive me? Now, you must meet us tonight at the Savoy. Seven-thirty. No, I shall *not* take no for an answer; we're going to the most *fabulous* party—it's in an opium den."

It was already four-thirty. I had spent the morning trying to write, the afternoon with my horrifying pupil; Edward wasn't due back for another two hours, and when he arrived, what would we do? Drink tea, read, have a fuck . . . It all seemed, suddenly, so boring, so cozy and domestic! (How angrily I thought those words, not knowing a day would come—this one—when cozy domesticity would be the thing I longed for most!)

I had a bath and shaved, wondering the whole time how I might best resolve the situation. What if I brought Edward along? I tried to envision the group that would result—me, Louise, her undoubtedly very sophisticated Paris friends, and Edward, in his ungainly, ugly, too-small suit. Surely he would throw the rhythm off, make everyone uncomfortable. They would look down on him, which would pain me—and Edward as well. On the other hand, he might regard the evening as a grand adventure; Louise might find him rustic, charming; her Parisian friends might flirt with him . . .

No, under either circumstance, it would never do.

I put on a suit and brilliantined my hair—I looked quite dapper, I thought—then headed down to the station to have a talk with Edward and catch the train.

"Well, what a surprise," he said when he saw me. "Are you going out somewhere, then?"

"I'm afraid so. Remember I told you about my friend Louise? Well, she's come into town on the spur of the moment. I'm to meet her at the Savoy, and then we're going to a party."

A whole spectrum of emotions passed over Edward's face as he realized I wouldn't be inviting him along: regret, anxiety, jealousy, anger, envy.

"All right, then," he said. "I was wondering why you were so dressed up."

"Sorry not to have given you any advance warning. Louise just called this afternoon."

"No, it's no problem. Anyway, I planned to go out myself tonight. Visit Mum and the girls, call in at the old pub."

He said this so hesitantly I knew it couldn't possibly be true. Nonetheless I smiled. "Well, that's lucky, isn't it? Do give them my love."

"Of course."

A strangled second passed.

"Well, I must be off, then. Goodbye."

"Goodbye."

We shook hands.

"Brian!" Edward called as I passed.

"What?"

"I may just stay the night in Upney, if I'm out too late. So don't be surprised if you come home and I'm not there."

"Whatever you think is best."

The train was at the platform. As I approached it, I turned and saw Edward staring after me. I got on. The doors shut.

I found and took a seat. I was trying to excite myself about the prospect of my reunion with Louise; really, there was no one in the world I had more fun with. And yet I also felt guilty about Edward, and frustrated to be feeling guilty. He and I were adults, after all, free to do as we pleased. If he'd chosen to go out by himself, *I* wouldn't have cared. (Or would I have? And of course he never did choose.) Really, I felt like saying, enough of this. You're not a child; you're a man.

Still, the image of his crestfallen face haunted me. And what would he have for supper? Fish and chips, grease and vinegar soaking the paper cone? I hoped he really would go to Upney, to the comforting arms of his mother. Anyway, it would never have done for him to come along. He would never have "fit in."

At seven-fifteen I arrived at the Savoy. It seems to me to be my fate always to be early and to have for friends, exclusively, the sort of people who always arrive late. Louise sailed in around ten past eight. She was swathed in black crepe and silk and doused with perfume, had smeared kohl on her eyes and bobbed her hair and spit-curled it over her forehead. In her florid, aromatic wake trailed two thin men wearing fedoras.

"Darling, I'm spectacularly sorry," Louise said. "I just couldn't make up my mind what kind of outfit one ought to wear to an opium den, and then the keys to the room went and hid behind the dresser, and then there was the most extraordinarily long wait for the lift— someone must have been ravishing the lift-boy. You look glorious. Are you in love?"

"As a matter of fact—"

"Let me introduce you before my friends think I'm frightfully rude. This is Alexei, and this is Joseph."

"How do you do?" Alexei said, extending toward me a pale, elongated hand on which were displayed many heavy rings. Everything about Alexei was attenuated—his fingers, swanlike neck, nose. As for Joseph, he was in fact not a man at all, but a raven-haired woman, quite beautiful, dressed in a man's topcoat.

"Enchanté," Joseph said.

"Joseph ne parle pas anglais," Louise said.

"Ah," I said, then apologized in my schoolboy French for speaking only schoolboy French.

While Alexei ordered drinks, Louise told me everything that had happened to her since we'd last seen each other: a complicated litany of *fêtes, déjeuners, soirées,* evenings à *l'opéra.* How different her life in Paris had been from Nigel's!

"And have you seen Nigel?" I asked anxiously.

"Yes, once. At Café des Flores. The boy was there too: what was his name—Wolfgang?"

"Fritz."

"Yes, Fritz. Good-looking but common as dirt. Boys like that are a dime a dozen. Then again, Nigel has never exactly been what I would call discriminating. And he does like a waif type. Personally, I prefer rich men."

"How did he seem?"

"Who—Nigel?" She paused, as if to consider. "Well, he was happy to see *me*, which took me by surprise. I mean, darling, you must admit, I've never been his favorite. To be honest, I always suspected he was a bit jealous of my friendship with you. This time, though, he positively *ran* to me. It was as if he were so starved for gossip and conversation that he would have welcomed his worst enemy. You'd think he'd been exiled on Elba for the last twenty years! And in a sense he has. They've barely left their wretched little pension in weeks. This business of getting Fritz emigrated has positively *consumed* him. Now, if it were up to me I'd advise him to drop the boy altogether; it's costing him far too much—yes, yes, I know, I'm one to talk. And Fritz *is* quite pretty, if you like that type of blond, girlish boy. Still, it broke my heart. The things we do." She batted her eyelashes melodramatically, then cast a glance toward Joseph; in the course of her monologue a heated discussion—close to argument—had begun between her and Alexei. "They do this all the time," Louise confided in a low voice. "Bicker, bicker, bicker. So tiresome." Then, coming even closer: "Darling, I have the most wonderful confession to make. Joseph is my *lover*. Yes! She *seduced* me! And it's the most astonishing thing—they say only a woman can know what to do to a woman, and it's true! I'm putty in her hands! I've never known such pleasures! The other night I screamed so loudly the couple in the next room called the hotel detective!" She laughed in delight, then turned to make sure Joseph wasn't catching her words. "Now, I know what you're thinking, and it's just not true, I haven't become a lesbian. I'm afraid I'll always adore men and their *charming* organs. This is merely a *coup de foudre* for me. Unfortunately I'm afraid it may be a bit more than that for Joseph. Such a pity. Still, I must say, when I think back to some of the men I've had, what clumsy oafs they were—well, a woman of such, shall we say, skills as Joseph *is* to be recommended. Everyone should try it at least once, darling." She sipped her anisette, or whatever she was pretending to imbibe. (Louise liked encouraging other people to drink better than drinking herself.) "Brian, dear, don't you ever think what a pity it is that you'll never have the experience of being made love to as a woman by a woman?"

"Don't you ever think what a pity it is that you'll never have the experience of being made love to as a man by a man?"

"Life *is* unjust," Louise said, then lifted her glass. "To homosexuality, then."

"What are you toasting?" Alexei asked.

"Homosexuality. *Homosexualité.*"

We all lifted our glasses and clinked.

"Darling," Louise said, "I've been talking up a storm, as usual. You must promise next time we meet to bind my mouth with tape. Now tell me about you."

"Well, I—"

"Louise, we ought to be going," Alexei said. "We're already late."

"Oh, dear, yes. I suppose. Is the car waiting?"

Indeed it was: a black cab ordered in advance. Crowded together in the back, we drove for about half an hour. At first I tried to keep track of where we were heading—it was generally east—then gave up. Do not be fooled by the underground map's orderly network of colored lines: real London is a maze that circles and doubles back and folds in on itself. They say that to become a cab driver here, you must first acquire something called "the knowledge," which, once obtained, puts in the hands of its possessor the capacity to locate without maps even the obscurest Hampstead mews. (Shall we call the angel on the driver's shoulder, then, the "mews" of cartography?)

Conversation during the ride was conducted almost exclusively in French.. "We are speaking about Paulette," Alexei said in English at one point. "Have you met Paulette? She is the Marquise of—I cannot remember. Joseph . . ." But then he got caught up in the discussion and forgot to finish his translation.

Eventually we disembarked in a chilly region of fishhouses. The air was thick with salt and silt, and there was a moldering wetness to

the ground, as if it had been raining for years. We walked down a
shrimp-smelling street, empty except for a drunken man urinating
in a corner and a dog with bare patches in its coat like an old carpet.
Somewhere not too far off, ragtime music played on an out-of-tune
piano.

Alexei led us to a swollen wooden door with a brass knocker,
which he lifted. Eyes appeared through the peephole, unintelligible
words were uttered, we were admitted to a room crowded with noise
and light. Everyone was smoking; curls of smoke spiraled through
the air like the ghosts of snakes. Having deposited our coats in the
rather overstuffed little vestuary, we moved on into a large hall. Even
though chandeliers had been hung and a burnished mahogany bar
constructed, it was hard not to notice the collapsed state of the ceiling, the dirty plank floors.

In one corner a jazz band rattled away. There seemed to be a thousand people in the room, men and women, women dressed as men,
men dressed as women, all drunk and hysteric.

"Darling, can you imagine?" Louise said. "In *London!* It's positively *Berlin*. Let's dance, shall we?"

She grabbed my hand, pulled me onto the floor and began dancing
with euphoric abandon, her silk dress rippling like water, her hands
mercurially passing one over the other, knee to knee, until their
movement blurred and she was a puppet on a string, a piston firing, a
perpetual-motion machine. There were so many dancers, the loud
clomping of feet on floorboards became audible, like a stampede of
horses. Then the song ended. Louise jumped up and jackknifed my
waist with her legs, surprising me with the weight of her body. I
clamped her hips and started whirling like a dervish, and she put her
arms out and her head back and opened her mouth and crowed. We
staggered; I nearly dropped her. I lost strength, and we collapsed in a
heap on the floor, laughing and breathless and exhausted.

Collecting ourselves, we staggered to the bar, where she poured a gin and tonic down my gullet. "Oh, darling, isn't this marvelous?" she shouted above the din. "Like the old days!" Gin dribbling onto my suit *was* like the old days, as was Louise herself not drinking anything; she didn't have to.

"So where's the opium?" I asked.

"We'll have to ask Alexei about that! Apparently it's in another room, and you need to know the password, which of course he does! Alexei's slept with positively *everyone!* Let's find him, shall we?"

Grabbing me by the hand, she once again pulled me onto the dance floor. With great speed we navigated the room's complex human geography.

After several tours Alexei was located at last, chatting up a bearded chap in a turtleneck. Near him, Joseph leaned against the wall, looking supremely bored. Louise whispered something in Alexei's ear, at which point he smiled, bade adieu to his companion and led the three of us back through the crowd to a narrow corridor, along which several young women stood flirting. We knocked at a door, which opened; eyes peered out. Alexei muttered something and was admitted, but the guard barred the rest of us from entry.

"They're with me," Alexei said.

The guard—a narrow-eyed Indian—regarded us with suspicion before reluctantly allowing us to pass. The door was shut, the jazz music instantly muffled. We were in a stuffy, dark, windowless room filled with dust and the fetid smell of unwashed bed linens. The room's shadowed occupants—about fifteen of them—sat or lay on old velvet horsehair sofas and armchairs, the sort that if you took your fist and pounded their much-abused cushions, huge clouds of dust and skin flakes and God knows what else would puff up and hang in the air for hours.

There was sitar music. No one spoke, no one seemed even to notice us. Then a woman beckoned Joseph, handed her a pipe, which she began to suck on . . . Joseph sucked, then offered the pipe to Alexei, who sucked and offered it to me. I took the pipe and inhaled— the flavor was sickly sweet, like Nanny's jelly. There was no immediately discernible effect. I passed the pipe on to Louise. "Oh, no, darling, thank you," she said. "You go ahead, I'll just watch." Even though her voice seemed shockingly loud in this languorous atmosphere, it failed to rouse the room's inhabitants.

Alexei and Joseph continued to puff at the opium; I could see their eyelids growing heavy. "Louise," I said, "I think I'll go back out to the party—you don't mind, do you?"

"Oh, not at all, darling," Louise said. "In fact I'll join you." She whispered something in French to Joseph, who whispered something back. A brief argument ensued; Joseph turned her back. Grabbing me firmly by the arm, Louise led me out of the lair. "She knows I won't tolerate possessiveness," she whispered as we strode past the narrow-eyed guard and out the door, into the world, where light and noise once again engulfed us. I was squinting as I tried to adjust to the light, Louise nattering on about Joseph. Then I heard a voice calling my name—"Brian? Is that you?" —but I was still squinting and couldn't tell where it was coming from. I turned, forced my eyes open. The blurry girl before me coalesced. I knew her, but I couldn't say where from.

"Brian, whatever on earth are you doing here?" the girl said, and laughed, and then I knew. It was Lucy Phelan.

"Lucy!" I said. Nothing more, I was so surprised to see her. She stood before me and laughed and laughed, holding her cigarette into the distance. She was arm in arm with a heavy woman in a smoking jacket. "I told you I had a French friend!" Lucy said. "This is Paulette—the Marquise de Beaumesnil."

The marquise was, like Joseph, monocled. She had a fat, cherubic face and a wide grin.

"*Enchanté,*" I said, shaking her hand, then introduced Louise.

"The marquise and I go back years," Louise said archly. "How are you, darling?"

"It seems I can go nowhere without encountering you," the marquise said in a low, heavily accented voice.

"Dear Marquise, I *am* ubiquitous. And who's your little friend?"

"This is the dear sweet Lucy of whom I have spoken so often. Lucy, I would like you to meet Louise Haines. We know each other from Paris."

"What a delight," Louise said, and held out her hand to Lucy, who took it. Smiles etched on their faces, they appraised each other. I could tell each recognized something in the other, some unnamable commonality neither could bear to look at for too long. Women of their ilk, I have noticed, invariably despise each other for mirroring back those aspects of themselves they would really rather not confront.

"She *is* charming," Louise said to the marquise, letting go of Lucy's hand. Then, turning to me: "And how do you know this ravishing creature?"

"He's buggering my brother," Lucy piped in.

"Really," Louise said, baring her teeth. "How delightful. Why haven't you told me about this, Brian?"

I was going to answer her—I really was—but I suppose at that moment the single puff I'd taken of the opium kicked in, for I was suddenly stuporous and couldn't seem to formulate a sentence. In addition, I had become captivated by the charcoal-colored paisley swirls in the black fabric of Louise's dress and felt determined to follow them to their logical conclusions.

"Perhaps it's time for another drink," Louise said. "Will you excuse us?"

"Of course."

"Goodbye, Brian!" Lucy called. "Be sure to tell Edward you saw me!"

Louise steered me toward the bar. "Darling, I've been remiss. I haven't given you the slightest opportunity to fill me in on all your new friends."

"Oh, I hardly know Lucy," I said.

"And her brother?"

"He lives with me."

"That is news," Louise said, then ordered me another gin and tonic.

I told her briefly about Edward, then switched to what seemed to me at the moment the much more fascinating topic of the Piccadilly Line extension. "Forgive me for saying so," Louise interrupted at one point, "but your life does sound frightfully dull. You must get terribly envious of the characters in your novel—they seem to have so much more fun than you do! Anyway, no doubt as soon as you're finished with this one you'll begin writing a book about *me* and all *my* adventures, which will be an enormous success and earn you *pots* of money while I languish in some *gutter*!" She threw back her head and laughed. In fact the idea of writing a novel about her hadn't crossed my mind until that moment, but now that she suggested it, it seemed a rather good one.

The rest of the night is a blur. I have no idea how I got home—somehow, however, I must have, for at two o'clock the next afternoon I awoke in my own bed, my head pounding, convinced that I had committed sins of the flesh with someone other than Edward. (Who it was I could not for the life of me recall.) No one else was home, or in the bed with me, which was a good sign. I had a distant recollection of riding the underground, riding and riding, arriving at some remote destination, and then having to get on another train and ride back. What this destination was, however—Edgware? Cockfosters?—I couldn't have said.

I bathed, had a cup of strong tea and committed to paper the events of my extraordinary evening. Soon Edward would be home. How I longed to see him! At that moment no place on earth could have seemed more welcoming to me than this old-ladyish bedsitter, no prospect more appealing than to rest for hours in the arms of my big, bighearted boy—that is, assuming he wasn't angry. From that day on, I resolved, I would turn down all invitations; I would stay each night at home, with him.

He arrived just after five, his face a cipher.

"Edward," I said, "I'm sorry about last night. I—"

He shook his head. "It doesn't matter. Listen, I have something to tell you."

We sat down.

"You should know that after you left me at the station, I didn't go home to Upney at all."

"No?"

"No. I was in a funk, and jealous that you weren't taking me along to meet your friend—yes, I admit it—and was just going to go home and go to bed, when who should call from the train platform but that fellow from the meeting."

"Which fellow?"

"John Northrop! Of course it was quite a surprise that someone so important as him should remember me, but he did. He even knew I was living with you—what do you think of that? He asked me if I'd like to have a drink with him at the pub across from the station, and I figured, well, why not—I wasn't planning anything in particular—so I said yes, thank you, I would very much. He ordered the drinks and then he started talking. He's quite a speaker, I can tell you.

Mesmerizing, that's the word for it; I only wish I could talk half as good as he does. We drank down our pints and he ordered more just like that and went on telling me about the Republican struggle in Spain and the brave comrades giving up their lives—it sent chills up my spine, let me tell you, especially when he started on the terrible things the Fascists are up to, torturing women and the like. He'll be going over to Spain himself—he's going to be a leader of the International Brigade—and he wondered if I'd thought of joining up. Me? I said. Yes, you, he said. Somehow I get the feeling you might make a very fine soldier. That's very flattering, I said, but what makes you think so? Intuition, he said, and hit his head with his little finger. I've got a good eye for soldiers. Then he asked me if I'm a Communist. I said I'm not sure. He said given my background I must be quite aware of how the bourgeois class enemy exploits the workers. So I started telling him about Frank and all his talk of the workers of the world organizing and his getting killed in that factory accident. I don't remember exactly what happened after that—we had a couple more pints—but soon enough he was trying to convince me to join the Party and get you to join as well: how do you like that? He says given as you're going to be a well-known writer, no doubt they could certainly benefit by having someone of your capacities working with them. Your friend Nigel Dent too. He seemed especially keen on getting him to join. I told him I'll think about it for myself, but as for you, he'll have to speak to you personally, you've got your own opinions, and he says, I know, I know, and laughs. Then I started feeling a bit sick in the head from the beer and told him it was probably a good idea that I get home now and thank you very much. We shook hands and I came back and fell into bed, and when I woke up you still weren't home and I felt a bit cross with you—more than a bit! I was furious! And then, when I got to work, there was a package waiting for me—look at this, Brian, he gave me a book!"

He pulled from his satchel a copy of *The Communist Manifesto*. "I started reading it in my lunch hour. It's difficult, I can only read about a page every three minutes, which is slow for me, usually I can read a page in one and three-quarter minutes. But I'm getting the gist of it. And he inscribed it! Listen to this: 'To Edward Phelan, comrade in arms. With warmest wishes, John Northrop.' What do you think of that?"

"Edward, listen," I said. "I'm terribly sorry about last night; it *was* callous of me. I just didn't think you'd get along with Louise and her friends. They're very—"

"I know, I know, you were embarrassed because I'm the wrong class."

I flustered. "Now, Edward, it's nothing like that—"

"It's all right if that's what you think," Edward said airily.

"Edward, you must believe me, this has nothing to do with class." (But even as I spoke these words I doubted them.) "It's just that there are certain parts of my life—everyone's life, really—that don't necessarily mix well with other parts."

He looked blank.

"I mean, I love Nanny, but I wouldn't have her to a dinner party."

"Oh, so now I'm in a class with your nanny, is that what you're saying? The beloved old retainer in the room at the end of the house?"

"No, not at all—oh, let's not talk about it anymore, shall we? I have the most extraordinary news." And I told him about Joseph, the opium den, my encounter with his sister. This raised his eyebrows. "So Lucy's French friend *does* exist," he said. "Who is he?"

"It's not a he," I said. "It's a she. A marquise, in fact."

Edward looked amazed. "A lady?"

"I suppose you could call her that, yes."

"So do you suppose—" He burst into a smile and shook his head. "Lucy Phelan, you are full of surprises."

Another postcard came from Nigel. He and Fritz had been hounded out of Utrecht and were now in Stockholm. Nigel would arrive in London Thursday week.

Chapter Six

As if things were not confusing enough, the world seemed to have joined into a conspiracy to mirror back all my fears. One evening, for instance, I returned to the flat after a visit to some Charing Cross Road bookshops and found Edward drinking tea with John Northrop. Even though Northrop could not have been more cordial, there was also no way he could not have noticed there was only the one big bed. After he left I suggested to Edward that perhaps the next time he was thinking of having someone up to the flat, he consult me first. We quarreled. "I live here too," Edward said, quite rightly. "I'd just as soon move back to Upney if you're going to start telling me what to do."

"The last thing I want is to impinge upon your liberty," I said. "But, Edward, not everyone is going to be so understanding about the nature of our relationship as—"

"So you're ashamed to share the flat with me, is that what you're saying?"

"Nothing of the sort. I just think one has to be careful. Look, perhaps the simplest solution is to put in a second bed."

"Ah, so now you're ashamed that we sleep in one bed. I'll have you know my brother Frank and I slept in one bed for fifteen years, and no one said a word about it."

"We're not in Upney now."

"Oh, yes, I forgot. We're in Belgravia."

The next day Emma Leland's fiancé, Tim Sprigg, rang up and asked if I might like to have lunch with him. This surprised me, given that I'd met Sprigg only once. All I could guess was that Northrop had gotten to Emma, and Emma to Sprigg, for he began the lunch by confessing in a low voice that for years he himself had been a slave to "homosexual tendencies," until he met Emma and discovered in "the landscape of woman" a sense of "peace" and "well-being" his many trysts with boys had never given him. He now saw his homo-sexual years for what they were, he said: a wasted epoch of "imma-ture experimentation" that led only to "emptiness," "degradation" and, in one instance, a diagnosis of gonorrhea. "The love of a woman is enriching, nourishing," he said. "With men there is never love, only sex." And it was no coincidence that his conversion to hetero-sexuality had coincided with his conversion to Communism. "Just take a look at Oscar Wilde, or Radclyffe Hall—it's the ultimate expres-sion of a corrupt bourgeois mentality." I left the lunch more confused than ever, for though I found Sprigg's shopworn denunciations as spurious as most of the arguments the Communists use, his procla-mations of newfound happiness with Emma—not to mention vivid accounts of homosexual misery—reiterated my own fears too exactly for me to be able to ignore them.

The sad truth was I hardly knew myself. And if the way I'd always got to know other people was by writing about them, then logically, to know myself, I had to turn the lens upon myself, I had to view my own life from the same detached perspective from which I might view the lives of Nigel or Louise or Aunt Constance, only this time I would be the figure at the other end of the telescope. So: adjust the focus, refine the edge. What did I see? A young man of twenty-two, with a head of wiry dark hair. Is he handsome? Well, I couldn't say—he's not my type. Even so, I imagine he probably has his admirers. If only he could straighten up, really, he'd look much better! And a haircut would do him good.

"The other day," I wrote in my journal, "I was standing next to an old man at a public lavatory, an old codger, who watched while I pissed, all the while wanking furiously his pathetic limp willie in the hope of getting his nut off before the next bobby wandered in to arrest someone. His willie, his oldest and dearest friend, had not aged with the rest of his body, I noticed. Willie still looked exactly the way he looked when the old man was a young man and could do it five times a day without effort. And yet Willie was tired. He'd never had the chance to live out his biological destiny. Instead the million billion microscopic homunculi that churned inside his sagging balls had been wasted, they had taken their turn climbing into the giant slingshot and been ejected and found themselves landing—splat!—only on hairy stomachs and stubbly faces and dirty bed sheets, where they suffocated in seconds. These million miniature men must swim up-river to where the egg—that winking, blond, fur-bedecked Jean Harlow of an egg—beckons them; it is what they were born to do. But the old man never gave them a chance. Instead he just kept coming into urinals (disgusting), or his handkerchief (a tragic waste), or that convulsing tunnel that looks familiar but something is not quite right about it and at the end, instead of that sexy egg, is a piece of shit."

I did not mince my words, I see now. My disgust was visceral, vivid. Yet according to the journal it didn't stop me from fucking Edward against the wall the next afternoon.

*   *   *

That week Aunt Constance rang. Philippa Archibald was back in London.

It was mid-November. We met at the Hotel Lancaster, where Aunt Constance, as threatened, had booked a private dining room. Of course I made sure, for once, to arrive as late as possible.

"There you are!" Aunt Constance scolded as the prehistoric porter announced me. "We had nearly given up!" She stood, bustled over and gave me a "naughty boy" pat on the cheek, but the relief in her voice was audible.

"I'm sorry, Aunt Constance," I said. "Tube trouble, you know."

"Oh, you and your tubes! I will never for the life of me understand this childish passion of yours! To *prefer* riding dirty trains through smelly tunnels when you could just as easily take a taxi . . ."

"Taxis can be expensive, Aunt Constance."

"The bus, then! Ah, but I'm being rude. Now let me introduce you. Edith, may I present my nephew Brian Botsford. Brian, this is my dear friend Edith Archibald."

"How *do* you do," Edith Archibald exclaimed breathily, standing from the table and shaking my hand in what seemed to me an exces-sively energetic way. She was about sixty, with black eyes like raisins and the narrowest waist I had ever seen.

"And may *I* introduce my niece, Philippa? Philippa, Mr. Botsford."

"Hello," Philippa said, reaching out her hand. "I've heard a lot about you." Her half-crooked smile spoke volumes. It seemed to say, I don't like this any more than you do, but what can we do? We might as well make the best of a bad situation.

"How do you do?" I said, and took my seat. Perhaps it was not going to be such a dreadful evening after all.

A hostess came in with menus, the perusal of which provoked a heated discussion between our two elder stateswomen as to the extent to which large amounts of runner beans did or did not benefit the digestive system. I looked around. We were sitting at a square table in a small dark box of a room. Heavy velvet curtains enshrouded the windows. Across from me—directly over Aunt Constance's head, in fact—a huge landscape painting in a peeling gilt frame had been hung at a precarious angle. It was so dirty that in the dim light you could barely make out its subject: it seemed nothing more than a coffee-colored morass, from which, intermittently, a pair of human or animal eyes gleamed out.

"Brian," Aunt Constance said, "Philippa was at school with your sister Caroline."

"So I gather."

"How is Caroline?" Philippa asked.

"Oh, she keeps busy. Fixing everything up at the old house, you know. There's a lot of work since our parents died."

"I didn't realize they'd died," Philippa said. "I'm sorry."

"And I gather you two even met once," Aunt Constance went on. "When you were children."

"Did we?" Philippa asked. "To be honest, I can't recall. Can you?" She smiled at me quizzically.

"I'm afraid I can't," I said. "Sorry."

"Oh, it's perfectly all right."

Our aunts were now staring at us with such looks of concentrated panic that we both burst out laughing. This broke the ice, as it were. They laughed too. For the first time that evening I actually looked at Philippa. She was really very pretty, I thought: gray-eyed and fine-boned, with hair dyed the rich, burnished color of terra-cotta.

The soup arrived. Philippa was speaking with some animation about her job in book publishing, as all the while our aunts nodded and beamed at each other. How different Philippa was turning out to be from what I'd imagined! Aunt Constance had led me to expect a harelipped saint, one of those creatures hideous of face but bountiful of soul who spend their spare time doing things like taking care of maimed sparrows. Instead the real Philippa was knowing and self-assured and no doubt had men lining up outside her door. Even the harelip scar—a pale-red scallop on her upper lip—she carried with surprising panache.

We had much in common; among other things, Philippa was very knowledgeable about Spain, having spent quite a bit of time as a child in the company of a bachelor uncle who lived in Gibraltar. Now she kept actively abreast of events there, so we spoke about the PSOE and the Falangists, the threat of Franco and the Republican hope, our mutual disillusionment with the Party and our shared conviction that nonetheless it offered the greatest prospect of freedom for the greatest number. Aunt Constance interrupted periodically to say she found politics a bore, while Aunt Edith kept trying to finish an interminable anecdote about a bad oyster she'd eaten while on holiday in Santander. Every now and then they smiled or winked at each other conspiratorially, as if in congratulations for a job well done.

We had coffee in the lounge. Here a host of unhappy women besieged our chaperones in quest of Aunt Constance's autograph, giving Philippa and me a brief moment of privacy. I asked her where she lived. "Just off Sloane Square," she said. "I've got a little bed-sitter. And you?"

"Earl's Court." I neglected to mention Edward.

Philippa leaned confidingly over her coffee cup. "I must tell you, I'd been *dreading* this evening."

"So had I," I admitted.

"I tried and tried to put it off—"

"Me too!"

"I mean, my aunt's not a bad sort—goodness knows she always has the best intentions—but if you could see the men she'd set me up with before! Well! You'd certainly understand my hesitation."

"I must say Aunt Constance described you . . . rather differently than you are. I believe the adjective that kept coming up was 'responsible.' "

"Yes, yes, that is what they would all like me to be."

"And you're not?"

"Oh, hardly."

"Really!"

She cast me a rakish glance, then said, "Pleasant surprise, this evening, isn't it?"

"Yes," I said, smiling shyly. "Very pleasant."

"Now, that wasn't so bad, was it?" Aunt Constance asked as she buttoned up my collar. "All the fuss and bother you put up! And didn't I tell you you'd have a lovely time? Next time you should really trust your aunt Constance, dear. She does have your best interests at heart."

She tucked something into my pocket and sent me off into the night. Philippa had already left by taxi. Really, I was thinking as I rode the tube back, this *had* been pleasant. Philippa, after all, was quite pretty. And intelligent. I thought I'd quite like to see her again, though how much this feeling was the result of the fears that had recently been plaguing me, and how much a reaction to Philippa herself, I wasn't prepared to guess. Still, it did seem to me that one should follow instinctive attractions to their logical conclusions, especially if one was only twenty-two. One should hardly be expected to have the course of one's life predetermined when in fact it had barely begun.

Remembering, suddenly, Aunt Constance, I reached into my breast pocket and found a twenty-pound note stuffed there, folded in eighths.

*　　*　　*

When I got home that evening Edward kissed me brightly. He had gone out drinking with Northrop again and was full of gossip and chatter. I felt tired and said I thought I would go to bed early, but Edward said he was too wound up to sleep and that he would instead read his *Communist Manifesto* for a while. This was a relief to me, as I needed some time to sort out my reaction to meeting Philippa. Was I really attracted to her? I was wondering. Or was she just the first woman to come along since it had entered my head to start looking at—noticing—women?

After a while Edward got into bed. As always, he put his arms around me, kissed my neck, rubbed against me so that I could feel his erection. How annoying, I thought. He's distracting me from the very interesting train of thought on which I've embarked. I tried to push him off—"I've got a headache!" I shouted in a shrill Cockney falsetto—but he persisted, and when he started fumbling inside my pajamas, I lost my resistance. At first I thought we would just have a wank, but Edward wanted me to bugger him. "Please, Brian," he said. "I need it tonight." I said no, I was too tired. "Please?" he said again. "No," I said, then felt his fingers wrap around my cock and knew I was lost.

After that I fucked him ferociously—a rare nighttime fuck that culminated in my coming up his arse with unusual, growling abandon, at which point I worried: how might Philippa react if she found out what Edward and I did together? Might someone tell her?

We washed and got back in bed. Edward had already fallen asleep: his breath went in and out, sweet as a baby's. How content—how *easy*—he seemed to be with himself. He did not question, as I did. I suppose it was a matter of class.

To be honest, I envied his unproblematic capacity to accept.

And if he'd known what was going through my head—well, then, he wouldn't have slept half so peacefully, now would he?

*   *   *

Nigel arrived the next morning. He was to be in London only a few days, he told me, and would be occupied almost the entire time trying to raise the money for Fritz's emigration. No visits to his publishers or his old piano teacher? "Goodness no, I haven't the time for that! But listen, why not come by Mother's house for tea on Monday. Would that be all right?" I said that of course it would be.

I got to St. John's Wood around four-thirty. It was a sunny day of a type rare in England in winter; I smarted as I recalled Rupert Halliwell's fatal umbrella. Nigel's mother let me in—she wore on her face the look of a woman who has sold herself into prostitution for love of a worthless rake. "I must apologize for Nigel not being here yet," she said, leading me into the drawing room. "He had an appointment with that Mr. Greene, the solicitor who is supposedly going to help his friend emigrate to South America. Would you like some tea in the meanwhile? And I've put out some of Nigel's new music magazines for you to look at."

I thanked her and told her that would be lovely, then sat down to peruse the magazines. Mrs. Dent had arranged them in the shape of a fan.

Nigel blew in a few minutes later, breathless and cursing the underground. "For no good reason the train stopped—just *stopped*—between Oxford Circus and Regent's Park, and for a full quarter of an hour we sat there, we didn't move at all. So frustrating! Hello, Brian."

"Hello, Nigel."

We embraced. He had gained a bit of weight and needed a haircut; otherwise he looked fine.

Mrs. Dent brought in tea, then pattered off to parts unknown.

"How're things going with your book?" I asked.

"Supposed to have it finished next month. I won't, of course."

"And the piano?"

"Haven't been in one place long enough to practice. Frau Lemper is ready to disown me. Milk?"

"You know I take milk, Nigel."

"Yes, of course. Sorry. And no sugar, right?"

"Right."

"So tell me what's up. How're you earning your daily wage these days?"

I started explaining to him the details of my tutoring job. "Um," he said. And, "Ah." He kept raking his hand through his hair, looking over his shoulder as if he were expecting a messenger to arrive at any moment. Even the saga of Lady Abernathy—even the opium den— failed to capture his attention.

"By the way," I said, "John Northrop's been over quite a bit lately. Remember him? I think he's quite keen to get you into the Party."

"He thinks I'll bring them respectability," Nigel said. "Well, darling, my price is higher than he can afford. You can tell him *art* is my ideology and that I have no intention of writing for the Party."

"Right. Well, if that's how you feel about it."

Once again he glanced over his shoulder expectantly.

"Nigel," I said, "whatever's bothering you, you're not hiding it very well."

"I'm not."

"No, you're not."

He stared into his cup. "It's just a bit difficult for me, being away from Fritz," he said finally. "Of course I know he's perfectly safe— he's with Horst's brother and sister-in-law in Stockholm, and they're sure to take good care of him. Still, the poor boy's awfully frightened, and I don't blame him. There are terrible rumors coming out of Berlin. Remember old Dr. Hirschfeld, who ran that sexological institute? They say he's been shot. They say homosexuals are being rounded up and herded into concentration camps. His father won't accept what he is. Fritz thinks that if he can't reform him, his father will just throw him to the dogs. And this solicitor, this Greene—I know he comes highly recommended, but I just don't trust him. He's an old Jew and he works out of a grimy little office in Soho, and every time I ring him up he gets cross with me and tells me everything's in order, the papers should arrive any day, and please not to bother him anymore. But he's been saying that for weeks, and they haven't arrived! And on top of that I've still got to raise five hundred quid to pay the bastard off!" He lit a cigarette. "All that keeps me going—well, I imagine us in Ecuador. Far away from all this bloodletting. God willing, in a month we'll be there, and Fritz will finally be safe."

For several minutes we were silent, Nigel blowing out smoke.

"And what about Spain?" I said at last. "Everyone seems to be going. Even Emma Leland said she planned to motor down in her little roadster!"

This elicited, from Nigel, only a halfhearted laugh. "I suppose I've been so preoccupied with Germany I've missed Spain. By the way, have I shown you a picture of Fritz?"

"No."

For the first time all afternoon a look of something like hope flushed Nigel's face. "Oh, I have one right here. It's not really a very good likeness, but you'll have some idea."

He took from his pocket a blurry snapshot in which a boy with short-cropped blond hair and babyish cheeks, dressed in traditional Bavarian *lederhosen,* stood proudly on some sort of rock. "What a lovely summer that was!" Nigel said. "So much sunshine; everything seemed possible." A smile came over his face that reminded me of Nanny when she recalled the brief, blissful honeymoon she and her husband had had at Brighton before he went off and was killed by a tractor.

Love makes us young, but the world makes us old.

The oddest news came from Upney! Edward went to visit his family and when he came back announced that his sister Sarah no longer harbored amorous feelings toward Mr. Snapes at the post office; instead she had transferred her affections to me! "It's true," Edward said. "Lucy found her diary. She adores you and lives for your next visit, though of course she won't dare ask when that might be; she's terribly afraid of giving herself away, poor thing. So Lucy and I were thinking, really, you ought to come to supper another time. Sarah's a good girl, she really is—just simple—and you can't imagine what a thrill it would give her. Oh, don't worry, she won't expect anything of you. She'll just want to gaze at your manly profile . . . It'll make her month, that's what it'll do. Hell, it'll probably make her year!"

The next afternoon Philippa Archibald rang, inviting me to dinner at her flat the following Saturday.

Chapter Seven

A ll that week I debated whether to tell Edward the truth—that I had received a dinner invitation and was once again, in spite of my promises to the contrary, going off and leaving him alone. And in the end I lied. I said Nanny was sick and that I felt obliged to visit her in Richmond. He said he understood and insisted fervently that I bring Nanny his best wishes for a swift recovery, even though Nanny didn't know him from Adam, and I promised to do so, all the while wondering what other, more criminal lies this still innocent one might presage.

In the bathroom I shaved and washed. "Your good suit! You do love your old nanny," Edward said—heartbreakingly, in total innocence. "What other boy would get dolled up for an old woman that used to wipe his backside?"

"I like her to know she's appreciated," I said.

He saw me to the door. "What will you do with yourself tonight?" I asked.

"Oh, I don't know. Read. Have a wank with Northrop."

I looked at him.

"Just kidding," he said.

His smile, as he saw me off, threatened to do me in.

As usual, I overestimated how long it would take me to get to my destination by tube, and arrived at Philippa's building a full half hour early. So I wandered about the King's Road, looking in shop windows, until it seemed a decent hour to ring her bell.

"Come in," she said, kissing me jovially on the cheek. "I've just finished washing my hair."

"Am I early?"

"No, no, I'm late. Come on."

A trail of puddles led from where she stood to the open bathroom door. Soapy, slightly greenish water was still rocking in the tub.

"Talk to me while I dry off," Philippa said casually. She was wearing a Japanese kimono tied around the waist with a blood-red sash. Splotches of wet outlined her slightly protuberant stomach, her breasts and nipples, the curves of her upper thighs. A lingering odor of violets—her soap no doubt—overpowered the little flat, as did the steam that was wafting out of the bathroom. Harems, I thought, must have smelled like this.

I looked around myself. The flat was just one room, slightly smaller than mine, and so crammed with bibelots and odd, mismatched pieces of furniture one could barely walk: brightly colored pillows, creaking bookshelves, an Oriental rug dusted with cat hair (though no cats were to be seen), an old horsehair sofa, taken, I would later learn, from the library of her parents' country house.

Searching for a remark, I glanced toward the bathroom door and saw, to my amazement, that Philippa had shed her kimono and now stood naked, toweling herself. She had ample pubic hair, a darker color than the hair on her head.

"My," I said, "you certainly do have a lot of books. Are they as chaotic as mine, or do you keep them in some sort of order?"

"Oh, they're very carefully ordered, but according to a system so peculiar and personal that only I could possibly ever locate anything. I'd make a rather terrible librarian, I'm afraid; you see, I'd be inclined to put *The Mill on the Floss* next to *Bleak House* because I read them both in the summer of 1927 on Spanish trains."

"It seems to me as sensible a method for organizing a library as any."

"Do you think so?" She pulled a blue frock patterned with tiny roses over her head. "Button me up, will you?" I did. "I've only prepared the simplest supper, a sort of vegetably stewy messy thing, plus cheese and bread. I'm afraid I'm not much of a cook, but I'm told my seasonings are unusual."

"Anything would be preferable to the Hotel Lancaster."

"Wasn't that food appallingly bland? When I got home I had to cook myself a curry."

"Did you? I would have liked to have done, but we—I didn't have anything in the house."

We sat down to table. The fact that we had met through our well-meaning aunts was lending to the evening a thrilling quality of forbiddenness that under normal circumstances it would never have had. That, plus the fact that Philippa, as far as I knew, had no idea I was homosexual, a lack of knowledge on her part I found liberating, until Edward's happy face appeared in the looking glass across the room, accusing me.

Philippa really had had the most extraordinary life. For example, her father was seventy when he married her mother, who was twenty-two. He was a widower at the time, with grandchildren—some of them older than his new wife. He died only a few months after Philippa was born, at which point her mother was married again, this time to a tea merchant somewhat closer to her own age. They had three more children. Philippa never knew her older siblings very well—"they were more like distant aunts and uncles"— while the younger ones, all girls, lived in a world of secret languages and doll intrigues from which Philippa, home on holiday, found herself necessarily excluded. Only during the summers she spent with Uncle Teddy in Gibraltar did she feel welcomed. Uncle Teddy, she said, was a single man of means, independent, intelligent, reckless. He took Philippa to all kinds of unsavory places—gambling houses and brothels—as well as to the palaces of dukes, one of whom tried to feel her breasts.

They spent weeks exploring the wild back regions of Spain, and toured the Balearic Islands; Philippa said she would never forget Minorca, with its miles of crisscrossed stone walls that went on forever and had no apparent purpose and had been there since the beginning of time. Nor would she forget the primitive *pueblos* of Aragon, the markets where women stood on the streets selling clay pots big enough for a child to sleep in. They had stayed at a *fonda* in Beceite, the proprietress of which, Tia Cinta, had a gangrenous leg. Tia Cinta took a fancy to them. "Send me a postcard from England," she said. "Of course," Philippa said in her schoolgirl Spanish. "To whom should it be addressed?" "Just send it to Tia Cinta, Beceite," the old woman said. "But aren't there other Tia Cintas in Beceite?" "Yes, three others, but none of them ever gets mail!"

Philippa's tone, as she told these stories, was measured, even. Not a hint of rancor or resentment; indeed, she seemed to go to great lengths to avoid placing blame—her mother, she said, really *had* tried her hardest not to favor her new little girls, her stepfather treated her as if she were his own daughter, even her three sisters made every effort they could to include her. It was not their fault that the intimate world of the nursery left no place for her; it was nobody's fault; she harbored no bitterness. And yet I could detect in her voice, if not bitterness, then a faint cynicism, even a fatalism. For instance, when we spoke of Spain, she shook her head and smiled slightly. "Of course," she said, "there is no hope."

"No hope?"

She stared into her wineglass. "I'm afraid not. You see, the Republicans are fatally divided. They pretend to present a united front, but behind the battlements the Anarchists are plotting against the Communists and the Communists are plotting against the Anarchists, and in the middle are so many foreigners drawn by idealism, who somehow imagine that if they can liberate Spain, they can save Europe."

She rotated the wineglass and coolly appraised the resulting red waves.

"But the enemy is known," I interjected. "And if the enemy is known, and the goal—that enemy's defeat—is clear, there's no reason that people with philosophical differences can't fight alongside one another. No one could possibly stomach the Fascist barbarities—"

"There are Republican barbarities as well. Perhaps not as many, but still—"

"I think the reports of priests being murdered are exaggerated."

"I hope you're right," Philippa said, "and doubt it."

Later, on the horsehair sofa, she asked about my life. So I described for her the house in Richmond, the deaths of my parents, my unhappiness at Cambridge and first encounters with Nigel. I did not mention my homosexuality, did not mention Edward or Digby Grafton or any lovers, for that matter (though I confess I dwelt on my friendship with Louise in a way that suggested it was more than a friendship). What a liar I was becoming! I had lied to Edward, and now I was lying to Philippa.

Then, quite casually, Philippa hoisted her legs over my lap. I stopped talking. I looked at her. Her expression hadn't changed at all. What it suggested, if truth be told, was a kind of monumental indifference: if I responded to her, she seemed to be saying, fine; if not, so much the better.

I, on the other hand, for my own reasons, felt it to be of the utmost importance that I respond to Philippa—and enjoy it.

So I kissed her. I was a little drunk—I suppose we both were. She took down her hair, and all I could think was that it flowed over her back like water, and I reached to touch it, wondering if it would slip through my fingers. She closed her eyes and kissed me back. Her mouth seemed so small, compared to Edward's! Small and delicate and hungry.

Her clothes fell open, the buttons on the back of her dress pulling free like a glissando, uninterrupted. She was barefoot, wore no brassiere, only the simplest white cotton knickers. By comparison, I had on a jacket, tie, wristwatch, shirt, vest, drawers, socks and garters and shoes, the laces of which I had tied in double knots. "You're wrapped up like a Christmas package," Philippa said as she struggled to undo it all. I only hoped, once unwrapped, I wouldn't prove disappointing.

How different her body was from a man's! She had, for instance, tiny hands and feet, but her wine-red nipples were huge and hard and purposeful—such a contrast to the pale-pink buds on Edward's chest, with their coronas of chaff-colored hair! She had very pretty breasts, round and firm, about the size of pin-cushions. Her sexual parts eluded my powers of description. I thought of envelopes within envelopes, lined with scented paper; envelopes made of flesh; or lettuce leaves, darker on the outside and paler within. Entering her was not so different, really, from entering a man: a bit wetter and silkier, perhaps. And as Nigel once remarked, you have to be more polite at the front door than the back.

We lay motionless on the sofa for some moments after the act was finished, glued together by sweat and semen and the fluids that seeped from between Philippa's legs. Finally she rose and went into the bathroom. I heard water running. When she came out again, she was wearing the kimono with the red sash and carrying an oyster-colored dressing gown, which she handed to me. I wrapped it around myself. I had started shaking.

"Are you cold?" Philippa asked, putting her arm around me.

"I'm fine," I said.

"You're sure." Like a worried mother, she felt my head for fever, then went into the kitchen and came back with hot tea. I drank it down, and within a few minutes the shaking subsided.

"I don't know what came over me," I said. "Excitement, I suppose."

"It's natural," she said. "Now just relax."

I told her I would try.

Postcoitally, Philippa spoke more freely and easily than before. I learned, for instance, that she had had a lover since she was fifteen. The same boy. Simon something; he was with the foreign office. They had met in France on a summer holiday and were at Oxford at the same time. Of course she always assumed they would marry. But then they came to London, embarked on their different careers, and mysteriously, a gulf seemed to open between them. "We'd been inseparable practically since we were children," was how she put it. "Our lives had been one life. And then, suddenly, they weren't."

She lit two cigarettes and handed one to me.

"And have there been others?"

"Others?"

"Besides Simon—and me."

"Oh, goodness, yes. Are you shocked? I shouldn't think you would be. After all, it must have been clear from the beginning that I wasn't what your aunt described." She puffed out rings of smoke. "To tell the truth, I'm seeing someone now, but I don't think it'll amount to much. He's married, you see."

"Really."

"Well, yes. Actually, to be completely honest, it's worse than that. He's my boss, at the publishing house. Not much to speak of in terms of looks. The tiniest willie, but he has a certain *authority* I find attractive. Anyway, it's just one or two afternoons a week at a Pimlico hotel."

"And what's that like?"

"Well, that's the surprising thing. One's supposed to feel cheap and sullied, isn't one? But once I'd actually done it, I didn't at all. I considered it a grand adventure, an episode from the novel of my life, you know: this is the chapter where Philippa goes to a Pimlico hotel with her powerful, handsome, alluring boss, for an afternoon of love she will never forget. Except that I will forget it. It was quite forgettable, really. Quite . . . *drab*. I ought to break it off." She laughed, then ruffled my hair. "I suspect," she went on, "that you have something to confess to me as well."

I looked away.

"Well," I said, "it's true that . . . I've never been with a woman before."

"That was obvious," Philippa said. "Oh, please don't take that remark the wrong way. You're wonderful. I adore you. It's just that I could tell you didn't quite know your way around. Yet. It was as if you were constantly having to consult a map."

I blushed, and laughed.

"No, Brian, actually what I was referring to was—well, it *is* fairly well known—that you're homosexual."

I gulped. I hadn't known it was well known.

"But I want to say that doesn't bother me, because I for one don't perceive sexuality as something rigid. I'm sure under the proper circumstances I could very happily make love with a woman, and will."

"Philippa, I hope you don't think I was trying to hide anything from you."

"Of course not."

"I always intended to end up with a woman—no, not intended, that's not what I mean. What I mean is, I always felt it was my *destiny* that I should fall in love with a woman. Which is not to say there's anything wrong with love between men—only I always suspected it wasn't the end of the road for me. Do you understand?"

"As far as I'm concerned," Philippa said, "love occurs between people, not sexes. Why limit ourselves? It's 1936; it's practically the future."

"Or on the other hand, it's practically the end of the world."

"In that case, we should gather our rosebuds while we may, shouldn't we?"

"Exactly."

She offered me another cigarette. The romantic mood had passed; we were both, as the French say, *pensif*.

I looked at the clock; it was nearly eleven-thirty. I would have to rush if I was going to catch the underground before it shut down for the night.

"You're welcome to stay," Philippa said.

"I'd love to," I said. "But I've got an engagement early tomorrow morning."

A shadow passed over her face—disappointment, or else relief. I dressed. Indeed, it was only as I descended the stairs from her flat that I began to fathom the potential consequences of what I'd just done. One rarely becomes conscious of betrayal until after the act is finished.

As I went into the tube station I realized I was still carrying her strong smell on my hands, so I stopped to wash. A youth slouched near the urinals. He glanced at me in a way that was impossible to misinterpret. To my great astonishment and shame I had an instant erection—not surprising, really; I am often most excitable just after sex. "Quite a big one," the youth said. "Want me to take care of it?"

I didn't answer him. He unbuttoned me, pulled my cock from my trousers and began to stroke it.

Right there in the middle of the tube station lavatory, where anyone could have walked in and seen us.

He knelt in front of me to get a better look, and I came ferociously, all over his face.

We finished just in time to catch the last train. While he spat and washed his face, I buttoned up and headed onto the platform.

"Hey, where're you rushing off to?" he shouted after me. "What's your name? Mine's Sydney."

I didn't answer him. I hurried away as fast as I could.

"Hello! I'm talking to you! Hey! What's the matter, you think you're too good to talk to me? Well, you can stick it up your bum, mate. Frigging snob, I'd like to knock your frigging teeth in."

But he did not follow me onto the train. I was going west, of course. He was going east.

At the flat, breath whistled, sweet as ever, through sleeping Edward's slightly parted teeth.

Chapter Eight

The world was ending, but in London women gossiped and argued over the price of mutton, men drank ale and wanked each other in public lavatories before going home to eat the mutton their wives had argued over. Meanwhile, across a sliver of water, much of Madrid had been destroyed; in Seville, Quiepo di Lieno filled the radio waves with his private hatred; in Irún, Republican refugees, defeated, scuttled across the water to France. As for the Republican side—our side—it was becoming each day more crippled by its own internal warfare. We were losing. Death upon death, and still Anthony Eden preached "non-intervention." The fool! Couldn't he see he was playing into Hitler's hands? (Then again, Lady Abernathy hadn't seen; many in England didn't see, for which they would one day suffer.)

Chaos reigned in the little theater of my private life as well, but I pretended everything was fine. Who was it said the denial of corruption signals the deepest corruption? It's true. Only in the journal did I dare report the truth, with the result that what was once a source of pleasure became bitter medicine. I dreaded touching the pen to those pages where conscience obligated me, for once, to speak things as they were.

The irony was that in spite of all the lying I did, I never became proficient at it. I was an inept liar. Then again, I suspect there is rarely such a thing as a *good* liar; there are just people who want, and people who do not want, to believe.

That I managed to pull it off as long as I did, in retrospect, astonishes me.

Most nights I still spent with Edward; we talked and read and made love. Other nights I dined with Philippa, either at her flat or at a restaurant, before or after a concert; or we lingered at a club she belonged to near Oxford Circus; or we took long walks along the Embankment, or on Hampstead Heath. We had begun to have a reputation as a couple; indeed, Emma Leland commented on how good we looked together—"both of you so literary, like the young Woolfs!"

We spent a lot of time laughing at Emma Leland.

One evening Anne Cheney rang to invite me to a dinner party she was planning to host. "And bring that lovely Philippa," she added.

It was eight o'clock, and Edward and I were reading on the sofa, and even though he had his eyes in his book, I knew he was listening—fiercely.

I slipped up only once: I said, "I'll check with her and let you know."

"Who was that?" Edward asked afterwards.

"That was Anne Cheney. George Cheney's sister. She's invited me to supper next week."

"Ah." A beat of silence. "And who is it you're supposed to check with?"

"Caroline."

"I see."

He went back to his *Communist Manifesto*, I to my novel.

Then, a few minutes later: "Couldn't she have called Caroline herself?"

"What?"

"Anne Cheney. Couldn't she have called Caroline and asked her directly?"

"She didn't know the number," I said.

"I see," Edward said again, before returning to his reading.

Of course I told just as many lies to Philippa. I told her I lived alone. I told her I'd never had a real male lover, just a series of nameless partners with whom I engaged in uncomplicated, never terribly satisfying sex.

"And what exactly do men do together? Do you mind my asking? I've always wondered."

"Really, Philippa—"

"Don't be flustered. Just tell me."

"A lot of wanking, mostly."

"Have you ever buggered anyone?"

"No. Never."

"When you walk down the street do beautiful men take your breath away?"

"To tell the truth, I've always had more of an eye for beautiful women."

"Actually so have I. Does that make me a lesbian?"

"I don't think so."

I lied about the evenings I didn't spend with her. I told her I spent them in Richmond, with Channing and Caroline. I also told her I couldn't ever sleep at her flat because of my tutoring job, and that she couldn't ever sleep at my bed-sitter because of the landlady.

Only once did she ring me in the evening, when Edward was home. I said she was Nigel's sister.

Shuttling between them left me sexually exhausted. At no time in my life have I had so much sex, or enjoyed sex less. Afterwards, in Los Angeles, it became my ambition for a few years to fuck as many men as I possibly could in a week. *Then* it was for pleasure. But in London, in 1936, I found myself making love to both Philippa and Edward primarily in order to ward off any suspicions either of them might have as to the existence of the other.

Sex too, in other words, became a lie, part of a vast scaffolding of lies that in the end existed only to support itself: whatever it had initially been intended to bolster had long since fallen away.

With Edward I had trouble maintaining an erection. It wasn't so much that my attraction to him had lessened as that guilt and terror had undermined it. Thus my body—its new smells, fatigue and depletion—betrayed me. Since Philippa was a woman, the problems with her were more endemic, the largest of them being that in order to achieve climax, I found myself having to summon into my mind images of fornicating men. Of course the instant I felt the orgasm beginning I'd hurl these images from my head, I'd open my eyes and stare into Philippa's face or at her breasts, and while this method sometimes worked and I'd come in what seemed an agony of love for her, more often the orgasm subsided, forcing me to close my eyes and start the process all over again. Oh, don't think I felt *nothing*. Touching her breasts and sexual parts, I could perceive rising inside me, very remotely, some vestige of heterosexual desire—a feeling barely felt, rather like touching the bedpost when your right arm has gone to sleep. So why couldn't I, with time and concentration, coax that desire out of its hiding place, into the forefront? Why couldn't I transform my lust for hairy chests into a lust for pincushion breasts? It seemed entirely within reason.

If Philippa perceived my imaginative betrayals, she never let on. To be honest, in my deluded state, I took relief from the calm surface she presented without ever considering what eruptions might be brewing beneath it; as long as Philippa *seemed* to accept things as they were, I assumed that she *did* accept things as they were. It was necessary to believe I was falling in love with her, if for no other reason than because being in love with Philippa was proving to have significant financial benefits. Ample checks from Aunt Constance were pouring in at a steady rate. "Consider the enclosed *mad money*, since *Betty Brennan* is selling *briskly*, "she wrote. "By the by, can I expect to be hearing an *announcement* any time soon? Edith Archibald has a quite *marvelous* champagne at the ready." Normally I laughed at Aunt Constance's delusions, but this time they meshed with my own so exactly that I wrote back to her with great haste, informing her that things between me and Philippa were becoming "serious." The next day she rang to say she would come into town that afternoon to help me shop for an engagement ring, the cost of which she would of course help to defray.

Today I shake my head in appalled horror as I recall that ludicrous expedition, the two of us giddily traipsing from jewelry shop to jewelry shop, looking at ring after ring, and I convinced at every turn we'd run into Edward. (What I'd say to him I pushed to the back of my mind, refused to contemplate.) Finally we settled on a simple gold band embedded with two tiny diamonds, after which we lunched at the Lancaster, where I extracted from Aunt Constance a promise not to mention my intentions to anyone until Philippa had in fact accepted my proposal. "Oh, but of course," she averred, her eyes twinkling with conspiratorial glee.

She insisted on giving me taxi fare, which I used not to ride home but rather to go to a public lavatory in Shepherd's Bush notorious for its "activities."

Astonishing, isn't it, that given the fullness of my dance card, I still found time to go cottaging? How did I have the stamina for it? I ask myself now. But I was only twenty-two. I could come five or six times a day without trouble. And I needed sex for pleasure, sex for its own sake—something I wasn't getting from either of my lovers.

I visited the lavatories in the afternoons, when Edward was at work, or in the evenings, after seeing Philippa. Sometimes even on the nights I spent with Edward. I'd tell him I felt restless, that I needed to have a walk and think about my novel, but in fact I'd steal over to Dartmoor Walk, a long narrow pathway that aligned Dartmoor Park and was a notorious homosexual meeting place. There were always good-looking men and boys lingering around Dartmoor Walk in the evenings. I'd find a partner (or two, or three), and we'd hoist each other over the fence into the dark murmuring treescape of the park, which was closed at night: the park with its gravel paths and soft animal stirrings. And what rare, elusive camaraderie we experienced during those moonlit escapades! We were boys lost in the forest, boys from a novel we'd read as boys. Treasure hunters. And the treasure was that rapture among the fallen leaves, sealed in its own moment, cocooned from the rush and whistle of time.

As for the engagement ring, I put it away. I locked it away in the locked drawer in my desk, the same drawer in which I kept the journal. It is a man's delusion—never a woman's—to think he can partition his life, like the famous bigamist who managed to juggle five wives in four cities for ten years without any of them catching on.

He must have been a very good liar, the bigamist—either that or his wives really loved him.

At first I made excuses when I went out with Philippa; then I stopped making excuses; then I not only stopped making excuses, I stopped even offering explanations. Edward, prideful creature that he was, never asked for any. We still made love, but less often, and only at his instigation. I think he realized this at a certain point and stopped instigating things in order to test if his hypothesis might be correct. Then we didn't make love at all.

One night I arrived home from dining with Philippa to find him reading on the sofa. As soon as I walked in the door he dropped his book, stood, and put his arms around my waist; Philippa lingered in my mind and on my hands, however, so I told him I wasn't feeling well and took to bed.

I was still awake when he climbed in with me an hour or so later. He did not touch me at first but instead lay flat on his back, his body as far away from mine as he could manage. Then I turned over; my foot brushed his. He must have taken this accidental contact as a signal, for a few seconds later he rolled over onto his side and put his arms around my chest. I neither said a word nor moved. I lay perfectly still while he pressed against me, nuzzled my neck, kissed my hair-line. Finally he reached inside my pajamas, but my penis was shriveled and cold, as far indrawn as possible, and he pulled his hand away as if he'd been bit.

The next evening I dined with Philippa in an Indian restaurant. A young man with a rather elaborately coiffed mustache approached our table. Philippa's face went red.

"Simon," she said grimly.

"Philippa."

"I must say it's a surprise running into you here," Philippa said after a pause. "I wouldn't have thought this place nearly grand enough for you."

"You know I like something hot now and then."

She smiled and looked away. I coughed.

"Oh, forgive me. Simon Napier, Brian Botsford."

I stood. "A pleasure," Simon said manfully. He was taller than me by at least four inches and had absolutely immense hands, which led me to wonder about other parts of him. "I've certainly heard a lot about you," Simon went on, looking into my eyes in a way that gave me an instant erection.

"And I about you," I responded, wondering from whom he'd heard whatever he'd heard—and what it was. I doubted the source was Philippa, since as far as she'd let on she hadn't kept up much contact with Simon.

"Well, I must be off. A friend's waiting. Delightful to see you, Philippa—and to meet you, Brian." Then he was gone, rushing toward a back table at which a pretty young woman sat playing with her rings.

"So that's the famous Simon," I said after he had left.

Philippa looked away. "He does rather enjoy scenes."

"How long has it been since you last saw him?"

"What? Oh, let's see—it was Saturday."

"Saturday!"

"Yes, at Jane Caldicott's drinks party—remember the one I told you about?"

"You didn't mention Simon having been there."

She shrugged. "Nothing much happened. It's just a bit hard to resist Simon; he does have such a—such an air. I'm sure you recognized it."

"Yes, I suppose I did." I drummed the table.

"What, are you jealous?" Philippa laughed. "But don't worry, we didn't actually *sleep* together. Anyway, it was for old time's sake, nothing more."

I opened my mouth to say something more, then stopped myself. I had no right to complain.

"Well, Philippa, I suppose I'm just a bit more old-fashioned than you are," I said. (One of the few *true* things I'd said in weeks.)

"You are quite charming," Philippa said. "I could get used to you."
She patted my hand in a maternal way.

"Could you?"

"Oh, yes."

Relief flushed my heart. "I'm glad to hear that," I said. "I really am."

Philippa smiled beneficently and fussed for something in her
purse.

Aunt Constance rang. Did I have any news? "All in good time," I said.

Edward, sitting across from me on the sofa, never took his eyes
out of his book.

In the middle of the night, Edward woke me—his hands on my stomach. I knew what he wanted: a kiss, an embrace; reassurance. And I
lay stone still. I couldn't give it to him.

Eventually he took his hands away. His breathing—steady,
anxious—kept me awake, however, so I got out of bed.

"Where are you going?" he called.

"Just to the sofa."

"Why?"

"I don't want to keep you awake."

I lay down on the sofa. I could hear him across the room thrashing, twisting. I closed my eyes, counted my breaths, fell eventually
into a troubled sleep. Then it was morning; the bed was made;
Edward had gone to work. I had an early date with Philippa in the
evening, which required me to leave the flat an hour or so before he
got home. (Uncharacteristically, I traveled by bus.) When I returned—
well after midnight—he had already gone to bed. Once again I made
my bed on the sofa. Once again I slept through his morning departure. Thus twenty-four hours passed in which we literally never
spoke to each other.

The next night I dined with Philippa, then went cottaging, and didn't get home until four in the morning. There Edward sat, fully dressed, on the edge of our caved-in bed. He had switched on all the lights in the flat, even the ceiling light. Under its cruel unflinching gaze every stain on the coverlet was illuminated: salmon spread and tea, mineral oil and snot and piss and spunk.

Edward looked up at me. In his lap he held his precious copy of *The Communist Manifesto*. A thin streak of blood ran down his cheek from where he'd cut himself shaving (shaving at this hour?), and sitting down next to him, I wiped it away with my finger, noticing how the blood illuminated, briefly, the coiled rings of identity around the tip.

"Edward," I said.

"Where were you?"

"Out to dinner. We got to talking rather late, that's all."

"Late! It's four in the bloody morning."

I lifted the book from his lap, put it down on the bed, took his face in my hands and stroked his cheeks so that tears came into his eyes.

"What's happening?" he asked, his voice hushed, desperate.

"Quiet," I said, touching my lips to his forehead. "Everything's fine."

"What—"

I kissed him. I pushed him down on the bed, pulled his trousers and his drawers down, took the bottle of mineral oil from the drawer and smeared it over his cock and started rubbing. But his cock was soft, and when I lifted his legs and tried to bugger him, my cock was soft too and kept slipping out.

Finally I rolled off him. We lay like this for some minutes, quite still, our faces to opposite walls. He still had on his black socks, his shirt and tie and sweater.

"What is it I've done?" he asked after a while.

"You haven't done anything."

"Have I irritated you? Taken too much of your time?"

"No, of course not."

"Is it that I had John Northrop up to tea? I've been thinking about that, and I've decided, really, perhaps I stepped out of bounds, this is your flat—"

"No!"

Brutal silence.

"Are you in love with someone else, then?"

I sat up. "What?"

"Are you? You must tell me if you are. You must."

"Edward, what gave you that idea? Of course I'm not. And what's 'in love' anyway? Are we 'in love'?"

"I thought we were."

"I never said it."

"No, you didn't, did you? So perhaps I was a bloody fool."

I leaned away from him. "Edward—everyone has his own way of saying things. The point is, we're still young, we're too young to be— to be having this conversation. I need—we need—to be freer with each other."

"Freer! You never let me go anywhere with you or do anything with you. More and more your life's out there, while I sit in this bloody bed-sitter listening to the water pipes rattle."

"Edward, you're making too much of this. It's natural that I should want to have my own social life. It has nothing to do with my feelings for you. Nothing."

He looked away. It was as if he suddenly understood that we could talk and talk and it would do no good, because one of us was lying.

The blood on his face, I noticed, had started scabbing.

"Look, it's late," I said finally. "Let's go to sleep."

"As if that's any solution."

"I'm just going to wash."

I went into the bathroom, where I ran the tap, splashed cold water on my face, examined it in the looking glass. This cannot be happening, I told the looking glass. I am altogether too young for this to be happening. Fuck off, the looking glass answered. You are not, and it is.

I went back in. During the interval Edward had unmade the bed and taken off the rest of his clothes. He was now lying, eyes clenched closed, body S-shaped, tightly packed beneath sheet and blanket.

Very quietly I picked up my pillow and tiptoed to the sofa.

As if it mattered. As if he weren't watching my every move.

Chapter Nine

O f course, when the end came, it came hard, and suddenly.

First Philippa asked me to a weekend at her family's house in Oxfordshire. Two of her younger sisters would be there, she said, as well as some school friends.

Thinking that this would be an ideal opportunity to make my marriage proposal, I accepted immediately. (Edward, I'd decided, I would deal with only once I'd received Philippa's answer.)

With great trepidation I told Edward "a friend" had invited me to the country, but by this time he'd become so used to my going off without him that instead of becoming angry he reacted with a kind of glum resignation. "And what weekend would that be?" was all he asked.

"This next one."

Suddenly his expression changed. "But, Brian, that's the Friday you promised you'd come to Upney for dinner! If you don't, it'll break Sarah's heart!"

I reassured him that as I wasn't expected at my friend's until lunchtime on Saturday, there would be no need to cancel the dinner with his family.

"All right, then," he answered in a tone that suggested he'd have been happier if I *had* canceled and thus given him a good reason to be cross with me.

We took the tube out to Upney on Friday evening. It had not been such a long time since our last District Line journey together—Edward scrubbed and nervous, me stinking of Aunt Constance's cheeses. *Then* I'd been eager; now I only wanted the dinner over and done with, and Edward could tell. So we just sat there, side by side, not speaking.

After a long time we pulled into Upney station. We got off. Once again Edward led me along the circuitous network of small, drab streets that led to his home. Everything was as I remembered, except that now it was almost Christmas, so wreaths and nativity scenes had been set up in front windows, hesitant displays that suggested a fear of "putting on airs," as if Christmas belonged, by rights, only to other streets, better neighborhoods.

At Lil's house we hung our coats on the coatrack. This time the never-seen dog did not bark. Perhaps he had gone to Walthamstow with Headley and Pearlene. (Two weeks before, their mother had finally come back from Glasgow and reclaimed them.) We slunk into the kitchen, and Lil—overburdened and influenzaed the last time we'd met—stepped forward from the stove, the picture of womanly vigor. She had her blond hair neatly done up in a bun, had rouged her cheeks, and wore a clean white apron over a black frock. Real or fake, the pearls that rested contentedly on her bosom seemed to confirm the old myth that the oils of a woman's skin will give to those jewels a special luster. She kissed me with a warmth that suggested Edward had told her nothing of our troubles, then sat me down at the table with a glass of sherry. Across from me, silent Sarah furiously peeled potatoes. Someone had taken a curling iron to her flat brown hair, which now scalloped upward in large, artificial-looking waves. Sarah too had makeup on, though applied in a childish and inexpert way, as well as incongruous seahorse-shaped earrings that weighted down the lobes of her ears. She wore a brown party dress patterned with bluebells. When I said hello she blushed furiously and continued peeling.

"Now, Sarah," Lil said, "what do you say?"

Sarah mumbled something inaudible.

"I didn't hear you."

"Very pleased you could come to supper," Sarah enunciated through clenched teeth.

Suddenly her nervous knife slipped; she scraped her knuckle and began sucking on it furiously.

A pale pink bloodstain spread out over the potato she had been peeling.

"Did you hurt yourself?" I asked.

"It's nothing," she murmured, looking me in the eye for the first time and, knuckle in mouth, smiling.

Lucy traipsed in. Her hair was longer than the last time I'd seen her. Once again she had on her face that look of aloof disinterest that appeared to be her trademark.

"Edward!" she said in mock surprise. "To what do we owe the honor of a visit from the likes of you?"

"Just missed Mum's cooking," Edward said quietly.

"Missed Mum's cooking! That's a laugh!"

"I'll thank you not to bite the hand that feeds you," Lil said.

"Oh, Mum, I'm just joking." She turned to me. "Hello, Brian. Been out much lately?"

"A bit."

"How's that lovely girlfriend of yours."

Edward shot me a glance.

"Girlfriend? I don't have a girlfriend."

"Yes you do. What was her name—Lulu?"

"Oh, Louise," I said with relief. "She's gone back to Paris."

"What a pity! I'll be arriving in Paris next week." She lit a cigarette.

"It's true," Lil said from the stove. "My little linnet is flying the nest. Soon it'll just be Sarah and me left here to guard the old house, ain't that right, Sarah?"

Sarah said nothing.

"And what will you be doing in Paris?" I asked.

"I shall be an artist's model," Lucy said. "Paulette is taking up sculpture."

"Imagine!" Lil said. "I'm jealous, I am. It's not every girl what gets to go to Paris and be an artist's model. And this marquise—well, I thought, who does she think she is, stealing my little girl just because she never had one of her own? But then I met Paulette—imagine that, she wanted me to call her by her Christian name—and she couldn't have been more polite. Not like those earls and dukes and what have you here in England, who won't so much as give you the time of day if you've got the wrong accent. The marquise—Paulette—treated me like her oldest friend. It put my heart at ease, let me tell you."

"How are the children?" I asked.

"Not here anymore, thank God," Lucy said.

"Lucy!" Lil said. "The way you talk about your own niece and nephew! In fact, Brian, they're back with their mother, and it's very considerate of you to ask. And they seem fine over there in Walthamstow. Children want to be with their mother, even if she's an unreliable one like that Nellie. Imagine, running off when you've got two little angels like those!"

"But I thought her grandmother was sick."

"Don't believe it! She had a fellow there, that was the truth of it. He must have caught on to her, too, because quick as a flash she was back, just the way she left."

"And not a moment too soon," Lucy said.

"Bite your tongue, missy! I'm tired of your attitude, I am. You should be grateful to have them, your brother's only babies. They're all he's left us, after all."

Suddenly Lil stopped cooking; tears welled in her eyes. "Now, Mum," Edward said. He put his hands on her shoulders to comfort her.

"I'm sorry," Lil said. "It's been two years, but the wound's as fresh as the day I heard the news. I doubt I shall ever get over it."

For a moment, everyone was silent in honor of mothers who have lost their sons. Even Sarah stopped peeling.

"Have you got a picture of Frank?" I asked, once it seemed decent to do so.

Immediately Lil brightened. "Why, yes, lots. I'll go and get them." Taking off her apron, she bustled into the dining room.

"Now you've done it," Lucy said. "We'll be looking at pictures all night."

Edward laughed—it seemed as if it were the first time in years— and then Lil came back with picture albums that she spread out on the table. We looked at Frank as a baby, held in the arms of his father. Frank throwing a ball. Frank and Nellie at a dance. Then all four of the children as children, gathered nervously around a small, ratlike terrier. The little girls on horseback. The entire family posed formally in their Sunday best, staring at the camera with that particu- lar gravity—almost terror—that seems so typical to photographic portraits of the working class: as if, by the mere fact of sitting before this imposing shutter-eyed machine and recording their existence, they feared they were "putting on airs."

A quiet descended, the hush of a roomful of beings suddenly lost in collective memory, familial memory. Things fleeting, and gone. Children grown, brothers dead. "That was the year the dog got hit by a milk truck—remember, Sarah? I'll never forget the poor little thing waddling around, up to its neck in snow." A chorus of "Yes, ah, yes." Clear as morning. Close as you're standing. As if it were yesterday.

Edward was smiling. He had his hand on his sister's shoulder, and he was smiling. And I knew that for the first time in days, perhaps even in weeks, he was thinking not about me but of other, older things, here in his family's house, this house he'd been raised in, this house with its cache of experience that dwarfed my brief tenure in his life. This house where everyone loved him and would gladly say what I, in Earl's Court, would not.

We went in to dinner. I was seated between Sarah, who ate methodically and would not look up from her plate, and Lucy, who smoked cigarette after cigarette, complained about the meat, swirled her potatoes around with her fork. There was both wine and beer. It seemed that every time I emptied my glass it was refilled before I had a chance to ask. The extent to which I was enjoying myself surprised me—I hadn't expected to. It was as if, after weeks of self-imposed misery, Edward and I were being given a holiday, a chance to forget our troubles, to talk of other, incidental things and feel at home. From reluctance and poutiness Edward's hardy, happy, optimistic old self reemerged, the way a desiccated flower, given water, comes back to life; his first hesitant bites gave way to faithful appetite. Such bashful hopefulness in his green eyes that I couldn't help but wonder if he and his family had conspired in planning this evening, to remind me of everything I stood to lose along with him.

And of course, by the time the dinner was over, it was too late— and we were both too drunk—to catch the last train back to Earl's Court. I protested; I had to be in Oxfordshire in the morning. "Never mind," Edward said. "We'll get up early and I'll take you to the station." It seemed I had no choice.

Once again, we put away the dining room furniture; once again, Edward dragged out the narrow cot. The women bid us good night. When I kissed Sarah on the cheek she smiled and blushed bright crimson.

And then the door closed. We undressed tenuously, as if, in the absence of those cheer-inspiring women, in the wearing away of the liquor, the old misery might return at any moment, might fall like a sheet, muffling and silencing and separating. But it did not.

Cautiously we got into the narrow bed. There was not enough room not to touch. It had been a week since we'd last made love. Instinctively we reached for each other, we kissed, groped, burrowed inside each other's pajamas, our hands laying claim to whatever flesh they could find.

Later, I held Edward while he slept—peacefully again, the way he used to—and stared at the odd bits of furniture silhouetted in the moonlight: the crib from which that silvery-eyed child had gazed at me; the sideboard with its smell of mutton; the little cabinet where Lil kept her photograph albums. I thought how nice it was to see Edward sleeping again. I thought that I could love this family more than my own, given half a chance. And yet it seemed beyond question that the next morning we would wake up very early, that I would catch that train to Oxford, that I would leave him.

It started to rain: just a few drops at first, then a downpour, sheets heavy enough to bend and break the fragile young stems in the window boxes. Spring in London often brought cruel surprises: a last late frost that would kill them all. But of course it wasn't spring. The window boxes were empty.

Still, I took comfort in the rain and held Edward tightly as it beat its old drums around us.

*   *   *

The bells on the alarm clock went off at six, boring into our sleep. Edward's body spasmed. Even though I knew he'd woken up, he pretended he hadn't; he kept his arms clutched tightly around my chest so that I had to push and wriggle, until reluctantly he relinquished his embrace.

I staggered out of bed and peered through the curtains. It was still raining; the sky was the color of cold porridge. Anyone who would willingly drag himself out of a warm, sticky bed and a warm pair of arms on such a grim morning as this had to be mad, which I suppose I was.

I sat on a chair, pulled on my socks, stood, felt suddenly and acutely dizzy and had to sit back down.

"Are you all right?" Edward asked. (He had stopped pretending to be asleep.) I nodded and stood again, this time successfully.

I pulled on my drawers and trousers. Edward got out of bed and started to dress as well.

"You know you don't have to go with me," I said. "Really, I'll be fine on my own. You can stay here and get a few more hours' sleep."

"Don't be silly," Edward said. "I told you I'd see you off at the station, and I'm going to."

"But really, it's not necessary."

"What, don't you want me to?"

"Yes, of course—"

Edward turned away. "I don't think you do. I think you'd rather go alone, in case one of the other guests at your smart weekend party sees you at the station."

"Edward, please. I just don't want you to have to go to the bother—"

"It's no bother."

"All right, then. Fine."

And I strode into the kitchen. There was Lil, in her dressing gown, making tea. "Hello, lovey," she said sunnily. "Did you have a good sleep, then?"

"Yes, thank you."

"A bit headachy, ain't you? Never mind. A little tea will do the trick."

She handed me the steaming cup. How fresh she smelled! Amazing, considering the indecent hour and the cold.

"Are you always such an early bird?" I asked.

"I've never needed much sleep. A blessing, I suppose. More time to live. Good morning, Edward."

"Good morning."

Lil handed him his tea, which he took without a word. She raised her eyebrows.

For a few moments the three of us just sat there, silently sipping. Even for Lil it was perhaps too early to say much. And Edward seemed peeved.

Finally I announced I had better go if I was going to get to Paddington in time to catch my train.

We bade Lil goodbye and walked to the underground. On the train, sad-looking East End girls sat all around us, barmaids on their way to Knightsbridge to look at things they could never afford to buy. Those who expected nothing, I was learning, could be content to breathe in the steam that rises off the accoutrements of other people's wealth. They all got off at South Ken to switch to the Piccadilly.

Rain was still plunging when we got back to the flat, where I pulled a few clothes and books into a suitcase. We would have to hurry, I realized, if I was going to make the train I'd told Philippa I'd be arriving on. Of course I would rather have made the trip to the station alone, but after the morning's scene I didn't dare ask Edward *not* to accompany me. So once I had my things collected we got back on the tube and rode to Paddington.

And then, at the station, I had a vivid premonition that this would be the last time we would see each other in a very long time.

I looked at Edward. As I recall, I felt the need to take him in, fix him in memory. He had on a black-and-red-striped waistcoat, a wrinkled blue shirt misbuttoned by one button, my red-and-yellow school tie. His leather satchel kept slipping off his shoulder, so that he kept having to hike it up. He hadn't combed his hair.

"And what will you do with yourself this weekend?" I asked him.

"Oh, I don't know," he said. "Read. Potter about."

I looked at the ground; the lace on one of his black work shoes was undone. And very spontaneously I got on my knees and did it up. There I was, on my knees at Paddington station, staring up at Edward's foreshortened figure, his befuddled face, while I laced his shoe.

A voice over the loudspeaker announced that the nine forty-five to Oxford would be leaving from platform number six.

I stood. "Well, that's my train," I said. "I'd better run."

"Goodbye," Edward said.

"Goodbye."

I patted him on the shoulder, turned around and headed for platform number six. Some impulse, however—perhaps, again, that premonition of finality—turned me back. Edward got bigger and bigger, more and more surprised-looking, as I strode toward him; when I got there, I kissed him on the mouth. He didn't say anything, nor did I hear any particular reaction from the crowd, though I noticed an old lady putting on her spectacles and peering at us as if we were fornicating monkeys at a zoo. "Goodbye," I said again, and left.

From the front of the platform I looked to see if he was still there. He was. Staring after me, his green eyes wide, his lips parted. The battered satchel had fallen off his shoulder, its contents spilling out over the tiled station floor: a pen, an underground map, a toothbrush, and a copy of *The Communist Manifesto*, which fluttered open in the wind of fleeing trains.

Chapter Ten

A driver—not Philippa—met me at the station. Me and a big-toothed couple from Highgate, whose favorite adjective was "sporting." The wife said she'd known Philippa since they were two.

The sun had briefly emerged. We drove through fields of wheat and verdant loping hills from which erupted occasional villages, farms, quaint old cloches that looked like roofs without houses. Hale, oddly springlike weather. Rotting marrows littered the ground, split apart, spilling their seeds. Then we were on the long drive leading up to the manor. Cypresses lined it like sentries, and at its terminus stood Philippa, waving wildly.

The house was huge, elegant, freezing cold, with rooms opening onto rooms, and all of them filled with heavy specimens of Louis XIV furniture—sofas with claws, burnished armoires it would have taken five men to lift. There were servants—fewer than there had been ten years earlier, more than most people in those days could afford. Philippa's younger sisters, in my mind, blur together into a single ringleted unit wearing a pinafore and at one point announcing,

"Father, *I* should like someday to ride in an airplane." "And very soon you shall, my dear," the bearded father jovially assured her. His wife—Philippa's mother—behaved perfectly but seemed indrawn, as if she were obliged to meditate every moment on private troubles her good breeding forbade her to mention. As for the school friends, they were, as school friends tend to be, charming, opinionless, given to drink. Two boys and a girl, in addition to the couple from Highgate. I have lost their names.

After lunch Philippa and I took a walk in the grounds. It really was a lovely place. There was a rose garden, trellised and fragrant, a pond filled with ancient carp, perhaps most notably a topiary garden that re-created the Sermon on the Mount. Rows of carefully sculpted bushes ascended in staggered hierarchy to the bush that was Jesus, above which loomed only hills, hills so smooth they might have been upholstered in green velvet: more furniture than geology.

On the sloping lawn that led up to this monument we sat. The wind was brisk, unseasonably warm. Philippa took her hat off and lay back to look at the sky.

"When I was a child," she said, "this was my favorite place. The topiary, I thought, would protect me."

"Protect you?"

"Yes. I was very frightened of dying, then. Dying, or being abandoned. I used to walk around all day in the clutches of a nameless dread." She hoisted herself up on her elbows and gazed at the garden. "We didn't build it, of course. Believe it or not, it dates back to the eighteenth century. It was commissioned by some wife of an earl who was rich and terribly pious. Unlike me. I was utterly impious. I loved to hide in Jesus' shadow. And once I stood in front of Jesus and pulled down my knickers and played with myself. I felt so dreadfully wicked."

She picked a blade of grass and began shredding it. In truth I could hardly hear her for the thumping of my heart. You see, I was trying to find just the right words to ask her to marry me . . .

"Brian, is something wrong?"

"Wrong?"

"You seem nervous, suddenly."

"Do I? Perhaps that's because there's something I want to ask you."

"Oh?"

"Yes." A strangled pause. "Philippa, for a long time now—that is, since we met—" I looked away, agonized. "I'm afraid I'm not very good at this."

"Brian, is something the matter?" Taking my hand.

"I'm sorry," I said. Then I reached into my pocket for the ring. "This is for you."

"For me! Brian!" She opened the box. "Brian, it's lovely."

Then she looked at me.

"What does this mean?"

"It means I'm asking you to marry me."

She snapped the box shut.

"Is something wrong?"

"Well, no, it's just—I'm just a bit taken aback, that's all."

"I don't see why you should be. After all, I think I've made my feelings fairly obvious—"

"Of course, of course. It's just—it's the last thing on earth I was expecting." She brushed a hand against her hair. "Look, it's very sweet of you to ask me this, but—Brian, dear, I can't marry you."

"Why?"

"Well, first of all—because I don't intend *ever* to marry. And second of all—because I don't love you."

I gazed at her. She had said these words with such tenderness, so, well—*lovingly*, that at first I thought I'd misheard them. But I had not.

"I'm sorry," I said, standing hastily. "I must have misunderstood." And stumbled.

My leg, having fallen asleep under me, hummed with static. Philippa stood as well. "Brian," she said, "please listen. You're a charming young man, and very intelligent, but I have the impression you take our relationship, well, a bit more seriously than I do. I'm delighted to know you. But I'm not in love with you. Is that cruel of me?"

"Not cruel exactly. Just . . ."

"You must not take this personally. Nothing's wrong with you. It's more that something isn't *right* with *us*. Oh, I'm not making much sense, I know." She took my hand. "Dear Brian, have I hurt you horribly? Am I a beast?"

"No, of course not," I managed. "In fact, I'm sure you're right. I'm sure this will be best."

"Are you?"

"Yes. I think so."

"But you're not sure."

"No."

We started walking again. "You must think me a fool," I said.

"Oh, of course not, Brian. To be fair, in fact, I suppose I *have* led you on a bit. I suppose I really have given the impression—well, that I felt more than I did. But Brian! Marry! We're both much too young to marry, with the world as it is and so much to do!"

She picked a leaf off a tree and pretended to examine it.

"Anyway, you must admit, there wasn't really that passion, was there, between us, that we've had in other love affairs?"

"You mean you had more passion with Simon?"

"Oh, yes . . ." Seeing the stricken expression on my face, she added, "I'm sorry, Brian. But you must have felt it yourself. Really. You never did seem to enjoy yourself, for all the effort you put in."

"You didn't say anything."

"Women often don't know how to put these kinds of things into words."

A breeze came up, fluttering away the leaf she had been playing with. She handed me the box with the ring.

"Has it occurred to you," Philippa said next, "that you might be happier in a homosexual relationship? Oh, I know you've never tried one. But you might." She clasped my hand again. "I think you only thought you were happy with me, Brian. I could tell you weren't."

I looked her in the eyes. Her eyes seemed to me, at that moment, the intensest, most liquid, cruelest eyes I'd ever seen.

And then—I have no idea where he came from—another being claimed me. Some horrifying jolly chap who was like one of Philippa's school friends. "Now don't you worry," the jolly chap said. "Just my bad luck, in the end. I suppose you could say my loss is another fellow's gain. Tell you what: how does a nice cup of tea and a game of cards sound?"

"All right," Philippa said doubtfully. "If that's what you want."

"I could do with a rubber."

The jolly chap escorted Philippa to the house, whereupon she excused herself to take a nap.

Later, I tried ringing Edward. No answer.

I find it difficult, in retrospect, to sort out the many emotions that laid siege to me that afternoon. On the one hand there was a terrible dread, almost a grief, as if I had just failed one of those examinations the results of which determine the very outcome of one's life. Then there was embarrassment—acute embarrassment—at having misread Philippa so thoroughly. And finally, above and beyond both of these reactions, there was an overarching sensation of relief, because now, at least, I no longer had to lie; now I was face to face

with the truth, and the truth was proving in its own way to be a source
of comfort. Cold comfort, yes. But at least the chill hand of reality
against your cheek is steady.

I understood that I would never marry Philippa; I understood that
I would never marry *any* woman. Instead I would lead a homosexual
life, but it would be a life without lies. What folly to imagine one can
somehow transform the *idea* of desire into desire! Perhaps women
are capable of such Pygmalionism. Men are not. And while the prospect of a homosexual life still frightened me, I knew it could not be
worse than a life built around delusion. Lies corrupt you, they
provoke you to acts of cruelty your ordinary self would find shocking.
Yet you commit them. You hurt people desperately in order to protect
your lies, which have become like children to you—gnawing, desperate children not content to suck every drop of milk from your breast,
because they are always hungry. So they bite into the nipple itself,
they devour the flesh itself, and still you protect them. The problem
ceases to be that you cannot live without your lies so much as that
your lies cannot live without you.

Viscerally, as if for the first time, I realized just how much I
must have hurt Edward. I felt the sting of my own betrayal. I had
lied to protect him, but instead my lies ate away at his sense of
security until it must have seemed to him that even the ugliest
truth would have been preferable to this misery. Yet when he
pleaded with me to tell him the truth, I denied him even that
comfort, in effect saying, You must go on suffering. I will not let
you free. What kind of monster had I become? I wondered. And
what must come next?

At dinner that evening the food was tasteless. Nonetheless, by
dividing it into equal portions and forcing myself to put one forkful
into my mouth every minute, I made a respectable show of clearing
my plate. I also managed, I am proud to say, to keep track of the

conversations, even to utter a passably witty remark or two. No one guessed a waxwork sat with them at table.

We had drinks after dinner, which gave my obliviousness an excuse. Philippa looked very pretty, and a remote part of me thought that perhaps I should try to seduce her, but we had been placed in rooms at opposite ends of the house. I very much doubted that in my drunken state I'd be able to determine which door was hers.

Around eleven-thirty I excused myself and went to bed, where I must have slept, because when I woke it was just past seven. A strange, wordless panic had gripped me. Suddenly it seemed there was very little time. So I got up, tiptoed into the foyer and tried ringing Edward; once again, no answer. A railway timetable had been posted next to the telephone, presumably as a hint to guests who were thinking of overstaying their welcome. If I hurried, I saw, I could still catch the nine-thirty train to Oxford.

I went back to my room, packed my things and wrote a quick note to Philippa:

Very sorry to leave before Sunday lunch but a family crisis requires that I return immediately to London. Please thank your mother for her hospitality. B.

Other than the servants, no one had yet risen. I spoke only to the gardener on my way out. He was clipping leaves from the nose of the topiary Jesus. "Top of the morning," he said. "Top of the morning," I said.

And then the walk—five miles—to the village; the wait at the station; the very slow steam-driven ride to Oxford through wintry landscapes. Edward, poor Edward! I was thinking. How I longed to fling my arms around him, embrace the breath out of him! And yet can the inflicter of injury ever be the source of comfort? I could not undo the lies I had told Edward. Nor could I dissolve the membrane of class that separated us. Nor could I see my way clear to offering him the kind of "marriage" he seemed to want. (Indeed, though I had cast off my delusions about Philippa, it would be twenty years before I came around to the idea of "marriage" between men.) Still, tender feelings for Edward flooded me. (But dared I name them?) I wanted, more than anything else, to hold him and not let go, not for hours or even days. (But what about years?)

The train pulled late into Oxford station. With seconds to spare, I made my connection to Paddington, where I caught the tube. Even though it was only a five-minute walk from Earl's Court station to the flat, I had no patience: I ran the whole way, down the high street, where flowers bloomed along the pavement, through the door to my building, up the stairs, past my old neighbor, who was on her way back from church. "Good morning, Mr. Botsford," she said. "Good morning," I said, breathless, heaving, trying my key in the lock, stepping inside. "Edward?" I called. "Edward?" But of course there was no answer.

I suppose the first thing I took in—aside from the fact that Edward wasn't there—was that the flat was much cleaner than when I'd left it. The floor had been swept, the mantel polished. A shelf was empty on the bookcase—Edward's shelf. After that I checked his drawer, but of course by that time it had all come together in my mind; I knew what I *would* find—the journal, open on the desk where he had read it—as well as what I wouldn't: his clothes, his toothbrush, his razor and shaving mug, any proof that he had ever lived here or known me.

From the desk, the journal stared up at me indictingly. Had I forgotten it on purpose?

An unaddressed envelope sat on the kitchen counter. I tore it open. It contained a week's rent in cash and the following typewritten inventory:

Goods used during stay and not purchased by me (or jointly):

6 packets tea

2 bars soap

1½ boxes tooth powder (rounded off to 2)

4 Wall's sausages

2 boxes ginger biscuits

1 pair black socks

1 teacup (to replace teacup I broke)

1 copy *Howards End* (coffee spilled on page 143)

Each of these items was neatly displayed on the countertop.

I think, now, that I can imagine exactly how Edward must have sat as he read the journal: bolt upright, his back arched, the way he always sat when he read, as if he were in church. At one and three-quarter minutes a page, it would have taken him at least two hours, which meant that around the time I was being welcomed by Philippa's mother he would have just finished, he would have stood, stretched his legs and had a piss, before taking out his ledger and calculating exactly how much he owed me. Perhaps he had a nap then, or went to the pub and got drunk, or perhaps it was then that he headed out to the little grocery shop on the corner to buy the necessary provisions. (For the socks, the teacup and the copy of *Howards End* he would have had to go farther afield.) Next—or perhaps this was the morning, Sunday morning—the packing, the typing out of the note on my type-writer, the careful arrangement of the things he'd bought on the kitchen countertop. (I can't be sure, but somehow I assume this arrangement was careful.) Or perhaps I have the order wrong; perhaps he shopped first and cleaned later. Most likely he cleaned at night. One does, when the night is long. He cleaned with a venge-ance, as if to scrub all traces of himself from these rooms. He scoured the tub and mopped the floor. He even bleached the lovemaking stains out of the old coverlet.

Or tried. For at some point in that long day I walked over to the bed and, turning on the reading lamp, examined it. In fact, the biggest stain was still there—significantly faded, detectable only by careful examination, but still there. If you shone a bright light on it you could see it: vanilla-colored, about the size of a penny coin. If you ran your fingers over it you could feel it: a patch of scar tissue, pocked and risen, bumpy like a message in braille.

Chapter Eleven

I stayed home that night. I didn't go out and search for Edward; instead I listened for his footsteps. I might as well have walked to Upney, for all the pacing I did in that narrow flat, but I never stepped out the door. Why, I ask myself now, when this was my only chance to save him? All I can offer by way of an explanation is a memory of profound, almost paralyzing ambivalence. Yes, Philippa had forced me to confront the foolishness of my delusions; yes, I now recognized it was Edward whom I loved. And still I was afraid of what it would cost me, what people might say about it, this improbable union between writer and ticket taker, Richmond and Upney; worst of all, most frightening of all, two men. So I did nothing. For the eight crucial hours when I might—*might*—have done something, I did nothing.

A loud rapping noise jolted me from sleep. I leapt up, my heart racing, though whether with hope or dread I couldn't say.

"Edward!"

But it turned out only to be pipes knocking.

I looked at the clock: half past five. I got up, drank some tea from the cup Edward had bought, washed my face with the soap, put on the new socks. "Only Connect" said the *Howards End,* so at eight I went down to Earl's Court station.

He was nowhere to be seen.

At the ticket office, the stationmaster, an old man with long whiskers, regarded me through steel bars. "Phelan's quit, he has. Didn't give any notice, neither, just a letter saying his back pay could be sent to his mum and he was very sorry for the trouble. Left me a man short at the rush hour. He'll never work for London Transport again, I can tell you that."

"Cheap day return to Upney," I said.

The old man issued the necessary ticket, and I climbed onto a train packed tight with humanity, hats and noses and beard stubble and perfume and tweed. It was a very slow trip—or perhaps it just seemed slow—the train disgorging and taking on more masses at every stop. Finally we passed the last City station; we were now heading into East London, Plaistow and Barking and Becontree and Dagenham, and suddenly it was the platforms opposite that were full to bursting, the population of my own train having thinned out to just a handful. We were men and women who, like the train we rode, went against traffic, who worked nights, or had bedridden parents to tend to, or were on our way home after waking up in the flats of strangers—the westbound trains, in their normalness, seeming to go backward, to our view, though of course it was they, and not us, who were going forward, into the urban day. I closed my eyes. I was imagining I could join them, head home from this nightmare, toward Richmond, childhood, the light playing on the river. My mother, alive, with Nanny and Caroline: three women drinking coffee in the garden . . . then I opened my eyes again. We were pulling into Upney station.

I got out. Without Edward I had no idea how to negotiate the route to his mother's house, but as luck would have it, the ticket collector knew the Phelan family and gave me directions.

At Lil's house I rang the bell. No one answered. I rang again. Anxious footfalls sounded against linoleum.

"Who is it?"

"Sarah, is that you? It's Brian Botsford, Edward's friend."

No answer.

"Please let me in."

The door opened a crack.

"He's not here!"

"Do you know where he's gone? Is your mum here, or Lucy?"

"He's not here!" Sarah nearly shrieked.

She tried to shove the door shut. I pushed back. "Sarah, please—"

"Let him in," I heard Lil say.

Slowly the door creaked open again. Sarah stepped aside to make room for me in the narrow hall. By the entrance to the kitchen, Lil stood in her dressing gown, her hands on her hips, her hair chaotic.

"What do you want from us?"

"I'm looking for Edward. Is he here?"

"Here!"

"Yes. Or if he's not—do you know where he is?"

"As if you don't!"

"I don't."

She looked at me in puzzlement.

"I don't know where he is," I said again. "He cleared out of the flat this weekend while I was away. I assumed he'd come to you."

"You drove him to it!" Lil cried.

"What do you mean? Drove him to what? What are you saying—are you telling me he's done himself in?"

"Done himself in—that's a laugh! He might as well have!"

"Where is he, then?"

"Right now? I should imagine right now he's in the middle of the channel crossing."

"I don't understand," I said, even though I did.

"He's gone to Spain," Sarah said softly. "He's gone to save democracy in Spain."

Lil turned and walked back through the swinging door into the kitchen.

I stopped being young.

Somehow I found my way back to the underground station, and the flat, where I fell into a stuporous sleep.

When I woke it was teatime. A stubborn vine of cold late-afternoon light creeping through the closed curtains; the smell of bacon coming down from upstairs, along with the muffled drone of a wireless tuned to the BBC, cups clinking, old women chattering as they sorted through the day, who said what at the grocer's and what Mary wore to her daughter's wedding and the frost.

I stood and, like an infant on unreliable legs, stumbled to the lavatory. Where was Edward now? Near the frontier? The new language would daunt him. I imagined nervous soldiers stepping from their truck to have supper in some cheap restaurant; the dim light, a toothless old woman in the kitchen. Strange food is placed before him—he would like to ask for something else, but he doesn't know how; and so he gamely cleans his plate, though the seasonings make him long for his mother, for beef and biscuits and tea, and really, he thinks, swallowing hard, it isn't so bad, is it? Rather—interesting.

That is how he was raised: to clean his plate.

Or was he thinking about me?

Of course he would record it all dutifully in his little notebook, every meal he ate once he stepped off English soil.

His grand adventure, remembered in lists.

A week passed, then two weeks. I saw no one except the child I tutored. Philippa gone, Edward gone. Even Nigel had stopped writing to me—lost, no doubt, in his efforts to rescue his own beloved boy.

I turned down every invitation I received, until the invitations stopped coming. Most evenings, instead, I went cottaging. It became a ferocious addiction, that search for sex, for the soft, stroking hand that alone might bring a temporary relief. Or I'd show up at the house in Richmond, surprising my sister: "It's not often we're honored with a visit from the likes of you!" she'd say, trying to disguise her pleasure at seeing me. Of course she sensed something was wrong, but didn't know how to broach the subject.

"Might I sleep here tonight?" I asked her one evening. She seemed surprised but pleased, as did Nanny, who felt my head for fever before I went to bed. I remember lying awake, that night, in my childhood room, craving some comfort its old familiar walls could not give me, though outside the trees rustled familiarly, there was the familiar sound of foghorns out on the river, as well as the familiar smells: camphor, candle wax, my mother's face powder, its sweet aroma somehow still lingering.

Had Lil begged him to stay, her voice hoarse with rage?

If only I hadn't left the journal! (Or had I meant to?)

I pulled the pillow tight over my head, like a vise.

*   *   *

Aunt Constance rang. "My poor dear! Edith Archibald has told me what happened with Philippa! The impudence! I made no bones about what I thought to Edith; *she* at least was in tears, as she should be. Such a stupid woman! Do you still have the ring? We shall certainly be able to return it for credit. Now in the meantime, there is a lovely young lady who has recently come to work for my publisher. Shy, but a good girl. What would you say about a little dinner at the Lancaster next month, just the three of us . . ."

Anyway, *was* it my fault?

The facts: Edward was an adult, capable of making his own decisions. His genuine political convictions could not be underestimated as a motive for joining the brigade; nor could Northrop's influence. Edward was a hero, braver and better than I. Risking his life because of Spain was democracy's last best hope.

Just as Edward was my last best hope.

And if I hadn't fucked Philippa, gone cottaging, lied to him, left the journal about—what else?—he would have gone anyway, wouldn't he?

Wouldn't he?

I managed, on certain days, almost to convince myself of it.

Christmas and New Year's passed. I have no memory of them. In January, however, I gave up both my pupil and flat and moved back to Richmond. As I recall, I spent most of the winter sitting by the wireless, listening for news about the war.

Once on Dartmoor Walk I met a chap whose brother was in the brigade. He promised to find out anything he could for me about Edward, as well as to keep me abreast of developments on the front generally.

At the battle of Jarama, the International Brigade clashed with Moors fighting on the Fascist side, and most of them were slaughtered. I thought I didn't want to know if Edward had been among their number.

Then the letter came.

Chapter Twelve

February 25, 1937
Altaguera

Dear Brian:

Please forgive this interruption of your no doubt busy life. I would not be bothering you except as I can think of no one else to turn to at this moment when I find myself in quite a difficult situation here in Spain. To cut to the heart of the matter, things have not been as I was led to believe they would be by John Northrop. Training in the brigade was rigorous, even brutal. Still, it was nothing compared to what followed. To sum up, I have seen battle. A shell exploded twenty feet from me that nearly took off my arm. I escaped with merely a flesh wound and the local medic tells me I am lucky to be alive. In addition I had to watch fellow brigadiers—my friends—die next to me by the dozens. I also believe I may have killed or wounded a man fighting on the Fascist side—a thought that is repugnant to me.

We live under horrible conditions, with insufficient blankets and clothing; never in my life have I been so cold. In addition, food is scarce, and what we get nearly inedible. Disease is rampant in the barracks. We do not have anything close to sufficient weaponry. The Republic itself is quite divided up between Communists and Anarchists, and supports actions I cannot condone, specifically the murder of priests and other barbarities. Northrop and the other brigade leaders excuse these actions. Because the Fascists are aristocrats, they say, they must be held to a higher standard. I am a peasant, at least in their view. Am I therefore less than human?

In the event, I contacted Northrop hoping that he might help me to leave. He would not give me the chance, insisting rather that I must stay and that I would be grateful to him. But why must I give up my life for the victory of the Republic? In any case, I cannot go home, as the brigade has confiscated my passport, issuing a worthless brigade passport in its place.

I realize I left England rather suddenly, and in doing so no doubt caused you distress. Suffice it to say that I had the misfortune to come upon your journal and commit the unpardonable sin of reading it. No doubt by now you and Miss Archibald are engaged and I am the last thing on your mind. Nonetheless I am facing a difficult dilemma and know no one else who might be able to help me find a way out of it.

I should add that meeting the people of the Spanish culture has been a most edifying experience, bringing me into contact with things I never could have known in Upney.

In the event, any pity you might be able to muster for your old friend at this hour would be greatly appreciated. Again, let me apologize for the inconvenience I may be causing.

With very warmest regards, I remain yours sincerely,

Edward Joseph Phelan

I put the letter down. Nine o'clock in the morning, the old house quiet except for the sound of a maid polishing silver. Outside, boats on the water, sunlight filtering through clouds and spreading itself out over the river, and in my chest a wild trembling, half terror and half joy. The letter, having been sent to Earl's Court, then forwarded, had taken several weeks to reach me. Yet I did not think: was Edward still alive? I thought: Two weeks ago he was alive, scarred but alive. He wrote this letter. Two weeks ago he still lived.

It is odd, given my earlier ambivalence, that I never doubted for a minute what I had to do.

I rang up Emma Leland. I rang up the chap from Dartmoor Walk. I rang up everyone I knew who might possibly be able to get me an address for John Northrop, until finally I was put in touch with a brigade organizer from Putney, a fellow named Chambers, who had an address where he thought Northrop could be reached. The telegram—sent that afternoon—informed him of my desire to come to Spain as quickly as possible. If he still wished me to write a pamphlet, I was at his disposal . . .

Chambers called that afternoon. Northrop had wired him from Altaguera, the brigade's base, to tell him to thank me for the telegram and ask if I might consider going to Spain right away: apparently a position had been found. As for my request to join the Party, the pertinent card had been issued; I had only to sign the proper forms.

I assented immediately, having no idea that years later, in a different country, that letter—unearthed—would prove the undoing of my career.

Travel arrangements were finalized. Northrop, Chambers said, would meet me in Barcelona upon my arrival; at that point, having been briefed, I would be sent on to the town of —— to continue on my own. Couldn't I go directly to Altaguera? I asked. What would be the point? Chambers said. Altaguera was the opposite direction. Oh, of course, I said, not wanting to reveal my real motive; once I arrived in Spain, I decided, I'd find a way to Altaguera, and Edward.

It was the winter of 1937, and I was twenty-three years old.

Shadow of an Umbrella

Chapter Thirteen

B arcelona. Mountain and water.

I took a room at a pension in the old part of the city, off the Ramblas. It contained a sagging bed with a threadbare white spread; a table with a short leg; a cold-water sink; a chair; a chicken-scratched armoire; and a calendar reproduction of Velazquez's *Las Meninas*. The floor tiles were old, the same shade of gray as gray hair. My windows opened onto a street so narrow almost no light came through them. Only if I thrust my head out and looked up could I see a sliver of sky and make a guess as to what the weather would be like.

Barcelona's geography is itself a metaphor; the poorest people live downtown, by the port. Then, as the long avenues steepen toward Mount Tibidabo, the apartments grow extra corridors and bath-rooms, the shops fill with elegant clothes, the people's faces take on that ruddy look faces have when people have always been well fed, warm and clean. Some streets are so steep, there are escalators on the pavements.

Downtown, by contrast, was a delirium. On the Ramblas, elderly whores, their cheeks and lips painted crudely as clowns', offered sex for a few pesetas. A transvestite with huge false eyelashes winked at passersby and thrust out a breast as hard and spherical as a coconut. Another whore, in a tight red dress, flitted through a café, singing and periodically shoving her breasts (real) into the faces of gawking foreigners.

On the Ramblas, I passed booths where you could buy orchids, houseplants, chickens and parrots, dogs and cats and mice. There was a booth where a monkey wearing a bow tie picked envelopes that told your fortune out of a jar. There was a swallower of flaming swords and an elderly flamenco dancer and a contortionist who could tie himself into a bow.

Even though it was winter, the sun shone brazenly. It would never have dared shine that way in London, which went a long way toward explaining my own skin, ludicrously pallid in this land of dark vigor. Smoke hung heavy in the streets; everywhere there was the odor of potatoes, frying oil, horse manure.

I saw an old woman knitting a pink sweater as she walked down the street.

The first two days, I ate lunch in empty restaurants, wondering if their emptiness signaled that they were second-rate, until I caught on that no one here had lunch before three. This was then followed by siesta, two hours during which the city became a ghost town, every shop shuttered. Around dusk, things came alive again and didn't stop. The Ramblas were up all night; you could buy a parrot that said "I love you" in four languages at three in the morning; everywhere there were soldiers, brigadiers, the color red. The Spanish call the mysterious hours between midnight and dawn *la madrugada;* if you stay awake through it, you are said to *madrugar,* and most people I met *madrugar*ed every night. But working hours were no different than anywhere else. When did they sleep? Did they hibernate in the winter, like bears?

Every couple of hours, news from the front shot through the city. Women thrust wirelesses out their windows and turned them up full blast; old men dragged blackboards to the streets, on which they scrawled hastily received dispatches. Usually these had to do with battles in Aragon. The actual facts—who had won, how many had died—got through only after several days' worth of unsubstantiated and contradictory rumors. Then came funeral processions, huddled clusters of mourners bearing sepia-toned photographs of young soldiers wreathed in flowers. And the mothers wailed their grief, grief on a Mediterranean scale, showing none of the restraint for which the English are famous. They tore open their blouses until the buttons popped, they scratched at their chests; if they could have, they would have torn out their own hearts.

Word spread that there had been heavy brigade losses at Guadalajara. But when I visited the local Communist Party headquarters and asked for information about casualties, the depressed-looking lackey at the desk merely shook his head and said he was sorry but he had no news.

The grand dining room of the Ritz Hotel, meanwhile, had been converted by the hotel trade unions into a canteen; the Anarchist leader Federica Montseny, who wanted to outlaw marriage, was appointed minister of health; and on posters all over the city a bare-chested fellow appeared with whom I might easily have fallen in love. "The Spanish workers struggle for the liberty and the cultures of all countries!" he pleaded. "Solidarity with them!" Barcelona, it seemed, was revolution central, while down the coast in Málaga the Fascists ruled; vendors sold postcards on which Hitler, Franco and Mussolini shared equal billing, like a demented Three Stooges. (Hitler did look like Moe.) "Viva España!" the captions read. "Viva

Italia! Heil Hitler!" And how long would it be, I wondered, before the Führer's Mediterranean *confrères* emulated him further, dispensing with nationalism, demanding allegiance not to the mother country but to its holy generalissimo, its prodigal son?

Two days passed, and still I had received no word from Northrop. Finally I decided to go myself to Altaguera.

I was in the middle of packing when the old woman who ran my pension rapped on the door. Northrop had sent a message to say he would be in Barcelona that evening. Could I meet him at ten o'clock at Bar Bristol on Plaza Madrid?

I got there half an hour early. Bar Bristol turned out to be a simple *bodega*, barnlike, with big communal tables and, instead of chairs, warped benches designed to hold ten people but squeezed, that night, with as many as twenty. (Once, one of the benches collapsed under the pressure, spilling its occupants onto the stone floor.) The owners, a young couple of weather-beaten beauty, appeared to speak the same four languages that the parrots on the Ramblas spoke, with only slightly more fluency.

I stood near the entrance. The bar was so crowded, people were literally bursting out the doors onto the streets. Music might have been playing, but you couldn't hear it; it was completely drowned out by a huge human noise like a hive of bees, men and women shouting about politics, or demanding tables. While the husband balanced trays filled with wine and *cerveza, tapas* and *empanadas* and *bocadillos,* his wife simultaneously sliced ham, pulled a bottle from an ice chest and wrote up a bill. They had no employees; the two of them managed the unruly crowd by themselves. They seemed to be the sort of people who could do a dozen things at once, perfectly, without ever losing their otherworldly composure.

In a dozen different languages, the patrons at the bar were arguing—Communists with Anarchists, Catalans with Castilians—which went a long way toward explaining the divided condition of the left. Spaniards enjoy argument and practice it as a sport, something I witnessed frequently during my days there, restaurateurs duking it out with customers over the honor of an insulted salad. Even those who stood on the same side of the fence could work themselves into such a frenzy over fine points, they might come to blows.

Across the room some soldiers started singing a drinking song. With each verse they raised their glasses higher into the air, until, on the twelfth verse, one of them lifted his glass so high the beer splashed a bare light bulb on the ceiling, which fizzled out. *"Coño,"* the wife said, then went into the kitchen, emerging with a ladder and a new bulb, which she held between her teeth like a rose. She climbed the ladder and began removing the old bulb. The soldiers, still sing-ing, surrounded her and lifted the ladder in the air, and taking the bulb out of her mouth, she told them to put her down, but they would not put her down; instead they started twirling the ladder as if it were a chair that carries the bride at a wedding. Then she smiled, she threw back her head so that her hair flew out in a fan, as the ladder swayed, and the crowd applauded, and she let herself be lost in the pleasure of motion.

I heard a voice, loud and distinctly English: "Excuse me, excuse me, passing through." It was Northrop, looking quite hale in his brigade uniform. "Botsford," he said, "how good to see you!"

He thrust out one of his huge hands to shake mine; the other, I noticed, was swathed in bandages. "Sorry about the delay," he said. "We took a bit of a drubbing at Guadalajara. No one emerged unscathed, not even yours truly, though in the end I'm happy to say our side managed to prevail."

"Were losses heavy?"

"Depends on your definition of 'heavy'. Let's get a table, shall we? Manu!"

The husband put down his tray and came over to greet Northrop. For some moments they conducted a gushing conversation in Spanish, the result of which was our being ferried immediately to two open places at a table, much to the chagrin of the people who had been waiting. Northrop, it appeared, had become a figure of importance.

Two *cervezas* arrived—pale and urine-colored, nothing like English beer. "Drink, drink," Northrop said. "I know it looks pissy, but it's the best you'll find over here." I drank. "Cheers, I forgot to say. Anyway, I was delighted to get your telegram, though I can't say it surprised me. I knew you'd come around sooner or later."

"Northrop, I must ask you about Edward," I interrupted.

"Edward?"

"Edward Phelan. The fellow who shared my flat."

"Ah, Phelan, yes." He shook his head.

"Well—is he all right?"

"I wish I knew."

"But I presumed—" My heart was racing. "Northrop, has something happened to Edward?"

"Easy, old boy! It's just that he's deserted."

"Deserted!"

"Yes. It's been almost a week now."

So Edward wasn't dead. I closed my eyes in a silent prayer of thanks.

"But we'll find him," Northrop went on. "Mark my words, we'll find him. A thing like that can't go unpunished. If men desert and get away with it—well, what then of the republic? What then of the cause?"

"But how? Why did he leave?"

Northrop shrugged. "I suppose he just didn't like the fighting. Not that anyone does. Anyway, he came to me and asked to be relieved. I said no. The next morning"—he snapped his fingers—"gone."

I stared into my beer.

"And no one has any idea where?"

"Oh, we've got leads. Nothing I can talk about, of course. In any case he hasn't got his passport, so he won't be able to leave the country. It may take a few days but we'll track him down."

"Well, really, what's the point? Why not just let him go?"

Northrop's eyes widened. "This is an army, my friend! Not some rugby club! Things like this can't just be overlooked. Phelan is a soldier, and as such subject to military law."

"So you'll just hunt him down like an animal, is that what you're saying?"

"Don't confuse what's happening here with one of your novels. We will not hunt him down like an animal. The police will simply search for him and when they find him turn him over."

"And then?"

"There'll be a hearing. A fair one. He'll be judged by his comrades."

"And what might they decide?"

"Well, he *could* be sent home, though that's unlikely. Or they could assign him a few months' duty in a prison camp, after which he'd probably be put back into the battalion. The firing squad is a possibility as well, though I tend to doubt—"

"The firing squad! The boy's a volunteer! What kind of barbarians are you, to shoot a boy who'd volunteered?"

"If you'll let me finish, I was saying the firing squad is a *possibility.* An extremely unlikely possibility." He brushed his fingers through his hair.

"I hope for his sake he makes it to France."

Northrop eyed me narrowly. "Look, what is it with you and this boy? Phelan knew what he was getting into when he signed up; I made it all very plain to him. He welcomed the opportunity. And a soldier can't just leave a war because he's changed his mind. If we allowed that, where would we be? Just where Franco wants us. Just where Hitler wants us."

"But he's twenty years old!"

"They're all twenty years old."

"Well, that's my point! There's no draft here, Northrop. These boys came by choice, out of a sense of idealism. Surely you can be easier on them than the Royal Marines."

He slammed down his beer and leaned closer. "I don't think you understand what's happening here, Botsford. This is class *struggle*. Class *warfare*. Individual lives don't matter. I would give up my life gladly for the cause. We'd all give up our lives, just as so many millions of our comrades gave up their lives so the rich could—"

"*You* are the rich!"

"Botsford—"

"Don't give me this party line shit. I know you! Christ, you grew up in fucking Eaton Square! You went to Oxford! Your father's an earl, for Christ's sake!"

"Are you done?"

"Well—yes."

"Good. And now that you've had this little opportunity to vent your frustrations, may I speak frankly as well?"

"Of course."

Then he looked me in the eye and said, "You're a buggerer. And for the last several months you've been buggering that boy, until finally he decided he'd had enough and he had to get away from you."

"That's ridiculous—"

"Maybe you thought I didn't know what was happening. Maybe you think I'm stupid generally. Well, I'm not. Oh, I know we've never discussed what went on in school, but that doesn't mean I don't remember. It was normal—back then. Now's a different story. A lot of people wouldn't stand for it, but my feeling is, what a fellow does in his bedroom is his business, so I kept my mouth shut. Now it's wartime. I'm in charge of a battalion, and where the morale of my men is concerned I've got to put my foot down."

I looked away. "You don't understand, Edward and I—"

"Oh, I think I understand perfectly. You used him. You exploited him sexually the same way the bourgeoisie has been sexually exploiting the working class for generations. And Phelan went along with it, because he didn't know any better. That's the sad part. They've been trained to think it's good for them too. Probably Phelan figured he'd make a quid or two that he could spend standing his mates a few pints at the pub, or getting Mum a new dress. Only soon he was in over his head. I guessed from the minute he rang what it was he wanted, and to be honest, my first reaction was, well, it's the best thing for him. The chance to get out of England and prove he's a man on the battlefield, with other, normal blokes. Now, if you want my advice, you'll stay out of it. Don't worry anymore about Phelan; you'll only bring him trouble, and believe me, he's got enough as it is."

He smiled at me: a jaunty, old-school smile. I wanted to smash his teeth in. You idiot, I wanted to say. You fucking self-satisfied idiot. It wasn't like that!

"If I were you," Northrop went on, "I'd stop worrying about Phelan and start thinking about yourself. You're right: you *do* know me. Your world is my world. For years people have been telling us it's us that matters, us above all else, the privileged sons of the English privileged classes. Everything revolves around us. Servants have no existence beyond serving us. The world was created so that we could exploit it. And of course we came to believe them. How couldn't we when it was all so convenient? You may say you're a Communist now, Botsford, but it's obvious you're still in the thrall of the Capitalist reward system. Not that I blame you. It took me years to overcome my upbringing, but I did it. You can too. I'll help you."

His voice had grown honeyed, almost seductive.

"First off, you've got to recognize that your homosexuality is merely a corrupt bourgeois aberration—"

"Oh, piss off!" And I stood, upsetting a glass of beer. The stream of yellow liquid raced toward the table edge. Northrop leapt out of its path just in time.

He looked at me as if I were mad but I stared him down.

"I have only one thing to say to you, Northrop, and it's this: if anything should happen to Edward—anything at all—I'll hold you personally responsible."

"I'm going to forget this conversation," Northrop shouted. "I'm going to forget this conversation ever happened—"

But I was already turning, pushing my way through the crowd, hurrying out the door into the lamplight, the moonlight, the moist, deserted streets.

Chapter Fourteen

I spent the next several days waiting—hungering—for news that never came. When I wasn't listening for gossip in Bar Bristol, I was wandering the city, hallucinating Edward's face into the most outlandish and improbable circumstances. Not that I had any good reason to suspect he might be in Barcelona; it was as likely—and unlikely—as his being in France, or Upney, or dead. Still, I had to believe something. So I drew upon my creaky draftsman's skills and worked up a likeness of Edward in black ink, which I showed to the patrons at Bar Bristol, to soldiers, to strangers in the street. An old woman on Calle del Carmen thought she'd seen him selling fruit at the *boquería*, the huge open-air market near the port—a purported sighting that sent me running frantically through that maze of stalls and peddlers where openmouthed fish gaped up from beds of ice, and the guillotined heads of boars and rabbits leered behind glass partitions, and pretty girls in dresses patterned with bluebells wiped their bloody knives with their aprons. The Spanish do not fear looking death in the face. There were chickens, half plucked like poodles, still wearing their crowns. But alas, no Edward, not even beheaded behind a counter, mouth and eyes open, bewildered, appalled. One young man looked like him from behind, but when he turned around he had cheeks scarred with acne, a missing front tooth.

Various other sightings were reported. A soldier at Bar Bristol said he thought he'd seen Edward the day before walking a dog on Plaza d'España. A woman was sure he'd been at a meeting she'd attended in December. Another woman said he had a shave twice a week at a barbershop on Calle Aribau.

In my madness I followed each of these leads to its inevitable fruitless conclusion. Don't think, however, that I required the prompting of strangers to start a wild-goose chase. I could do it just as well on my own. Thus one afternoon I hailed a taxi and had it follow a fruit truck thirty blocks through the rain, because I was convinced I'd seen Edward's face steal a glance out the back of it. During a parade I tried—without success—to break into an apartment on the balcony of which I was sure I'd seen Edward watering some plants. I even wandered "by accident" into the kitchen of a restaurant in the old quarter where I was having lunch one day. But the boy chopping potatoes in the back corner—the boy whom I had glimpsed stumbling sleepily toward the toilet—wasn't Edward. He didn't even look like Edward.

A telegram arrived from Chambers. As my first assignment, I was to travel to the town of —— and interview the mayor. He, in turn, would explain to me how the town had flourished under a Communist government. As I had no compelling reason to stay on in Barcelona, I decided that I would travel to —— as quickly as possible, then hurry back to see if there was any word as to Edward's whereabouts. Besides, —— was just as likely a place for Edward to be hiding as Barcelona.

It was a long journey to ——, almost nineteen hours. Outside the window, scenes of unrelieved harshness unfolded. The land was knotty and windblown: all edge. Periodically the train slowed to a crawl as it passed through villages where old women leaned out windows and children stood immobile on cobbled streets, watching as the train crept along, segmented like a worm, huffing and huge, almost kingly. Then the town would be gone, the old women gone; we'd pick up speed through olive groves, thorny fields of rosemary, rice paddies in watery troughs. The Spanish landscape, so much more varied than films would have you believe; and yet the light was always the same—severe, unforgiving, as if the sun were a bare bulb screwed into a ceiling socket.

In ——, I announced myself, as requested, at the mayor's office, only to be told that no appointment had been made for me. Moreover, the mayor was in Barcelona that week. So I went to have a beer at a *cervecería*, where I met a British officer, one Colonel Parker-Dawes, who recognized my accent and insisted we have a drink together. This jaunty and garrulous young idiot went on to tell me that he was an official with the government in Gibraltar. He had a lot of opinions about the residents of the colony—in particular a Lady Something who made herself available to him on a regular basis.

"By the way," I said, "I have a friend whose uncle lives in Gibraltar. I was wondering if you knew him: Teddy Archibald?"

The mention of this gentleman's name sent Parker-Dawes into gales of uproarious laughter. It turned out that Philippa's uncle Teddy had a reputation around town for being a gambler and a rake, his parents, prominent members of the local polo-playing set, having died twenty years earlier and left him their entire fortune to squander. Most recently he had "gone red," shuttering up his house and leaving town: rumor had it he intended to offer his services to Republicans on the front. "If you can beat that," Parker-Dawes said.

"Although those Spanish soldiers will screw anything from what I've heard, even their own grandmothers. Even their own grandfathers! The fellow is, as they say, 'so.' Care for a cigar?" I declined, and he put his rather large feet up on the table. "It *is* refreshing to have visitors from home," he said, and I nodded, surprised and disturbed by the extent to which he saw me as one of his "kind."

Forgoing Parker-Dawes's invitation to join him for dinner, I went out to find a pension, where I spent a restless night. The next afternoon I was on my way back to Barcelona. The train was much more crowded than it had been going in the other direction, mostly with soldiers. Soldiers everywhere: smoking between the cars, lying on the floors of the corridors, their heads on each other's laps. My own carriage I had to share with three infantrymen, one of whom snored; a nun; and an immensely fat old woman, whose valise gave off a distinct odor of sausage. No matter: I couldn't have slept even if I'd wanted to. I was thinking about Edward. If he'd been captured, of course, Bar Bristol would be abuzz with the news. But what if he'd made it across the frontier? What if he was back in Upney? I needed desperately to know, yet I couldn't very well contact Lil without alerting her to the fact of his desertion, knowledge that—assuming he *wasn't* back in England—would cause her immense distress. Then there were the less palatable alternatives to consider: the possibility that Edward *had* been captured and was languishing in a prison somewhere; the possibility that he was dead.

So the train rolled on, through the interminable night, its rumble only partly muffling the snores and thrashings of the soldiers, the slow, regular wheeze of the old woman, who had fallen asleep with her head listing on my shoulder. I watched the window, partially curtained, for changes in the light. And then—it seemed eons later—dawn was breaking in blue streaks across the sky. The old woman lifted her lolling head. One of the soldiers raised the blinds of our sweaty carriage, filling it with a fevered radiance.

The nun got up, stumbled through the legs of the soldiers, came back awash with the sickly sweet odor of *eau de cologne*. I had to use the lavatory too, so I went out into the corridor. Everywhere soldiers were stretching, their hair rumpled, their cheeks dented with the imprint of whatever they had slept against. Looking out the window, I saw that we were passing through the distant outskirts of some city—I hoped it was Barcelona, then concluded from the talk in the corridor that it was Saragossa. Old neighborhoods of cobbled houses and stone streets passed us, going the other way. Opening the window a crack, I felt a rush of chill air and caught the distant odor of bread baking.

Eight torturous hours later, when we arrived in Barcelona, I had convinced myself that Edward—alive when I began this journey—would be dead by the time I ended it.

I got off the train. My stomach was hollow, but I did not eat. Instead—bypassing even my pension—I went to Bar Bristol. I had no idea if Northrop would be there, if he was even in town. Still, the place served as a kind of nerve center in those days; if I was going to find out anything, I reckoned, I would probably find it out there.

Almost as soon as I walked in the door I knew something had happened. It was as if, upon my arrival, the hum of the place had gone up a register. Strangers—people I barely knew—were looking at me and whispering.

A soldier approached me. *"Muchacho!"* he called. "You were looking for someone, an English soldier, right?"

"Yes?"

"I think they've found him."

"Where?" I cried.

"San Sebastián. Only now he's back in Altaguera, in the barracks brig."

"And is he all right?"

"I don't know; I just heard the rumor—that the English *maricón* who deserted had turned up. Then someone said he'd seen the *maricón*, and he looked just like the picture the other English fellow was showing—"

"Thank you," I said. "I'm sorry, I must go."

"Where? To Altaguera: *Qué loca*—" But I was already out the door. It was four o'clock in the afternoon, siesta just over, a mass of people hurrying down the narrow street toward the Ramblas with the directional intensity of a school of fish, a flock of birds, a wave: old women in mourning black, workers drunk on cheap lunchtime wine, young men whose beauty would stop your heart. The light— more generous, softer than it had been earlier in the day—had drawn them out from their curtained flats to browse at the book stalls or read the scribbled propaganda on the Ramblas. And I sailed among them, buoyed up by panic, by an impulse that could tolerate no distraction, it was so single-minded: for the first time in weeks, I knew where Edward was.

By metro, I went back to the station. I bought a ticket to Altaguera. There was no direct route, I discovered; instead I would have to retrace a substantial portion of the journey I'd just made—all the way to Saragossa. If I'd known, of course, I could have just got off at Saragossa in the first place. But I hadn't known.

I sat down on a hard bench to wait. Almost immediately the woman sitting next to me stood up and left. Only then did I realize I hadn't bathed, shaved or changed clothes in almost thirty-six hours.

All around me tragic partings were taking place: mothers rent from sons, wives from husbands. Uniformed soldiers laughing and waving as the dilapidated trains that would carry them to their deaths steamed off. The station had high, vaulted ceilings that, in their grandeur, only compounded the atmosphere of sepulchral gloom: it was a cathedral in which the train itself, the terrible voyage itself, presided like a god.

And in my exhaustion, I fell into a kind of stupor; slowly, inch by inch, I felt myself slipping off the bench—it seemed beyond my control—until the small of my back was where my rump should have been. Before me a panorama of busy life was spreading out, the sort you see when you lift a wet piece of wood. Vendors hawked newspapers and sweets, *chaperos* lounged casually near the lavatories, their cocks crudely outlined in their trousers. Dust and smoke everywhere, a film of blackness that even the desolate-looking chars, swishing their mops around, could never entirely eradicate.

Have you noticed how all war stories end up at a station? Think of the movies, the requisite scene where the train starts up, the soldier leans out the door to wave goodbye, his girl—desperate to prolong the moment of parting—chases after him, until the accelerating beast outruns her. There is no rest in a station; a station thrives on motion, and war usually necessitates a journey: the enforced transport of soldiers to the front, the panicked exodus of refugees, the surreptitious flight of exiles. Soldier, refugee, exile. Who has not, at one time or another, played one of these roles, or all three?

The time arrived for the train to depart. I stood, collected my bags, stumbled over to where the impatient crowd—my fellow travelers—had gathered.

But the hour of departure came and went, and no train pulled up to the announced platform.

Twenty more minutes passed. A voice came over the loudspeaker, announcing that the train to Saragossa would be indefinitely delayed.

Because it was wartime, the crowd greeted this bad news not with anger but relief. The soldiers' mothers, thanking God for the stay of execution, rushed their sons home for makeshift farewell meals.

As for me, I went to the station baths and had a shower.

And finally, around midnight, we pulled out. I remember droplets of rain slithering down the window, clinging to the glass as we picked up speed, then being snatched away by the hungry air. Saragossa—where I spent two hours—survives in my memory only as another hard bench, a fog of half sleep perpetually interrupted by unintelligible voices announcing delays. Nothing ever arrives on time during a war.

It rained for a long, long time, the rain thudding against the station's tin roof.

Three hours and fifteen minutes late, the local to Altaguera made its departure from Saragossa.

Six hours and thirty minutes after that, we arrived in Altaguera.

I got out; I was standing with some soldiers on a bare platform in the middle of a flat, dusty plain. Early afternoon, the sun hammering, in spite of the cold.

Hoisting up my bags, I walked into town. Altaguera had no charm to speak of; its streets and squares were flat and geometrical, with few trees and little shade. Old, low buildings forged from swollen bricks listed and crumbled onto barely paved streets. Donkeys mingled with the military trucks; women carried things on their heads.

I did not stop to find a pension, to drop off my bags or bathe or have something to eat. Instead I went directly to the barracks: a clump of jerry-built flat-roofed shacks laid out on a ragged field. Two soldiers stood guard at the gate.

I asked for Northrop. They appeared not to recognize his name. The head of the British battalion, I said. The soldiers looked me over for a minute, and then one of them made a call on a walkie-talkie. After a few minutes he received what I gathered was a favorable reply and motioned me through the gate, where another soldier escorted me through the barracks buildings to an old one-room farmhouse that appeared to have been converted into a kind of central command. And there Northrop sat, in full uniform, behind an empty desk on which a clock ticked mercilessly: Northrop, with whom I had frolicked on the bucolic grounds of an English public school, whose fat cock I'd stroked—how long ago had it been? Five years? Six years? Childhood.

"Botsford! Jesus, man, you look awful!"

"I haven't slept much," I said. "I've spent the last several days on trains."

"Well, sit down." I sat. "I gather you must have heard about Phelan, then."

"I have. I've come to ask if I could see him."

"Now, Botsford, I told you—"

"You must let me see him, John. Please. You must."

He looked away. "I don't see how it could possibly—"

"I'm not asking you to let him go. I'm not even asking you to understand or tolerate. I'm just asking, as someone you've known since you were a boy, to let me see him. A half hour, fifteen minutes. That's all."

He stared at his desk.

"Please, John."

"Oh, Christ. Look, this goes against every rule."

"I'm aware of that. And I'm prepared to take full responsibility if any blame should be leveled."

"All right," he said. "Fifteen minutes. But not a second more."

"Thank you," I said.

We stood.

At the door, Northrop turned to me and said, "I just want to say I can't see how this is going to possibly do any good—for either of you."

"You can't, I know. Still, you must let us speak."

He held the door for me, and I passed through. We walked between the barracks buildings until we arrived at a stone structure with blacked-out windows, outside which two armed soldiers stood guard. Northrop saluted them, and they made way to let us pass.

Inside, the building smelled of sweat and urine. We were in a mean little room, unadorned except for a table, two chairs, the ubiquitous bare bulb and a portrait of Lenin. Another armed soldier stood beneath the portrait.

"Wait here," Northrop said.

Taking a key ring from his pocket, he let himself through a second door, an inner door.

I sat down at the table.

What seemed like hours passed.

Then the door opened again.

Northrop and a soldier came through, between them Edward, his wrists handcuffed.

I stood.

"Edward," I said.

He looked at me. His eyes widened with surprise.

"Edward, I'm here."

The soldier sat him down at one end of the table. Northrop then waved the soldier out of the room.

"Fifteen minutes," he said from the doorway.

He stepped out.

The door clicked shut.

An expression of utter surprise gripped Edward's face.

I took his handcuffed hand in mine and burst into tears.

"Brian," Edward said, "it's all right. I'm all right. Don't cry—"

"It's just it took me so long to find you—I've been searching and searching."

"Take a deep breath. You've got to pull yourself together."

"You're right. I'm sorry." I breathed. "Ridiculous, your having to calm *me* down. Anyway, how are you?"

"I've been better."

"You're thin."

"Haven't had much to eat."

"Well, you look wonderful to me."

"Glad you think so." He leaned closer. "Brian—what are you doing here?"

"I got your letter. I came as soon as I got your letter."

"Oh. I wondered if you had. It seems like decades since I wrote that letter." He attempted a smile. "I suppose I'm in a lot of trouble, eh?"

"A little," I said, smiling as well, wiping my eyes. "Edward—what happened?"

"Well, like I said in that letter, I reached a point where I couldn't bear it anymore. The fighting, that is. So when Northrop wouldn't let me leave, I stole off. I got as far as San Sebastián, where I met this fellow in a bar. You must know him by now—Mr. Archibald."

"Philippa's uncle?"

"I knew who he was, Brian, on account of reading your journal, which of course I shouldn't have done. And in spite of—well, in spite of his relation to you, he was still someone familiar. Believe me, over here I would have welcomed my worst enemy if only he'd been English. Anyway, he was nice and civil to me, and I thought I could trust him. What a joke that turned out to be! Still, I confessed and told him what was up. Oh, at first he couldn't have been more cordial: he let me stay in his hotel with him, he gave me fruit and milk and coffee—things I hadn't had for weeks! And he said he'd take me back to England with him. He said he could arrange things, knew who to bribe to get me across the border. But first he wanted to stay a bit longer in San Sebastián on account of he had some business to finish there.

"Five days we stayed in the hotel. Nothing happened. I had my own room. And though I could tell this fellow *wanted* something from me, I pretended I couldn't, on account of—well, I just didn't fancy him. Anyway, how could I have done that, with anyone but you? I'm sorry to say it, Brian, believe me, but it's how I felt. And then the last night he came into my room, and I had to tell him point-blank I wasn't about to do anything with him. Well, you can imagine his reaction. Hurt and angry all at once. 'After all I did for you, after everything I've risked for you.' Finally he stormed out. And then the next morning we were having breakfast, all very tense and silent-like, when the doorbell rang and it was the police. Apparently they'd tracked me down from a photo. And he just let them right in, like they were coming to breakfast, stood by while they put the cuffs on, saying how sorry he was that he wouldn't be able to help me after all. As I left, he wouldn't meet my eye." Edward looked into his sleeve. "My own stupidity. I thought I could trust him, him being Miss Archibald's uncle—or is it Mrs. Botsford now?"

"Oh, God," I said, laying my head on the table. "Everything is my fault."

"You haven't answered my question."

"What? Oh. No. No, of course not."

"You did ask her to marry you."

"Yes—but, Edward, it was a dreadful mistake. A mad fantasy. She laughed at me."

Edward raised his eyebrows. "I'm sorry," he said.

"Well, never mind about that. The point is to get you out of here. Are you feeling all right? You look pale."

"I think I've got influenza."

"But are they treating you all right? Have you got enough food?"

"If you can call it that. They've got four of us right now—a Pole, two Russians and me. They're decent fellows, the others, though we can't say a word to each other. One of them had a deck of cards, and we play with that, day in, day out. And it's clean—well, I mean, it's not the

Savoy Hotel, but compared to the police cell . . . Makes our flat—your flat—seem like paradise. Still, I'd rather be here than on the battle-field." He looked behind himself, as if to make sure no one was listening. "Brian," he said, "it's not like they said at the meetings. Nothing is nearly so simple. Most of the blokes in my battalion are upper-class boys out to prove they can be rebels. Even so, if you've got an accent like mine they treat you like a servant. The leaders, the ones like Northrop, they see us as expendable on account of us mostly being from the lower classes. And the fighting—it's horrible, Brian! Those Moors would shoot you just as soon as shake your hand. I've had to kill; there wasn't any choice." He leaned closer. "Is there anything you can do? I'm sorry to trouble you, I know I'm of no concern to you now, but you're my only hope. All I want is to go home."

"Edward, don't say these things. I care about you more than anyone."

He stiffened. "If that's true, why did you ask her to marry you?"

"I was confused—"

He laughed. "*I* was the idiot. I should have seen the signs." Suddenly his face grew harsh. "You never did say you loved me, did you?"

"Edward—"

"I never was disloyal to you, Brian, not once! I'd never have done that to you! Whereas you . . . But there, I've said it. It's off my chest now."

I laid my head on the table. "Oh, Edward," I said. "If you told me right now you'd never forgive me, I'd say you have every right."

He leaned back and shook his head. "I loved you, Brian," he said quietly. "I really loved you. How could you have done that to me?"

"If only there was some way to make it up to you—some way to show you—"

"It doesn't matter anymore," Edward said. "*This* matters: I don't want to die."

And suddenly I realized I must get control of myself. So I sat up, held my head erect. "You're not going to die," I said. "I'll go to the consulate. You're a British subject; they can't just hold you against your will. I promise you, Edward, something will work out."

The door opened; Northrop and the soldier came back in.

Immediately I felt Edward's body tense.

We pulled our hands apart.

"Fifteen minutes," Northrop said.

We stood. Taking Edward firmly by the arm, the soldier motioned him back toward the door.

"I'll do what I can," I called again hopelessly.

I thought he smiled. I couldn't be sure. Then they were through the door, the door was closing behind them.

The door clicked shut. Edward was gone.

I stumbled back toward the station. Dusk was settling; the streets were crowded with shoppers: men and women whose faces were marked by a kind of uniform savage austerity. Every cheek had a scar on it, every lip a boil, every hand seemed to have been maimed in some horrible industrial accident. Even the children looked old, darting as they did among the market stalls, which were colorless, drab, all cabbages and root vegetables—a desiccated parody of the *boquería*. Nowhere had the slightest concession been made to pleasure or comfort; there were no parks or fountains or playgrounds, just church after church. Still, one had the sense these people would hang on forever, as their town did, teetering but not falling, while frailer, pleasure-seeking souls gave up the ghost.

I took a room at the first pension I saw, pulled off my clothes, lay down and tried to sleep. But the bed was narrow, the mattress straw-filled, sagging in the middle. The room—tiny and spare, lit by a single ceiling bulb—had the severity of a monk's cell. Through the tiny window I could hear dinner conversation, smell dinner smells: boiled meat, potatoes frying in rancid oil. A baby wailed, its parents argued. Then windows clattered open, another voice started up, this one high and thin and furious, screaming at the top of its lungs, an endless monologue that was more complaint than lament and the contents of which I could barely make out. Next the neighbors' windows: *"Cállate, puta!" "Señora, por favor!"* But she went on and on.

I closed my eyes. I must have slept then, because when I bolted up and looked at the clock, three hours had passed. Amazingly the same thin, high voice was still shrilling, pouring out its enraged miseries to indifferent ears.

Dizzily I got up, got dressed again, stumbled out into the streets. What I felt was not dread but lust, which can be the *doppelgänger* of dread: panic and grief translating into an itch in the fingers, an erection that wouldn't quit. Luckily the streets were full of soldiers, a steady stream that led to a café near the hotel in the center of town. Thank God, I thought, for soldiers.

I entered the café. It was dark, hectic. Flamenco music played on an old wind-up gramophone, cigarette smoke hung in the air like a fog. I ordered a beer. There were almost no women in the café, aside from a few beleaguered-looking whores. Russian soldiers, Polish soldiers, English and American soldiers, mingled with the Spanish.

I would have taken any of them at that terrible moment; any man who had approached me, grabbed me by the arm and led me away, I would have gone with.

I cast my eyes over the crowd; I cast and cast, like a fisherman, until they locked, for a millisecond, with another pair of eyes. The soldier in question had curly dark-blond hair, a bracingly clean face, black eyes. He was standing alone, smoking, at the opposite end of the bar.

I moved nearer. Next to him a whore sat on a barstool, regaling the bartender with stories about her days as a maid in Barcelona. "Every place I worked in I got fired," she said. "And why? Only because I had affairs with the heads of the houses! Well, don't look at me that way; is it my fault if they found me irresistible? Big houses, these were, up in Bonanova. Listen to me: if I've learned one thing over the years, it's that the rich are always the sickest. One of these gentlemen wanted me to whip him, another liked me to bark like a dog, another asked me to rub marmalade into his head while he masturbated. The wives, of course, got jealous and showed me the door. Farther and farther downtown I went, to poorer and poorer houses, until the men just wanted an ordinary fuck, and I ended up in the Barrio Chino. Now, *carino*, couldn't you give me just a little more whiskey? You know I'll pay you tomorrow. All I want is half a glass—"

The bartender merrily refused her, and cursing him, she got up from her stool, thrusting out her breasts for good measure. *"Maricón!"* she shouted at me, laughing, and her laughter rang out, getting softer as she rounded the corners of the streets.

I sat down on the barstool she had vacated, next to where the soldier was standing. The cracked black leather was warm and slightly damp from her sweat. The soldier smiled at me.

"Do you want another beer?" I asked him in Spanish.

"Ah," he said in perfect English, "so you're English."

"It's that obvious?"

"I'm afraid so."

"And do you accept offers of beer from Englishmen?"

"Well, it would depend. This is the first one I've received. In this case, yes, with gratitude."

Relieved, I called for the beer. The soldier's name was Joaquim, and as it turned out, he was part English himself, his mother's father having been born in Warwickshire. But he had grown up in Gerona and had never visited England. Now he was a captain with the Republican forces.

"And what are you doing in this horrible place?" he asked me. "You're not with the brigade, so you must be a journalist."

"More or less."

"And do you stay near here?"

"Down the street, at a pension."

"And what brings you out tonight?"

I looked at him. He smiled.

"You really want to know?"

"Yes."

"Well, to be perfectly honest, I was looking for sex."

"How convenient," he said. "So was I."

I laughed. He laughed. "Too bad the whore's gone," I said.

"A pity," he said.

"Unless of course—"

"Yes?"

"Well—we could go to my room."

"What a good idea," he said. He finished his beer in a single swallow. "Are you ready?"

I said that I was, and together we headed out into the street. The building where my pension was located had a huge ancient wooden door out of which a smaller, human-sized door had been jaggedly carved. Through this we passed. There was no light in the stair, and we had to grope our way.

On the fourth-floor landing Joaquim suddenly stopped me, reached his arms around my waist, pulled my face toward his and kissed me.

For a few minutes we groped each other there in the dark, my body pushed by his against the chilly stone wall. His mouth tasted of the honey and almond nougat Spaniards eat at Christmas.

As soon as we were inside my room I started stripping off my clothes. Taking my cue, Joaquim followed suit. We watched each other intently as jackets, ties, shoes, belts, shirts, vests, trousers, socks, and finally drawers fell in a heap on the floor. Then we were naked. He had a line of hair running from between his nipples to his navel, an erection that looked cumbersome, almost painful to maintain, bobbing up and down.

I got on my knees and sucked him. He moaned, gripped my head in his hands. Then I stood again, lay on the bed, put my legs in the air. I did not have to tell him what I wanted; he knew. Taking my legs in his hands, he pushed his cock against me, eager for entry, but I was too dry, so I told him to hand me some lotion that was in my case. As if I were he, I slathered my fingers and inserted them inside myself until the channel was wet enough for them to slide in and out easily. Then I took his cock and made it slick with my hand and guided it inside. The pain, at first, was enormous; I closed my eyes, counted to ten, tried to obliterate it, and found I could do so by wanking ferociously. "Are you all the way in?" I asked. "Yes," he said. "Good," I said. Cautiously he started moving, but it was too much; I cried out. He loomed over me, stone hard, a frozen statue. Then, once again, he started moving. He slid out and eased in again and hit something, some region of fire. Suddenly there was sensation, a flaring pleasure that seemed to radiate out in waves, that seemed initially to exist alongside the pain I was feeling, and then, miraculously, seemed part of the pain, and then swallowed the pain up. My eyes bulged out, my mouth opened into an uncontrollable shout. I understood, suddenly, what had driven Edward so mad those times I'd done it to him; it was this, this quadrant of pleasure hidden deep up inside. And Joaquim thrust harder, and with each thrust the radiating pleasure revived, flailing my limbs and rolling my head and twitching the length of my cock until it seemed I might come from it, from this thrusting, I might not even have to touch myself or be touched by him, but I did not want to come, I wanted this to last, I wanted to say things, filthy things, utter words I'd never uttered, and I did, I said, "Fuck me," I said, "Come inside me," and with a loud shout Joaquim thrust one final time and the warm flood of his semen was pouring down my legs like tears.

He pulled out, rolled over, heaved breath like someone rescued from drowning. I felt a chilly film of perspiration forming on my back.

I had to crap. Bolting from the bed, I pulled on my drawers and ran into the little water closet at the end of the hall, where I got on the toilet just in time. Gas erupted from me in loud explosive grunts. I put my head in my hands and, letting it drop, watched the checkerboard on the linoleum floor dissolve, reform, dissolve. I was so dizzy I thought, for a moment, I could feel the rotation of the earth.

When I got back, Joaquim was lying on the bed, smoking. I lay down next to him. Under our combined weight the bed sagged nearly to the floor.

"Cigarette?" he offered.

"No, thanks," I said. And closed my eyes. I was terribly, terribly sleepy.

With a screech of hinges, my mad neighbor threw open her windows again and launched into another tirade.

"What's she saying?" I asked Joaquim. "I can't understand."

"It's hard to make out; she has a very strange accent." He frowned in concentration. "Mostly it's about a baby. 'The baby needs to be bathed, and I don't have time! There are dishes to be done, so many dishes! The mother just wants a rest, but the baby keeps screaming!'

She repeats the same names: Manolo, Begona. Her children, I'd guess. Probably they've been gone for years." He shook his head. "People think madness is romantic, but it's not. Madness is boring, it's like cleaning and cleaning a room and it's never clean."

He cocked his ears attentively.

"What?" I asked.

"It's nothing. It's just that now she's shouting so loudly, and what she's saying is, 'Why do people say I shout in the middle of the night? I never shout in the middle of the night!' In such a voice!"

We both laughed.

"You know," Joaquim said, "you never explained to me what you were doing in Altaguera."

"What I'm doing here?" I smiled. "Trying to save someone I love. Or should have loved. Someone who loved me."

"Save him from what?"

"From being killed."

Then I told Joaquim the story. He listened thoughtfully, without remark, until I was finished. "The lesson here," I concluded, "is my own unworthiness, compared to Edward's sterling loyalty. I mean, look at me! I'm shameless! No sooner do I find him than what do I do? Betray him again."

"My friend, you're too hard on yourself," Joaquim said. "Yes, you made a mistake. But consider all you've done. You've come all this way for him. I would call that extraordinary. Brave, in fact." He extinguished his cigarette. "As for making love, what choice do we have, in these times? If you don't mind my saying so, you did it grievously, almost as if you were seeking an exorcism. And that, I think, is something he would understand."

Joaquim left soon after that. I never saw him again. I can't tell you if he died in battle, or survived and married, if he's a famous poet now, or a laborer, or a judge. So why is it that he survives so vividly in my memory—this boy I knew only for a night?

How hesitantly human souls brush against each other! Like the ads one sometimes sees in the lonely hearts column in the newspaper: "4/12: We spoke in front of the library. You were wearing a scarf, I was carrying a newspaper. I would like to see you again, love you, marry you!"

Well, Joaquim, if someday, by some miracle, you read these pages, consider this my own lonely hearts letter. Know that I remember that night in Altaguera. It's eighteen years later now. I'm middle-aged, blacklisted, broke. Edward is under, and I am across, the sea.

Still, if you read this, call me.

Chapter Fifteen

Altaguera, by morning light, looked even bleaker than it had in the afternoon. Grime caked the walls of the buildings; dust tornadoed from the unpaved streets every time a truck lumbered by. I was walking down a commercial block filled with butcher shops and *charcuterías*, the doorways of which were hung with strings of colorful beads. These bead strings stretched out when you pushed through them, then dropped back, raking your shoulders sensually, like long fingers. Inside, however, one found only the meagerest provisions, nothing remotely appetizing or appealing, though whether this was due to the war or to Altagueran asceticism I couldn't tell.

Needing to eat *something*, I went into a bakery. I wanted a sweet roll or a bun, but the proprietress had only loaves of dry bread, one of which I bought and tore into as soon as I was out on the street. Witnessing this, a group of women frowned and shook their heads judgmentally. (I learned only later that the Altaguerans considered eating in the streets a *faux pas* of the highest order.) Meanwhile some children were torturing a kitten. When I approached them they ran off, leaving the rheumy-eyed creature to bite at its flea-infested hide. And now I saw there were cats everywhere; the streets were filled with cats: tabbies with distended, low-hanging teats, packs of kittens gnawing at foul-smelling scraps, fearsome toms who wore their shredded ears and gouged eyes like medals. A sky mysteriously empty of birds. Perhaps that was why. Perhaps the cats had eaten them all.

Having finished most of the loaf, I set out once again toward the brigade headquarters. Once again I asked to speak with Northrop. I don't know what I had in mind—perhaps to beg, perhaps to make another attempt at convincing him to let Edward go. But Northrop wasn't in. No one was in. No one would see me.

Well, when would Northrop be in? I asked.

Northrop had gone to Barcelona. He returned in three days.

Thanking the anonymous figure that dispensed this information, I left.

For three days after that I waited.

I managed to convince myself that things were looking up. I wired Channing, explaining I was short on cash and could he do anything to extort some from Aunt Constance; wrote a fawning letter to the beldam herself, a reassuring letter to Nanny and an honest letter to Nigel; caught up on my journal. I even explored the town of Altaguera a bit, determined, before I left, to root out *some* bit of beauty, some pearl, amid all its studied austerity. And I did find something: there was, near the center, a very small, very old church, the oldest in the region. It had been built during the reign of Charlemagne, had walls of swollen, uneven brick, and displayed on its façade images of Christ and His disciples, the faces of which the hard winds of Altaguera had long since eaten away. Nothing spectacular about the church; rather, its very humility charmed me. It was like a beautiful girl before she learns she is beautiful, before she learns the power beauty carries.

The church had a unique history. Adjoining it was a convent whose sisters had been cloistered for more than five hundred years. A large balcony above the nave connected the two buildings, and it was from here and here alone that five hundred years of nuns had borne witness to the outside world. You could often see them when you went in: lofty figures in heavy habits, clinging to the shadows as if they feared, above all else, being seen by those they watched over.

I went to the church frequently during those days, not so much to pray as to reflect, to contemplate. In its hushed chambers, I could hear my own voice better; the questions that plagued me—if not answerable—at least became articulate. What would happen if Edward *was* freed? I wanted to know. Would we take up where we had left off, he and I? Or would he return to Upney, and I to Richmond? Yes, my bungled efforts with Philippa had resulted only in my own humiliation, but the fears that prompted them still lingered. Home was now as uncertain a prospect as Spain; I had no idea where I'd live upon returning, if I'd spend my nights scouring public lavatories for sex, or reading in bed with Edward, or some new Edward. As for England, she might not be a haven very much longer: there was every chance that soon both of us would be compelled to go to war again— the big war this time, the war that threatened in Germany and for which this one would prove, in the end, merely to be the prologue.

But of course, there was every chance in the world that Edward *wouldn't* make it back home, every chance that all my speculations were for nothing.

And of course dawn, the fourth day, the day of Northrop's scheduled return, found me at the gate to the barracks. Northrop, I was told, had been delayed.

"Well, then, might I speak with someone else?"

Doubts. Murmured consultations by walkie-talkie.

Finally a decision was reached: two other comrades, both familiar with Edward's case, would speak with me. If I might come this way . . .

And I did, following a claque of brigadiers back to the same office in which I had earlier met with Northrop.

They closed the door behind me. In the corner two figures stood in huddled conference, their faces shadowed. They were apparitions that, as I neared them, became more recognizably human: one dark, with alarming, almost spectral eyes and a drooping mustache; the other pale, plump, a youth who—

I stopped in my tracks, winded by recognition, the breath literally knocked out of my chest.

The two turned.

"Brian," the youth said. "What on earth . . ."

And suddenly it was as if that fatal umbrella, lost in another life, had blown open, casting its vast shadow over all of us: a darkness so huge it could never be defeated.

"Rupert Halliwell," I murmured. For it was he.

Not until years later would I learn what had happened: how Rupert, seemingly out of the blue, had one day woken up, put on his dressing gown, walked quietly downstairs and one by one smashed every precious teacup, every fluted crystal vase, every glass. Then he poured lye all over the Indian silk sofa. Then he went and said irrevocable things to his mother, and then he got in a taxi, rode to the London offices of the Communist Party, knocked on the door, and prostrated himself before the befuddled secretary who happened to answer: a piteous specimen of the corrupt bourgeoisie. "Reform me!" he cried. And they did.

"You know each other?" asked the man with the drooping mustache. He was French, by his accent.

Rupert looked away.

"Yes," I said. "We do."

The Frenchman smiled, so that the ends of his mustache curled upward. "England must be a very small country," he said. "And may I introduce myself? I am Comrade Bonet."

"Brian Botsford," I said, putting out a hand.

"A pleasure," Bonet said. "Won't you have a seat?"

The three of us sat. From his corner of the desk Rupert eyed me nervously.

"And how may we help you, Mr. Botsford?"

"I've come to inquire about my friend Mr. Phelan," I began.

"Ah, Phelan," Bonet answered, smiling. "What a sad morning it was when he deserted."

"I understand his case has yet to be resolved, and I was wondering if I might say a few words on his behalf."

"Of course. Not that *we* have any say in the matter—"

"Even so, if there is anything you could do . . ."

"Go ahead."

I steadied myself. "First of all, I don't contest the fact that Mr. Phelan deserted. Nor do I contest that desertion is a serious crime. However, in this instance there are extenuating circumstances that need to be taken into account."

"Such as?"

"Mr. Phelan is a young man of limited education who had the fortune—or perhaps the misfortune—to come within my circle. His decision to travel to Spain might well be said to have resulted from his exposure to that circle. But he hadn't fully thought through the consequences of his actions. As a result, when he arrived, he had second thoughts. For this reason, I would ask that you let him go home."

I stopped speaking. Bonet had laced his fingers into a temple over his mouth, while Rupert's eyes remained fixed on the wall.

"Mr. Botsford," Bonet said finally, "forgive me if I sound stupid or unreasonable, but I believe I have missed your point. Are you suggesting Comrade Phelan is so impressionable—so, if you will, unformed—that he cannot be held accountable for his actions?"

"No—not exactly. But he *is* young. And the fact is, if it hadn't been for me, he wouldn't be in this trouble now. He'd be at home, working for the London Transport."

"I understand. Nonetheless I fail to see why this should affect our treatment of him. Because he was under your influence, the pledge he made to the brigade—to the cause—is no less binding."

"It is I who should be going to prison. Not Edward."

"Mr. Botsford, you are not a brigadier. You made no pledge."

"No. No, I didn't. And I agree with you, pledges to a cause cannot be taken lightly. But what if a boy takes that pledge rashly—without thinking it through? What if there were other factors involved? Things that were going on at home that had nothing to do with the war but that might have prompted him to do something on the spur of the moment, something he'd later regret?"

"By other factors you mean, I presume, something such as, for instance, Comrade Phelan having a sweetheart who left him for another man."

"Well—yes."

"And did Comrade Phelan have a sweetheart?"

I looked down. "No. No, he did not."

"Then what type of other factors are you suggesting, Mr. Botsford?"

"I'm—I'm not sure. I'm just saying if there were—"

"But apparently there were not."

Outside something crashed. A cat howled. Tortures proceeded.

Bonet leaned forward and cracked his knuckles.

"Mr. Botsford, what exactly is your relationship to Comrade Phelan?" he asked.

Rupert, who had been silent up to this point, coughed loudly and recrossed his legs.

"He is my friend," I said, after a few seconds.

"Your friend."

"Yes."

"I see."

A palpable silence. Rupert pushed his stubby fingers through his hair.

"Mr. Botsford, may I ask you something, if you don't mind?"

"Of course."

"Do you consider yourself a Communist?"

"Yes. Fundamentally."

"And Comrade Phelan?"

"I couldn't presume to say."

"Well. We are brothers, then. No? We agree that the Spanish republic must be defended against the Fascist threat. That must be our priority. My comrades demand obedience, but we are not barbarians—"

"Then he won't be shot."

"That is not for me to decide."

"Then who must I speak to? For God's sake, who's deciding this boy's fate? Is he to have a trial? Is he—"

"Mr. Botsford, please calm yourself. There's no need for you to be so frightened. The firing squad is a remote—an extreme—possibility. More likely your friend will be sent to a prison camp, or back into battle—"

"I could go to the press, you know. The British press. I could—"

"Or he might be freed. In any case, contacting the British would do him little good. He no longer holds a British passport. He is a citizen of the brigade now."

"But he's not well!" Then, in a softer voice: "He says he's got a temperature. He says he's having pains."

"We have a doctor here."

"I don't want to make it worse for him. I hope my speaking to you like this won't make it worse for him. I'm simply trying to help Edward. I hope you understand."

"If I might make an observation," Bonet said.

"Of course."

"You care too much. He is not worthy of it. He is a coward. Let him go."

And he smiled. And suddenly, in that smile, I saw something. He had penetrated to the truth of my relationship *too* skillfully. His huddling intimacy with Rupert, as I'd entered, made a new sense, as did his interrogative eyes, his "England must be a very small country." England was not the only small country. *You are one of us too,* I might have said to him—Nigel would have. Instead I met his smile with my own, I let my gaze travel down the length of his body, over his chest, groin, legs, to his shoes.

"I cannot let go what will not let me go," I said.

Bonet gulped. For the first time that afternoon he appeared to be nonplussed.

"Well, that is all then, I suppose," he said, rising, putting out his hand. "Good day, Mr. Botsford."

"And can I ask you something?"

"Of course."

"When something happens—when a decision is made—you will let me know. I'm staying at a pension in Altaguera. You can leave a message if I'm not in."

"I would be pleased."

He bowed.

"Goodbye, then," I said.

"Goodbye, Mr. Botsford."

"Goodbye, Brian," Rupert said very softly.

I looked into his eyes, but they were blank.

"Goodbye, Rupert."

A door swung open, revealing the claque of hovering guards.

The doors to the church, though heavy as trees, gave gently, at the slightest pressure. I stepped inside. Candles, lit for the dead, glowed in niches, illuminating ancient frescoes, as well as a hideous diorama: a plaster Christ impaled on the Cross, while nearby Mary prayed and wept—Mary, her hair wiry and red, was in fact a porcelain doll with glass eyes. A scent of must and roses wafted from an open door. My footsteps, as I trod the aisle, reverberated, a muffled throb that filtered through the church the way the candlelight and the rose scent did, seeming to blanket and protect. There was no one else there except an immense elderly nun who sat on the balcony, snoring quietly, her head listing to one side.

I knelt, as if to pray, on the stone floor. But I did not pray. Instead I thought of Rupert. How he got there—what strange twists of fortune had carried him from Cadogan Square to Altaguera—concerned me, at the moment, not a jot. Rather, his umbrella haunted me; that and the memory of those times I'd rejected—even humiliated—him. Might he still hold a grudge? I wondered. Might he use this opportunity to avenge himself—through Edward—on me?

When my knees began to ache, I pulled myself up, leaned back against a hard bench. Above me the old nun snored on, so huge and immobile she seemed at that moment almost to have taken root.

Light surged in as the doors to the church creaked open; a woman in black crossed herself and sank to her knees. And from her lips a flutter of Ave Marias took flight, gentle as birdsong, scattering into echo as they rose toward the vaulted ceiling.

Chapter Sixteen

The next morning I was back at the barracks. This time I asked for Bonet instead of Northrop. Bonet was unavailable. So was Rupert. Nonetheless I was shown into the same office, to the same desk, where now one Comrade West held reign. He had ragged blond hair and bitten nails. American.

"I spoke yesterday with your associate Comrade Bonet," I said. "He promised he would let me know what judgment was reached regarding my friend Mr. Phelan, who is in the brig. But I haven't heard from him. I was wondering if anything had transpired."

West scratched his head. "Phelan . . . oh yes, the deserter! I'm afraid the news isn't good. They say he's to be shot two days from now."

"Shot! But Bonet—"

"It's a serious matter, desertion. We can't have the other men thinking they can just—"

"He's a boy!" I lunged out of my seat. "How can you shoot him? A boy?"

"Hey, it wasn't *my* decision. I'm only telling you what I was told. You'll have to speak to Northrop if you want to know more."

"Is Northrop back from Barcelona?"

"Yes, but he's not on the barracks. Now if you'll excuse me—"

"When will he be back?"

"This afternoon, probably."

He pretended to file papers.

As if on cue, two soldiers arrived to escort me—haul me—to the gate.

From the corner of my eye, I caught a glimpse of the brig—deadbolted, guarded on both sides.

I was back at the barracks gate at three.

This time I asked for West. He was unavailable. Bonet? No. Northrop? No. Rupert? Yes.

I had no idea what I was going to say. All that was certain was this: if a life was to be taken, it would not be Edward's. Perhaps mine. Perhaps someone else's. But not Edward's.

Once again I was shown into the same office. Behind the desk Rupert writhed, his legs twined one round the other like pipe cleaners.

As soon as the door had closed, however, he rose from his chair and crouched next to me.

"Brian, what on earth are you doing here?" he whispered.

"I could ask you the same question."

"Not so loud, please! I think what I'm doing is obvious. But you—"

"I'm trying to save a friend," I said. "A boy. And probably you've never forgiven me, Rupert, for everything that happened—the umbrella and Lady Abernathy—and if that's the case, I can't blame you, but still, you must help me, for there's no choice. A life is at stake. You must help me."

Rupert looked perplexed. "But I don't understand! What's Phelan got to do with you? Or how—"

"He's my friend. You understand? I love him. Or he loves me. Or rather, we lived together. And the point is, he wouldn't be here if it weren't for me. If he dies his blood will be on my hands, and so you must help me, Rupert, no matter how you feel about what I did, you must—"

"I'm not the same as when you knew me before, Brian. I'm a Communist now."

"I see that."

"And in other ways I'm—not the same." Suddenly his face brightened. "For instance, I'm engaged to be married. A nurse in the ambulance corps."

"I don't see what that's got—"

Rupert's lower lip quavered.

I saw.

From under heavy lids timid eyes glanced up.

I leaned back from him.

Well, why not? I thought. Why not blackmail, if through blackmail I might save Edward?

Like Bonet, I cracked my knuckles.

"Comrade Bonet is quite handsome," I said loudly. "Don't you think?"

"Brian!"

The door opened again. Northrop walked in.

Immediately Rupert leapt from his crouch, saluted.

"Comrade Halliwell."

"Comrade Northrop."

"Ah, Botsford. Somehow I'm not surprised to be seeing you again."

Northrop took the chair Rupert had vacated.

Where he stood against the wall, Rupert wrung his hands.

"That'll be all, then. I'll handle this from here."

"Goodbye, then."

"Goodbye, Rupert."

"Goodbye."

Throwing me a last tortured glance, Rupert left.

"I hoped it wouldn't come to this, Botsford," Northrop said. "Really, I did everything I could to keep it from coming to this. But in the end it was out of my hands."

"Everyone says that. A boy is to die, and everyone says it's out of his hands."

"Boys die every day. This is war."

"They're not killed by their countrymen."

"As I said, there's nothing I can do."

"I don't believe you."

"Is it my responsibility to convince you?"

I stood up. "I shall notify the press," I said. "I shall notify the press in England that an English boy is to be killed by his peers. And I shall name you as his killer."

Northrop coughed.

"And are you aware of what repercussions that sort of . . . outburst might have?"

"Perfectly."

"I'm not talking about the war anymore, Botsford. I'm not even talking about what happens to Phelan. I'm talking about you."

"What about me?"

"Don't think journalists are pushovers. They'll nose around, and what do you think they'll find? That you and Phelan lived together, that you shared a bed-sitter with a double bed. That's very odd, they'll think, a university-educated fellow like you sharing a bed-sitter with a ticket collector from the underground! I wonder if Mr. Botsford might be a buggerer—"

"Shut up!"

"I wonder if he might have been buggering that boy—"

"Enough, Northrop!"

"And soon enough your family knows, his family knows. What about your writing career then? What's your old nanny going to think if you get arrested? Not very nice for her to read in the paper that her beloved little boy is—"

I lunged at him. We wrestled, frantic, silent, the way we had when, as boys, we needed some prelude to grabbing at each other's cocks. I could smell his hair tonic, smell the tobacco on his breath.

Then he was on top of me, with a single thrust he was hoisting me into the air, hurling me against the opposite wall.

My skull smacked the plaster. I dropped to the floor.

"Jesus, man, are you mad?" Northrop was shouting. "Are you completely barmy? Well, fuck it, then! Call your newspapers, wire the fucking BBC. I've had it up to here with both of you! The whole lot of you!"

He sat down again, scratched at his skull.

"You bastard," I said.

"I do what I must do. There's a war going on, in case you don't remember."

"But you brought him here! Jesus, you even gave him his fucking precious copy of *The Communist Manifesto*. He worshiped you!"

Northrop clawed at his own hair. "Don't you see? He doesn't matter! None of *us* matters!"

I looked at him. He appeared, suddenly, to be on the verge of tears.

For a few moments we just sat there.

I pulled myself up from the ground.

"I *shall* wire the press," I said. "They're sure to be more interested in what you're doing than in what I've done. And I'm not frightened by your threats, nor do I accept your—your ludicrous logic. You may be willing to sacrifice Edward, but I'm not."

"You don't care about anyone but yourself, do you?"

"I care about Edward."

Northrop looked away. "Oh, do your damnedest! Now get out. I'm sick to death of the sight of you."

I left. Dust clouds rose outside. Church bells rang all over the city.

I wrote out the telegram. I carried it to the telegraph office. I stood nearly two hours in front of the telegraph office, while dust churned up around me, powdering my shoes, my clothes, my hair.

I stood there until the sun was low in the sky, the streets silent except for the sounds of a cat taking pleasure in the slow dismemberment of a bird.

The office closed. I turned around.

I never sent the telegram.

I suppose on some level I believed Northrop. I believed that they mattered more than we did. Their victories, their wars. Their loves.

I went to the station, where a huge yellow timetable charted departures and arrivals all over Spain.

Unfortunately the next train for anywhere wasn't due out until four o'clock in the morning.

I bought a ticket for that train.

Back in my room I vomited violently.

Later, I looked out the room's tiny window. Across the alley my mad neighbor ranted. It got dark. I hurled myself into bed, tried to will sleep upon myself. But it did not come. I lay awake for what seemed hours, moving restlessly, reliving peculiar moments from my childhood, school hurts, my mother's death. For suddenly I wanted her—desperately. I wanted my mother. Oh, where was she now, that poor, befuddled woman? I had not appreciated her enough when she was alive. I had not. I had not grieved for her, as my brother and sister had, her abstractedness, her bountiful hair that seemed always about to fall from atop her head like a cigarette ash. Had she ever been happy? Had any of us? Father, silent in death as he was in life. Caroline, so rivalrous, though perhaps that is always the way with daughters. "Mother's bed's still warm, and Caroline's reorganizing the kitchen! That just isn't right!" And now Channing would be a doctor, like Father. "I shall cure cancer," he told me. "I shall cure the cancer that took our mother's life." How I longed to run back to them all, to be reclaimed, rolled up into the rug of childhood and spilled out again, fresh, unsullied! Never to have known, much less betrayed, another's love!

And then I was in the church basement. Edward, standing against the wall, shook his leg; his satchel slipped off his shoulder. And I thought, If I'd known then what I knew now, if I'd known what it would come to, would I still have approached him? Would I still have walked up and started talking to him?

Yes. Oh, yes.

I heard a loud rapping: Mother beating out the rugs. Mother! Why must you beat out the rugs in the middle of the night? But it continued. *"Señor! Señor!"*

I sat up. One-thirty in the morning.

"Señor! Señor!"

"Who is it?"

"La portera!"

I stumbled out of bed, opened the door. The proprietress of the pension stood before me in bathrobe and slippers, talking and talking, yelling almost, very fast, in Spanish. "I don't understand," I mumbled, and then I did. Two gentlemen were waiting for me in the foyer, and in the future would I please refrain from asking visitors up so late; people were trying to sleep . . .

I followed her down. The light in the foyer seemed blazing, blinding.

It was Rupert, with Edward.

"Thank God you haven't left," Rupert said.

"Rupert—"

"Hurry and get your bag. There isn't much time."

"What? What's happening?"

"Suffice it to say that bribes still carry some weight, even among Communists."

"Edward—"

"Hello, Brian. I'm afraid I'm not feeling too well."

He was sitting on a chair the proprietress had fetched for him. Sweat beaded his face. "Edward, what's wrong?"

"I've got a temperature."

"What on earth—"

"There's no time to waste," Rupert said. "You've got to get out of here before morning."

"All right, yes. I'll be right back." And I hustled up to my room to pack my bag. The proprietress was yelling something at me about charging an extra half day's pension for waking her up in the middle of the night.

"Are you all right?" I asked Edward when I got back to the foyer.

"I'm not sure. I haven't got a thermometer."

"But are you well enough to travel?"

"Not much choice, is there?"

"There's a lorry waiting downstairs," Rupert said. "I've paid the driver to take you to Valencia, to the port. There you're to ask for Captain López. The ship is called *El Pingüino*. It's a freighter. They sail at dawn for Bristol."

"Rupert, how did you arrange all this?"

"Someday I'll tell you. Now you've got to go."

Opening his wallet, Rupert handed some bills to the proprietress. She smiled and began thanking him profusely. Then Rupert and I helped Edward up, and the three of us headed out into the night.

A lorry was waiting in the street; its driver—bearded, pot-bellied—grunted in acknowledgment of our presence. His lorry gave off the faintest odor of orange blossoms.

I hoisted Edward up, through a canvas flap at the back of the lorry, where sacks of oranges had been piled. Then I turned to Rupert.

"I don't know what to say. I thought—"

"Never mind that. Just pray I don't get caught."

"Jesus, Rupert, you could be in terrible trouble!"

"I'm just joking. Don't worry, I've covered my tracks. Now get in."

"And I'll pay you back, I promise. As soon as I can."

"Get in the lorry!" Rupert said. "If you miss that sailing—"

I climbed into the lorry with Edward. "Thank you," I called from the back. He waved. The engine sputtered into life.

Rupert receded, growing smaller and smaller, until we turned a corner and he was gone.

I closed the canvas flap at the back of the lorry. It was dark and fertile back there, like a womb, peaceful almost, except that every time the lorry went over a pothole—and they were plentiful—my behind lifted quite literally into the air.

"Edward?" I whispered, but he was sleeping, snoring.

I took his head in my lap, I cradled his head, ran my fingers through his hair, which was moist and glassy.

"What?" Edward shouted as we went over yet another pothole. Then he looked at me in the dark. "Brian."

"How are you feeling?"

"Nauseous. I must say, I can think of places I'd rather be than this lorry."

"You must stay calm. Relax. Just relax."

"You got me out."

"No, Rupert got you out."

"But he explained to me. He said it was all because of you."

I closed my eyes. The train ticket I'd bought was still in my pocket. Its hard edge gouged my thigh.

We bumped on. After a while I opened the canvas a crack. A cool breeze hit my face, the smell of wheat mingling with the oranges and petrol. We were out of Altaguera now, in open country. In the darkness I thought I could make out fields, scarecrows, occasional modest houses.

I closed the flap again. "How did he get you out?" I asked. But Edward was once again sleeping.

I must sleep as well, I decided. So I leaned back against a sack of oranges and tried to get comfortable.

When I opened my eyes again it was to the sound of retching.

"Edward, dear God!" He was vomiting onto my lap, onto the oranges. Pushing open the canvas, I tried to get his head out, but it was too late.

Even after he stopped vomiting his throat kept convulsing. I held him until he could breathe again.

He started weeping. "I'm sorry, I'm sorry," he said. "Oh, God, I'm so sorry."

"Don't worry," I said. "You're ill, that's all." Opening my case, I took out a towel and started wiping up the vomit. To cover up the stench I split an orange, squeezed the juice out over where Edward had been sick. Then I threw the towel out the back of the lorry.

He had a stomach flu, I told myself. Or food poisoning. Nothing more serious than that. In the morning, I told myself, he'll be better.

We lay back against the oranges. Dawn was beginning to break by now, milky light illuminating the tattered canvas.

"Where am I?" Edward asked at one point. "Are we going to the camp?"

"No, Edward. We're going home."

I peered out the back of the lorry. We were passing through the most remote of Valencia's outskirts, a region where farmland alternated with small neighborhoods of neat white houses. A woman was taking up laundry from a line, sheets that rocked, nearly frozen in the predawn chill.

"We'll be there soon," I told Edward. "We'll be home soon."

Chapter Seventeen

At first Captain López didn't want to take us. "He's too ill," he said, looking at Edward, who sat shivering in his greatcoat, even though it was getting warm out.

"But you've been paid," I protested. "The arrangements have already been made."

"The arrangement was to take on two healthy men as crew. No one said anything about one of you being so sick."

"But he's not *that* sick."

"And what if he dies at sea? Then the police find out the captain of the *Pingüino* is transporting prisoners." He shook his head. "I can't risk that, amigo. It's not worth the money."

I looked at him, to see if I'd correctly caught his meaning.

"And how much would it be worth?" I asked.

He stroked his beard. "Well . . ." He named a figure.

It was everything I had left, and I gave it to him.

The *Pingüino* turned out to be a dilapidated freighter with a crew of fifteen. Apparently it had once been under Japanese registry, because all the instructions on the ship were written in Japanese.

We were given a small cabin—just two bunk beds, a porthole and a tiny, foldable sink. The nearest head was on another deck. It had a couple of chipped enamel urinals and a toilet that stank not only of shit and urine but also of the lye in which the shit and urine was supposed to decompose. Not a very pleasant place to be sick, and even more unpleasant when you consider that to get him there I had to drag Edward halfway across the boat. The night was cold and the waves rough.

I remember kneeling on the floor of that head while Edward sat on the toilet, the Japanese instructions seeming to dance in front of my eyes as I tried to determine how to flush the thing.

I put him to bed soon after. He lay in a fever, alternately sleeping and thrashing beneath the sheets.

Outside the porthole, Spain receded, until it was a thin brown line at the edge of the horizon. Little waves lapped the prow.

"Headley, stop crying!" Edward cried out.

"What? What did you say?"

"Stop that crying this instant!"

I felt his hot head. "Headley isn't here," I said. "You were dreaming."

"Where are we? Are we in the lorry?"

"No, we're on the boat. We're out of Spain now."

"I think I have a temperature."

"You do, but you'll be all right. Now try to eat something—a piece of orange?"

"No!"

"How about some soup?"

"I couldn't. I couldn't eat."

"Don't worry, then. You don't have to. Just lie back and rest."

"But what if I have to go to the lavatory?"

"Then I'll take you."

"But it's far!"

"It's not that far; just down the corridor and up the stairs."

"But I'm afraid I might not make it all the way, like that last time."

"Don't worry about that. The crewmen understand; they've all suffered from seasickness."

"Is that what this is, then, seasickness?"

"Probably in part."

"I hope that's all. You know, I *was* dreaming just now. About that night we spent with the babies, Headley and Pearlene. Remember?"

"Of course."

"I felt so happy that night."

"So did I."

"Really? I was never sure."

"Yes, I did. Now try to rest, Edward. You must rest."

He fell asleep again, gently snoring, the soiled bed sheets thrown about his feet.

I stepped out onto the deck for a cigarette. The wind had got strong. No land visible anywhere now, which was a relief.

"Have you got an extra one?" asked a sailor.

I gave it to him. We stood side by side, smoking, the water roiling beneath us.

"How's your friend?" the sailor asked after a moment.

"Tolerable, thanks."

"Most of the crew, they won't go near him. They think it's typhoid."

"What? That's ridiculous."

"He shows all the symptoms."

"He shows all the symptoms of a bad stomach flu."

"Perhaps. Even so, they're nervous. They don't want to catch it."

"And you?" I asked the sailor. "Aren't you nervous? Don't you think it's a mistake to be smoking my cigarettes?"

"Not for me. I never get ill. I've got a charm. My cousin had polio when I was a boy. My sister died from the cholera. Me, not even the influenza, not even once."

"You're lucky."

"My grandmother says it's unnatural. She thinks I must be a demon. "He smiled at me. "What do you think, *muchacho?* Do I look like a demon?"

"You *look* more like an angel."

He laughed, blew out smoke, threw the butt into the sea.

"Buenas noches," he said, and shambled away down the deck.

A full moon cast a path of light over the ocean. "Look, Edward," I said. "Look at the moonlight."

He lifted his head. His fever had gone down; he seemed to be feeling better.

"When I was a kid we went to Margate once," he said. "We'd never been to the seaside before. And Lucy and I, we'd go every night to look at that light. She called it the moon road. She said if you stepped out on the water you could walk along it all the way to the moon, where there was a great fat lady who'd give you sweets. 'Go on,' she said, 'go take a walk on the moon road.' So I did. You can imagine what happened next! I cried all night, and wouldn't go in the sea for years."

"That's a terrible story," I said.

"Funny. I suppose so. I hadn't thought about it."

The water got choppier.

"Brian," Edward said, "when we get back to England, what's going to happen?"

"We'll live together."

"But where? That same bed-sitter?"

"No, not there."

"I'd like it if we could find a flat with a garden. I do like to garden. I'd put in peas, cabbages, tomatoes, potatoes, onions, carrots. Only, as I recall, you're not partial to carrots."

"No, I find them too sweet."

"Then no carrots. But flowers. Daffodils, tulips, roses—"

"That would be lovely."

"—delphiniums, perhaps petunias. And pansies, of course, since we're a couple of them."

I laughed. Another ship passed by, its smokestack letting out a high, thin drone.

"What happened at your trial?" I asked.

"It wasn't much of a trial, really. Just a chat. With a Frenchman."

"You mean Northrop wasn't there? Rupert either?"

"What, the fellow who sprung me? No. In fact I didn't meet him until he came to get me the next evening. How long ago was that?"

"Two days."

"It feels like an eternity."

"I know."

I lay back.

"Brian."

"What?"

"If Rupert hadn't sprung me—what would you have done?"

"I—I would have wired the newspapers. They would have made an incident out of your imprisonment and embarrassed the brigade into letting you free."

"You know, by the time it was over, I'd pretty much given up. I'd got tired of arguing. I thought, well, if they're going to shoot me, they're going to shoot me. There's nothing I can do about it, so I might as well go with God."

"I wouldn't have let that happen, Edward," I said. "I would have got you out."

"Would you? I'm glad to know that." He yawned. "I feel a bit better."

"I can tell."

"You know, I was really in a rage when I read your diary that day. Really. If you'd been there I might have hit you."

I looked away, toward the water. "You had every right to be angry."

"I did. You cheated on me."

"And I lied to you."

"And treated me badly."

"And led you on."

"Yes. All those things."

"There's no reason for you to forgive me."

"Yes there is. This ship. This ocean. I probably owe you my life."

I closed my eyes.

"Edward," I said after a while.

He snored. He was asleep.

A stench woke me in the middle of the night. I stepped down from my bunk to find Edward shaking between drenched sheets. He had shit and vomited on himself.

I hoisted him out of the bed, and he cried out.

"We're just going to clean you up," I said, swinging open the cabin door.

"It hurts!"

"Here—just sit here."

I pulled the stinking sheets off the mattress, hauled the mattress out onto the deck.

"Brian, it hurts!" Edward cried.

"I know, Edward! It's all right, I'm here," I said—holding him, stroking his hair, while his body shook.

Outside our cabin, the captain paced, cursing, praying that Edward might last till he reached England.

He didn't care about Edward. He only cared about his own hide.

Meanwhile, inside, I parted Edward's lips, trickled water into his mouth, spoonful by spoonful, to keep him from dehydrating.

"Edward!"

"What?"

"Edward, listen to me. There's something I must tell you. I lied to you when I said I would have wired the newspapers. The truth is I never sent the wire. I was too afraid."

"Yes."

"And then I bought a ticket to Valencia. I was going to go back to London."

"Yes."

"You mean you knew?"

"Headley, stop crying!"

"Don't you understand anything I'm saying? Rupert, not me, is the hero of this story!"

"I understand."

"Edward, please hear me! You must hear me! I was going to abandon you! I was going to leave you there!"

"Stop crying! Jesus! Why won't he stop crying?"

I opened the cabin door, stepped out into flooding sunshine.

"What's happened?" the captain asked.

"He's died," I said. "He just died."

"*Madre de Dios.*"

"It was typhoid, I think."

"We will have burial at sea."

"What?"

"Burial at sea! And when you arrive in England, you will tell them all he died in Spain, before you got on the ship, *¿Entiende?* That is what you will tell them."

"I don't care," I said. "I'll tell them whatever you like."

I opened his bag, spilled its few contents onto the floor. He had managed to hold on to a few pairs of his drawers, his name sewn into the waistbands. There was a battered copy of *Journey to the Center of the Earth*, as well as *The Communist Manifesto* Northrop had given him, some tea in an envelope, some sugar in a paper bag, and his notebook.

This I opened.

March 6th [I read]. Breakfast: bread and coffee. Lunch: beans. Dinner: stringy meat and soup. Two bowel movements. No wanks. Read *CM* pp. 81–93.

March 7th. Breakfast: coffee only. Lunch: dried fish and rice. Dinner: beans. No bowel movements. Wanked once. Read *CM* pp. 93–102, plus reread chapter one of *JTCOE*.

March 8th. Breakfast: milk. Lunch: more beans(!). Dinner: tripe and potatoes. One bowel movement. No wanks. Read *CM* pp. 102–106, chapters two to five of *JTCOE*.

I pulled the sheet off his body. Looked at it. There was a small spray of pimples on his chin. These I ran my fingers over. Then I felt his hair, which was limp. Pulled open his eyes, which stared up at me, their greenness the greenness of marbles, suggestive of nothing.

His cock, deceptively small when not erect, was resting atop his balls. I touched it, and it twitched slightly. I pulled my hand back as if I'd been bitten.

He hadn't cut his toenails in ages, it appeared. So I took some scissors and sheared off the ragged ends. They were the same yellowed color as the blouse of the woman at the hotel in Altaguera; the shape of quarter moons.

"Edward," I said, smoothing his hair with my hand.

Then once again I covered his body.

With the coast of England just becoming visible, the captain and two of the crewmen wrapped Edward's body in a canvas blanket and dragged it onto the deck.

A sailor played "God Save the King" on a flute.

For thirty seconds we stood, heads bowed, in silence. Then the crewmen dragged the canvas-colored mass to the edge of the railing and hoisted it over.

Head over heels the body spiraled, until, with a splash, it hit the ocean. White foam spread out in rings; the canvas darkened as it sopped up water.

Who killed him? Me? The war?

The sea swallowed Edward.

Then I went home.

Moon and Water

Chapter Eighteen

How I got from Bristol to London I cannot tell you. Somehow, however, I must have, for the next thing I remember is Richmond: the smell of grass and petrol; boats on the river. Of Spain, George Orwell wrote: "I do not think I have ever seen a country where there were so few birds." England was full of birds: starlings, skylarks, doves, pigeons, gulls, robins, terns. The sky rang with their competing song, so much song, after the silence of Spain, that it seemed deafening.

I went to the foreign office to register the fact of Edward's death. A young man in Oxbridge spectacles took down the information. Name of deceased? Edward Phelan. Age? Twenty. Place of death? Valencia, Spain. Date of death? April 13, 1937. Cause of death? Typhoid.

"And were there any effects?"

I thought he meant "effects" as in consequences, and wasn't sure how to answer; then I realized my mistake.

"No, no effects."

"Who is the next of kin?"

"His mother, Lil—Sparks. Yes, Sparks."

"Do you have an address for her?"

"I believe so." I rooted in my wallet. "Seventeen Newbury Crescent, Upney."

"Is there a telephone?"

"I don't believe so, no."

"Would you like to inform her yourself, or shall we send a telegram?"

"I believe it would be better for you to send a telegram."

Afterwards I burned Edward's clothes without ceremony; I burned his duffel bag and his books. I kept his notebook. I almost kept his toenail parings, imagining I might enshrine them, the way Catholics enshrine the physical remains of saints. But in the end I burned these too.

For weeks I cocooned myself in Richmond; I saw no one but Nanny, my brother and my sister. They treated me solicitously, with care.

My journal mentions a celebration when Channing passed his medical examinations. I do not recall it. What I do recall are endless hours in the kitchen, playing cards with Caroline and Nanny. The whistle of the teakettle. The leafy late-afternoon light.

"Do you ever wonder," Caroline asked me once, "if people who are in physical pain every minute of their lives, from the minute they're born—if they know it's pain?"

In May, I started going out again: just a few minutes at first, to look at the boats on the river; then on brief walks into Richmond. It seemed an excessively sweet and guileless place, with its cottage gardens and teashops and jonquils. In the newspaper I read that Miss Flora Avery of Abinger Hammer, Dorking, had grown a seventy-five-pound marrow in her garden, that Mrs. Mabel Allen of

Basingstoke claimed to have seen the face of Jesus in the bark of an ancient elm. No one spoke of the war.

Caroline went to Bath to stay with some cousins, leaving Channing and me alone in the house. My brother had emerged from years of self-imposed asceticism to become, for the first and only time in his life, a social creature. He was forever trying to talk me into accompanying him to balls and weekend house parties. I didn't go, just as I didn't go to Upney, didn't sit down with Lil to tell her what had really happened. And if I had, would she have taken comfort in the truth? Or would she have thrown me out her door, cursed me as I hurried away from her, rushing down the Upney streets?

Aunt Constance took me to lunch at the Lancaster. I was very somber. To my surprise, she did not probe but instead regaled me with anecdotes about a trip to America she had taken in March. Afterwards she sent me a rather large check and a note the sympathetic nature of which took me by surprise: "What you have been through," she wrote, "redeem through the *nobility* of art."

I took her at her word. I sat down and wrote out what had happened, got so far as to describe my meeting with Edward and our first happy days together, then stopped. For the story I had to tell was not noble. Rather, it described the supremest moral failure. Not its transcendence, not its defeat: the failure itself. And what possible good could come from telling a story like that?

Instead I went back to my old novel. I finished it rather quickly, and within a few weeks Alderman had purchased it for the princely sum of forty-five pounds. *The Train to Cockfosters*, I titled it. It was dedicated (oh, coward!) "To E.P."

"Imagine Cockfosters," Avery says to Nicholas late in the novel, as he has said to him repeatedly. "What do you see?" This time Nicholas looks at "the elemental blue line snaking upwards towards a mysterious blue north. What he saw was ice-blue houses with ice-blue lawns perched on the brink of nothing, the air itself thinning out to a radiance too pure for human inhalation."

Hell, in other words, leads to heaven, which is numbness; the pain of existence dulled. That I should have craved such a state tells a lot about the way I was feeling back in those dark summer days of 1937.

In June, Channing finally got me to go to one of his parties. It was for an old chum of his, a girl named Polly Granger. Everyone at the party was terribly jolly, and having just a smashing time, as was I. Whenever I had the chance, though, I stole away to corners and drank.

At the bar a familiar voice accosted me. "Brian, is that you?"

I turned and saw standing behind me Philippa Archibald, or, rather, a new incarnation of Philippa Archibald: she had had her hair cropped much like Louise's and was wearing a sleeveless sheath.

"Philippa, what a surprise!" We kissed.

"How *are* you?" she asked emphatically.

"I'm all right. And you?"

"Couldn't be better. I gather you've been in Spain."

"Yes."

"And was it everything you hoped?"

I considered this question. "No," I finally said. "No, I can't say it was."

"Well, I'm sorry to hear that, Brian."

"Thank you."

A few nervous seconds passed.

"Myself, I've just returned from America," Philippa added brightly.

"Really!"

"Yes! New York City, Chicago, Los Angeles. Quite extraordinary; you really must go there. And when you do, be sure to visit the Grand Canyon. It's the most amazing—"

"Philippa, have you heard from your uncle Teddy?"

"Teddy? Not recently, no. Why do you ask?"

"Well, I heard some news of him in Spain. You know, he's become a Communist."

Philippa laughed. "Yes, yes. At the moment. Teddy is, shall we say, ideologically promiscuous—"

"He killed a boy."

"What?"

"No, I must correct myself. He didn't kill the boy. I killed him. He merely . . . facilitated his death."

Philippa put her long fingers over her heart. "Brian, perhaps you've had a bit much to drink—wouldn't you like to sit down?"

"Ask him," I said, "about Edward Phelan. He was a deserter from the brigade. He took him in, promised to get him a passage back to England. Then he betrayed him. They put him in prison, and he died."

Philippa's mouth remained open, not so much in a smile as in a rictus. "I'm not sure what to say," she answered at last, "except that I should imagine it was never Teddy's intention to cause anyone—"

Channing came by. "Brian, are you all right? I could hear you clear across the room."

"Channing, I'm Philippa Archibald. We met decades ago."

"Yes, of course. How are you?"

"Your brother was just telling me the most extraordinary story."

"So I gather. Brian, are you sure you're all right?"

I smoothed my tie.

"Yes," I said. "Fine."

The weather got better. During the night spiders spun webs atop the box hedge that by dawn were finely coated with moisture. Most mornings I woke without memory, as if in the course of the night my very self had been erased, and I was now a blank page, an empty vessel. Unfortunately this sensation lasted only a few seconds, before memory came pouring back in, blotting the page, spilling over the vessel's rim.

It was August. Caroline had not yet got back from Bath. Channing was off on one of his weekends. No one home except me and Nanny, who rattled about downstairs and had not enough to do. I, too, had not enough to do: had no one to eat dinner or lunch with, no books to read, nothing to write. So I rose; went into the bathroom; lathered the shaving soap and smeared the resulting foam over my face. I watched in the mirror the slow progress of the razor as it dragged down the length of my cheeks. If I applied just the smallest extra pressure, I knew, I could damage myself—and then, before I had a chance to think any more about it, a rose-red bloom was flowering on my cheek. I pushed again: another bloom. Three more. I pulled the blade away. Now blood was sliding down my cheeks like rivulets of rain on a window, the stubbly water in the basin was pinkening.

I heard a rapping on the door. "Who is it?" I called.

"There's someone here to see you," Nanny announced.

"Who?"

"He won't say."

"Oh, Christ. All right, tell him I'll be right down."

I wiped the blood off my face—almost immediately it started flowing again—then pulled on some clothes and headed downstairs.

"Yes, who is it?" I said when I got there.

In the hall stood Nigel.

"Good God, Brian, do you always slice yourself to ribbons when you shave?"

"I don't—that is, the razor must have been dull."

"Clearly." He gave me a once-over. "You're thinner than the last time I saw you."

"So are you."

We stared at each other uneasily.

"Well?" Nigel said. "Aren't you going to welcome me back?"

"What? Oh, Nigel!" And I fell—literally—into him.

He seemed bewildered, even dismayed, and didn't know what to do with his arms.

"Welcome back," I murmured into his stiff collar. "Oh, Nigel, welcome, welcome back."

We retreated to my bedroom, where I finished cleaning myself off. "Can you stay long?" I called from the bath. "Can you stay for lunch? Tea? Dinner?"

"I have no plans for the rest of my life," Nigel said.

"Good. Neither do I." I reentered the bedroom. "When did you get home?"

"Yesterday."

"From?"

"Stockholm."

"And Fritz? Where's he?"

"Fritz is—Fritz had—well, he's no longer with me, that's all." He closed his eyes.

"Nigel?" I said. "Nigel, what's wrong?" And sat down next to him on the bed.

"Don't worry," Nigel said, "he's not dead. Not yet anyway. But you know, it's been mad these last months! We'd settle in one country for a few weeks, try to start up a normal routine, only to get a call or a visit from Immigration. Holland, Sweden, Norway, Belgium. One after the other, Fritz's name turned up on one of those bloody unde-sirables lists, they found us and turned us out. It felt like we were being squeezed out of Europe. And all the while that lawyer, Greene, kept putting us off, promising us it would just be a matter of days before Fritz got his new papers. But the papers never came. Just bills. Bills and more bills. All kinds of unforeseen fees.

"Finally we ended up in Brussels. We were asleep one night at the hotel, when there was a loud rapping at the door. A telegram had arrived from Stuttgart, saying that Fritz's grandmother in Mainz was very sick, probably dying. Fritz started packing immediately. Of course I tried to talk him out of it—to go back to Germany, right then, was sheer madness. But he insisted. He said that if he didn't go and say farewell to his grandmother, he'd never forgive himself. In retrospect, I think he knew what was up. I think he was simply exhausted. He was tired of running. Oh, he said he'd be all right; he said if he'd got this far there must be a guardian angel protecting him, and in any case the world could not have become such an uncivilized place that a boy couldn't go home to see his grandmother when she was dying. Anyway, this was his mother's mother, and she was not on speaking terms with his father. She would hide him, he said. It turned out he'd got himself a false passport made up in Paris—rather a scrappy-looking document, I must say, but functional, in a pinch. This was the first I'd heard of it.

"I took him in the morning to the train. You can imagine the tension of our parting, knowing there was a good chance we'd never see each other again. Of course in the station like that we couldn't kiss; instead we hugged, and then he was off. He promised to wire me the next day to let me know he'd got through safely. But no wire came, not that day or the next. Finally Horst made some calls. It turned out that Fritz had been stopped by the Gestapo and arrested almost as soon as he'd crossed the border. The telegram was probably a hoax perpetrated by his father, or some rotten Nazi friend he'd confided to along the way. He did—does—have a habit of talking too much.

"And you know what I felt when I got that call? It was odd. Not grief. No, I felt relief. A peculiar mad relief. Because finally, after all these months, it was over. It was finally out of my hands. I packed up; I made plans to come home. Meanwhile I found out that Fritz had been charged with everything from attempting to change his citizenship to taking part in 'unnatural acts.' I went to Stockholm and waited with Horst for the outcome. Funny: I'd become so used to worrying every time I got on a train about passport checks and whatnot, I almost forgot that traveling alone, as an Englishman, I'd have no problem. Also, I had plenty of money for a change, not having to pay for Fritz.

"A few weeks later the news came in. Apparently Fritz's father had managed to use his influence to have him released, at which point he was immediately conscripted—which is what Herr —— wanted from the start, as if the army will make him less queer. More likely, Fritz'll end up getting buggered by his commanding officers. But it could have been worse. They could have put him in a concentration camp. They've put lots of homosexuals in concentration camps lately."

He lit a cigarette. I looked away, out the window.

"After that I got on a boat for London. I got home yesterday. Mother's very conciliatory, but somehow nothing seems real. The only thing I take comfort in is the thought that if Fritz dies, he'll at least have got out early. He'll have missed the worst of it, which we've got to look forward to."

"I'm sorry, Nigel," I said, after a decent interval had passed.

"And now, back in England, I feel so out of touch! It's as if while I was trying to save Fritz, everyone I knew somehow got miles ahead of me, and now I'm stranded, far, far behind them."

"I know exactly what you mean," I admitted.

"I would imagine you would. You've been in Spain, from what I hear."

"Yes."

"And what happened to you in Spain?"

"Something very similar to what happened to you in Brussels."

"Ah, yes. I gather there was a boy. He ran off and joined the brigade, isn't that right?"

"Yes."

"And then?"

"He died."

"I'm sorry, Brian."

"Well, it was months ago. Since then I finished my novel. It's to be published, you know. I'm sure you'll loathe it."

"Most likely."

"In the meantime I sit here all day. Sometimes I go cottaging. Just your run-of-the-mill wretched buggerer. You know what I was thinking about doing when you arrived?"

"What?"

"Slitting my wrists."

"Saved by the bell," Nigel said.

He stood then; stretched his legs. I stood as well. We were looking at each other, smiling fondly, when the strangest thing happened. Nigel touched me, on the shoulder. My mouth opened in surprise. "Ssh," he whispered. Very gradually his hand moved to my cheek, stroked the wounds there. I closed my eyes. He kissed me.

We made love. It was not the last time; we have made love sporadically, casually, at other odd moments, in the intervening years. No, what was different about that afternoon was that on it a rare note of tenderness entered into our fractious dialogue. It was as if, naked, we could remember we were young—boys, really. From Nigel's lips emerged not scathing witticisms but soft noises of pleasure. His head briefly ceased to be the receptacle for that monstrous, over-grown brain; instead it became a bumpy globe, a fur-covered medicine ball, a thing to hold and kiss. Knowing it was what he liked—we knew everything about each other—I smeared mineral oil over my cock and balls and belly and let him squirm and slide atop me. He came within a matter of seconds, as was his habit. (It later became a terrible problem for him.) And I held his head as he cried out, as he bit my shoulder, his strong hands gripping my arse.

"We both have fat arses," he said afterwards. "It is the fate of pianists—and writers—to have fat arses."

"Is it?"

"I'm afraid so."

It was noon. We lay together on my childhood bed and did not speak. And in a corner, not far but far enough from where we lay, grief crouched, fended off, at bay. I knew it would wait until we fell asleep before it pounced again; this time, however, when we woke in terror, we would at least not wake alone.

Chapter Nineteen

The Train to Cockfosters was published that winter. Despite Nigel's predictable condemnations, it got good reviews and even sold a few copies. In addition, Channing finally relented and allowed Caroline and me to rent our parents' house, bringing each of us some income in the process. For the first time in my life I had money of my own and did not have to depend on the caprices of Aunt Constance to get by.

I rented a small flat off the Edgware Road. I started work on my second novel. Then Channing and Caroline both got married, contradicting Aunt Constance's predictions. Only I was alone—no Edwards, no Philippas—though often in the evenings I went cottaging or hoisted myself over the fence into Dartmoor Park. I had affairs that year with many men, among them an Ethiopian dockworker, an accountant from Stanmore and a gardener from Leamington Spa, and though most of these affairs lasted only a matter of minutes, they meant something still. Who touches the body, however fleetingly, also touches the soul.

Meanwhile, in Spain, the Republicans were losing badly; in Germany, Hitler's progeny were savaging the Jews. Oddly, this imminence of disaster provoked not panic in me so much as a peculiar calm. So Europe would destroy herself, I remember thinking. What of it? We deserved what we got. I saw no reason why the rest of the human population should be spared, either. The young, in times of crisis, resent the happiness of strangers, just as the old take comfort in it.

Once, in the Charing Cross Road, I thought I saw Lil peering into the window of a bookshop. I turned and ran the other way. A few days later, I became so convinced Lucy Phelan was sitting at the other end of my underground carriage that I got off three stops before my own. Soon I was avoiding apparitions of the Phelans as assiduously as in Barcelona I had chased down apparitions of Edward. I went so far as to stop taking the District Line, simply because its trains went to Upney.

Then one cold afternoon, in the lavatory at Green Park station, I had a wank with a rather chatterboxy boy who followed me out afterwards, told me how much he fancied me and asked if I'd like to have a cup of tea. We repaired to a grimly decorated venue off Piccadilly, where he informed me that his name was Albert and that he worked for an insurance concern in the City, in the underwriting department. Although his family hailed from Yorkshire, his father and mother had moved to London in the twenties.

"What part?" I asked casually.

"Upney," he said.

I nearly spilled my tea.

"Or Downey, as I prefer to call it, since it is the arse end of nowhere."

"Yes, yes, I know it."

"You know Upney?"

"I met a family there once. The Phelans."

"Why, the Phelans lived three doors down from my mum and dad!"

"Lived?"

"Yes. They left a few months ago. After the son, Edward, got killed over in Spain."

I looked into my cup. You don't want to know any more, I told myself. You don't need to know any more.

"Where did they go?" I asked.

"So far as I know, the oldest daughter—Lucy—she's in Paris. And the younger one, Sarah, she's got herself engaged to a plumber's assistant from Barking. As for Mrs. Sparks—Lil—well, it's a sad story, the way my mum tells it. She had another son, see, who died in a factory accident a few years before. And losing her second—it was the straw that broke the camel's back, was how Mum put it. And since her husband ran out on her, and she only made money taking in sewing, after a time she couldn't afford to keep up the house anymore. So she moved to Tunbridge Wells. She's got a brother-in-law there who runs a baker's shop."

"A baker's shop."

"Yes."

I looked into my tea. Don't listen! I told myself. What you heard was only hearsay, gossip, corrosive neighborhood chitchat. Yes, most likely Lil had moved to Tunbridge Wells. But who was to say she hadn't done so gladly? Who was to say she didn't savor the change of scene, wasn't happy there, or, if not happy, at least comfortable, in that cheerful baker's, that pleasant, fresh town?

Bidding Albert adieu, I went back to my flat. I could not write, could not read. Instead I paced the floor, trying to convince myself, as I had a thousand times before, that it *wasn't* my fault, that in fact Edward had gone to Spain of his own volition, and become ill by a fluke. Unfortunately this effort only exacerbated the anxiety it was intended to allay. Soon I had reached a point where I thought I would go mad from panic. So I put on my coat and went to Dartmoor Park. The gates, as usual, were locked. It was a warm night, the sky gray-blue and velvety.

I waited until I was sure no one was looking, then hoisted myself over the fence, landing like a cat in the bushes. Immediately the sounds of the street receded, the stench of petrol fumes gave way to the scent of lavender. I crept out onto the gravel path. All around me shadows were moving, shadows of men seeking and making love. One of them beckoned me; I followed it, down a narrow way, into a clump of brush. He was a young man, so far as I could tell. He had hot breath and cold skin. His coat gave off a musty odor, as if it had got wet and not dried properly. I could not make out his face in the dark, only his contours: lean legs, narrow shoulders.

We did not speak. We were fumbling with each other's belts. Suddenly a streak of light passed over his face, fleeting as a moon-beam through a break in clouds. For a millisecond Edward's eyes stared into mine.

The light passed. "Edward?" I heard myself whispering. He broke away, running, into the night. "Edward!" And now the sound of foot-steps filled the air, the sound of pants being pulled up, of change jiggling in pockets and belts being redone. The bushes had come alive; everywhere men were abandoning their lovers of a few moments, hurrying toward the fence as they fled the torches that danced like fireflies and were getting closer. I crouched back down. I could hear boots on gravel, growing louder; then came the torch, flailing, causing me to squint . . . and all at once it was dark again. I opened my eyes. Through a crack in the branches I saw the backs of the two policemen, receding.

I stepped out of the bushes, onto the path. Over the course of minutes the park had grown eerily quiet, the only sound that of the crickets pulsing. It was a clear evening, a lovely evening. In the sky, a full moon hung, its creamy opalescence shot through with cloudings of blue.

But Edward—if he'd been there at all—was gone. And the men who just moments before were groping in the darkness, they were gone too; they had dispersed all over the neighborhood, blurring into the crowds that surged into the tube station, breaking out of trots, sweat running down their foreheads, their panicked hearts just starting to decelerate though their cocks were still half hard, caught in the flies of hastily pulled-up trousers. And what were they thinking? Nothing noble. Only: That was a close call. Might anyone have seen me? And of course the coward's eternal lie: Never again. How many thousands of times had they said those words, Never again, and still gone back: not the next day, probably not the next day after that, either; but soon enough.

I was alone now. Alone, I walked, until I came to a little lake where during the day you could rent a rowing boat or feed the carp. Once again the moon had cast its trembling path of light out over the water, that path that perhaps ghosts use when they make their earthly visitations. And here, just moments ago, Edward's ghost had trod—or perhaps I had merely invented him.

Meanwhile, outside the gates of the park, the innocent slept. They slept even though a dead boy's body could know no resting place, even though it drifted, drifted, among the reefs and seaweed, the eyeless fish and the great dark motions of the tides.

That night I didn't go home. Instead I wandered the park, I wandered the hushed streets of Notting Hill. Dawn found me outside Victoria station, where I caught the first train out to Tunbridge Wells. I remember watching, through my window, houses thinning out, fields of hops, box-hedged gardens from which old elms stretched their craggy branches. Sweet Kent! There is no countryside more kindly. Alternating squares of yellow and green spread out from the tracks, stitched together by fences, undulant with hills: a quilt thrown recklessly over an unmade bed. And yet in the early light women were folding sheets. A group of laborers was loading bales of hay into a nag-drawn cart.

The dull, the ordinary day.

We pulled into Tunbridge Wells. I got out. As luck would have it, one George Phelan had a baker's shop not far from the station, specializing, its placard said, in "Cream Cakes, Gateaux, Tarts and Breads for Every Day & Special Occasions." There was a butcher's on one side and a grocer's on the other, neither with beaded doorways.

And through the glass I saw Lil, aproned, packing something into a pink box, then tying it with ribbon. She had her hair in a net; otherwise she looked the same as before; the same color rose from her cheeks as she chatted up her customer, an old woman with a hump. Pearls rested on her bosom, which heaved appealingly. And what was she saying? Something about grandchildren, no doubt. Then she finished wrapping the box, the old woman paid, turned, wheezed out. From behind the counter Lil smiled after her, until she saw me lingering there; then her smile disappeared.

"Lil," I said. "Hello, Lil." And I moved toward her, but she ran to the door and tried to shut it in my face. "We're closed!" she cried. "Go away!"

"Wait!" I said, pushing against her.

"Go away!" she cried again.

I let go. The door slammed shut and locked, the shade flew down over the glass, the OPEN sign flipped to CLOSED. When I moved to the window, she switched off the lights, retreating to the shadows.

"Lil!" I called. "I did all I could! I tried to save him! Oh, Lil, please, please talk to me!" But she stuffed her fingers in her ears.

And I turned. I turned away from her. And then I whirled around and heaved my fist against the glass, so that she screamed, and the whole window rattled, but did not break. And then I was running toward the station, my hand swelling with a pain that seemed like cold, but also burned, as if I had just dipped it into some unimaginably icy water, the water, perhaps, of the moonlit sea where Edward's corpse was thrown.

It was April 1938, and I was twenty-four years old.

EPILOGUE: 1978

T he war we knew was coming came; I spent most of it holed up in
country houses, doing intelligence work, and only afterwards
learned about the horrors that had happened at Treblinka, the guard
dogs trained to attack men's genitals, the knives. When it was over,
the house in Richmond, the house I'd grown up in, had been bombed
to rubble. My sister and brother and I spent an afternoon sifting
through the blocks of wallpapered plaster and porcelain shards, but
we didn't end up taking anything away. Our ideas of what was worth
saving had changed. Those a generation ahead of us, who had grown
up under the watchful eye of the elderly Queen Victoria, proved less
resilient. They retreated to country houses, those that still stood,
heating what rooms they could afford to heat. Or they sought refuge
in rivers. Or, like Stephen Tennant, the brightest of the bright young
things, in pink furniture, mirrors, *maquillage*. Became anachro-
nisms. Resistance to change can produce that kind of madness.

Other things persisted: for instance, Scotland Yard's zealous
campaign to entrap homosexuals in public loos. It was just after V-E

Day that I had my own unfortunate encounter with one of its plain-clothes officers. During the trial I felt obliged to mention his rather tumescent state at the time of arrest; the young bobby stood up in court, red-faced, shouting, "That's a lie!" But I was acquitted. A few days later I fled England, my homosexuality now having been made public knowledge. Which was exactly what John Northrop had threatened might happen ten years earlier, except that this time no one's life might have got saved as a consequence.

The ship that took me to America rode, for a while, over the same waters into which Edward's body had been thrown. I felt better once we got out into the Atlantic. Not that I'd forgotten him, but my guilt had become manageable. Ask the hit-and-run driver, the nurse who injects her patient with the wrong hypodermic, the mother who has accidentally smothered her infant: they will tell you that after the first few years, you learn to live with blame. Your standards lower. The human capacity for pain being limited, you find you can't inflict nearly so much on yourself as you can on someone else (or as someone else can on you). Thus you run away from the pain inflicters, you go to a new place and, because it is new, try to convince yourself that the old place no longer exists; that distance erases history; that the boy who died because of you belonged only to your imagination and therefore never died, and therefore his mother, his sisters, his survivors, survive no one, nothing; they are just people getting on with their lives. And if you loved this boy, if you are his survivor as well as his killer, then you must sacrifice the memory of your love. You must bury grief if guilt is to be endured. As I did, in Los Angeles, for thirty-one years.

Did I succeed? When I look back, I recall mostly peaceful days, if not joyous ones. Oh, certainly there were bad moments, such as when I'd see a stranger on the street and think, That's what Edward would have looked like at thirty, at forty, at fifty. But they passed quickly and, as the years wore on, became more and more intermittent.

Don't think that I never knew love again, either. I did. Sandy Fairfax and I spent twenty-two happy years together, and while it would be incorrect to characterize our relationship as a grand passion, there was between us an easiness, a companionability, that in my opinion is a far rarer commodity. And when, eventually, it became necessary for Sandy to move on, I bore him no grudge. "Go in peace," I said. He lives now with Peter, a young dancer, and we three are great pals. Last year we even went on holiday together in Hawaii.

You see? Things end. Even the blacklist ended, when Kirk Douglas hired Dalton Trumbo to write *Spartacus*—under his own name. A few years later *Spartacus* was finished, and a group of us, all card-carrying members of the choir, not to mention the Communist Party, got together for a screening. You can imagine our reaction to that famous scene where Tony Curtis, as the slave boy Antoninus, gives the general Crassus, played by Laurence Olivier, a bath. "Do you eat oysters?" Crassus asks Antoninus. "When I have them, master." "Do you eat snails?" "No, master." "Do you consider the eating of oysters to be moral and the eating of snails to be immoral?" "No, master." "Of course not. It is all a matter of taste." "Yes, master." "And taste is not the same as appetite, and therefore not a question of morals." Antoninus says nothing, until Crassus turns toward him and emits a low, suggestive, "Hmm?" "It could be argued so, master." "My taste," Crassus says, "includes both snails and oysters." (Of course the scene was cut.)

The fifties slid into the sixties. I looked for, and occasionally found, work. Somehow, however, my career never quite kicked in again, or at least not to the extent it once had. It would have been pleasant to blame McCarthy for this, but the fact was, the sort of films I was good at writing had gone out of style. It would have happened anyway. And while I made a valiant effort to catch up with the times, in the end I just didn't have it in me to script psychedelic comedies in which girls wearing hoop earrings cry, "Don't be a square, grow your hair!" and try to seduce oafish businessmen. So I retired to a small house in the hills above Hollywood, where among palm fronds and statuettes of cartoon chipmunks I cultivated a cottage garden, as well as a reputation for foppishness and eccentricity. I was an old poofter with money, a relic of prewar England washed ashore on the beaches of Malibu. A dinosaur.

And that is how things stood in the autumn of 1978; the blacklist over, my career over, the secret novel hidden behind the clock. Still, I had little to complain about. A man who has known physical pleasure and has traveled the world and tasted its rich and exotic foods—what right has such a man to complain? Even if, in diabetic old age, those foods can be savored only in memory; even if love, thanks to prostate surgery and a widening waistline, must also remain a memory . . . But I liked living by myself. And when I got lonely for physical companionship, there were always those boys who for fifty bucks are glad to pop round and give a delightful massage.

As for the Phelans, I never heard a word from them. Funny: for years, whenever I approached my post box, an unspecified trepidation would seize me, which I later realized had entirely to do with them. I was afraid that they might track me down even here, impose their suffering on me, force me to suffer in kind. No letter came, however, and as the years passed, my trepidation gave way to an equally unspecified hopefulness. Just as before I'd dreaded a letter that blamed, I now longed for a letter that forgave. But nothing came.

In memory the Phelans ossified; they aged, but they didn't change. Sarah, at seventeen ugly and shy, turned into a maid at the Hotel

Lancaster; Lucy was a dyke with an Eton crop. Or Sarah was the officious telephone operator with whom I had just had such an unpleasant exchange; Lucy the proprietress of that odd antique shop on
Madison Avenue. My fantasies about them were never promiscuous,
they never strained credulity. Indeed, you might call them the fantasies of a dedicated realist.

Then one day a letter came. From England. A very battered letter
in a blue airmail envelope. It had been sent care of a film studio that
had gone out of business two decades earlier, then forwarded to an
agent who hadn't represented me in twenty years, who in turn
forwarded it to an agent who hadn't represented me in fifteen years,
who forwarded it to the agent who ostensibly represents me now,
who forwarded it to the house I briefly shared with Sandy, the house
Sandy now shares with Peter, who stuck the letter into another envelope (there was no longer any room on the first to write addresses)
before sending it on, finally, to me.

> 11 Wilcox Gardens
> London, EN4

Dear Mr. Botsford:

My name is George Ramsey. I am eighteen years old, live in
North London and hope, next year, to begin my studies at the
Central School of Drama. The reason I am writing to you is that
the other night I had the pleasure of watching a film you wrote,
The Prescotts Divorce, on television. When your name appeared in
the credits, my great-aunt Sarah, who lives with us, became
highly excited, then explained she had known you in her youth.
Apparently you were a friend of her brother's and came with him
twice to dine to my great-grandmother's house. She says that on
one of those occasions you brought as a gift some extremely
peculiar cheese.

Having watched and greatly enjoyed your film, my curiosity got the better of me. The next morning I visited our local library, where to my delight I found copies of all three of your novels. Am I correct in deducing that the "E.P." to whom *The Train to Cockfosters* is dedicated is, in fact, my great-uncle Edward Phelan?

As you may have surmised already, my ambition in life is to be an actor. So far my experience has been limited to school theatricals. Nevertheless I believe I have the potential to become a Hollywood film star, several of my friends having remarked on my resemblance to Roger Moore (a/k/a James Bond). In school I have so far played: "the butler" in *Don't Dress for Breakfast*; "Algernon" in *The Importance of Being Earnest*; and "a soldier" in *Hamlet*. However, I believe my potential has barely been tapped.

What I was hoping was that you might have a role for me in your next film. Undoubtedly, being a highly successful screenwriter, you receive hundreds of letters of this kind. Might I ask you to take mine a bit more seriously, given your connection to my family? I would certainly be grateful for any help you can offer, and have enclosed my photograph for your perusal, as well as that of any agents with whom you might care to share it.

Thank you, in advance, and very warmest wishes to you.

Yours sincerely,

Tony Morlock

P.S. This is my professional name.

P.P.S. My aunt Sarah has asked that I pass on to you her greetings, as well as an invitation to tea, should you visit London anytime in the near future. As she is somewhat infirm, it is difficult for her to leave the house.

A photo floated out of the envelope: what's known in the business as a "head shot." From inside the white frame a good-looking blond boy with a thick neck and outsize teeth smiled up at me. "Tony Morlock," a caption announced, "6´2", 183 lbs., 19 yrs. old. Reads French and has studied tap dancing." I smiled. So this, I thought, is Edward's great-nephew.

I put the letter down. Sat back. Tried to absorb it, the simple fact of its arrival. There was a time, you see, when such a letter would have saved me. And then there was a time, a long, long time, when such a letter would have ruined me, when I would have thrown it away unopened rather than allow the past to intrude upon my new life. And then there was an even longer time—during which the new life was proving itself to be the flimsiest of scarecrows, a thing of sticks and glue, giving only the illusion of permanency—when once again I dwelt upon the past. Odd: all those years I assumed the Phelans hated me. The truth was, they forgot me. They went on with their lives.

I picked up the photograph. I looked at this boy who was Pearlene's son (unless Lucy had had children). And did George Ramsey resemble his great-uncle? Slightly, perhaps—perhaps there was something in his chin, or eyes. Probably I was imagining things. The face is such a delicate map after all; and after forty-one years, who can know how much memory has eroded? And yet I remembered some things: I was certain, for instance, that I recognized the name of the street George Ramsey lived on, Wilcox Gardens. So I went into my study and took down from the shelf an old *London A to Z*. When I was a boy, I liked to spread the *A to Z* out side by side with the underground map in order to compare its duplication of reality with the map's inventive, even fictional rendering. The *A to Z* showed how the lines curved, though the map shows them straight; how Queensway and Bayswater stations, seemingly miles apart, were really next door to each other. It even indicated by means of a broken line where the train tracks came aboveground. Alas, my old *A to Z* hadn't aged well—the glue on the binding had dried, the pages had yellowed. Nonetheless I gently cracked it open, scanned the index for Wilcox Gardens, turned to the indicated page, narrowed in, found it.

The Phelans lived in Cockfosters.

Within blocks of the station. In Cockfosters.

I closed the *A to Z*. I was feeling . . . what to call it? A kind of ordering pleasure, a novelist's or mapmaker's pleasure. Cockfosters, the place the imagination stops and turns back, the place I never went lest its reality, once witnessed, should supersede its dream, was also, I saw now, a normal, middle-class, most probably rather dull North London neighborhood. Where George Ramsey lived. Where Sarah actually lived. And as I sat there, the guilt that had all these years threaded its way not through, but under, my life, came aboveground too, into the light. A weakened, elderly thing, pale as milk, squinting against the sun.

Then he saw me.

"Well, hello. What are you doing here?"

"Sheltering from the rain."

"It's pissing buckets, isn't it? What luck, though. I've been meaning to ring you up . . ."

There is no more to tell. Tonight, after I complete this little epilogue, I shall place the manuscript behind the cuckoo clock, never to be looked at again. Archaeologist of the future, remember only that in committing these events to paper, I never asked for absolution. I never asked for forgiveness. Edward's and mine was a commonplace story that, caught up in the war, turned tragic—but that too is a commonplace story. I believe what courage I have shown is in the telling.

I no longer regret that I will never again breathe the wet air of London, with its scent of baking bread. Nor do I waste my time wondering what our lives might have been like had Edward survived the crossing. I cannot change the past, and even if I could, I'm not sure I'd want to.

And yet he does not leave me. Indeed, sometimes, when I'm driving down the freeway, or along Sunset Boulevard, he comes back; just appears there, in the passenger seat of my car. Older, of course. Gray in his hair. Crow's-feet. But still handsome. And most important of all, still Edward. And as I drive I point things out to him: That's Forest Lawn Cemetery, Edward. And that's the famous Hollywood Bowl. And here, on this corner, I met the man I would live with for the next twenty-two years, until one night in this restaurant, this restaurant here, he told me he was leaving me. For hours we drive, through Brentwood and Bel Air, through Benedict Canyon and Pasadena and Beverly Hills, until we come to the house Sandy and Peter live in. Like spies, we park across the street, watch for signs of life: a light in a window, a door opening. Dusk begins to fall. And when, finally, Sandy's car pulls into the driveway, I switch on the ignition, pull away fast (though I know he's seen me), until we're far from that familiar cul-de-sac, winding our way over Laurel Canyon Boulevard. And that is when Edward begins to disappear. He lessens, somehow. Shadows invade the car. We cross Sunset. I know that by the time I pull into my own driveway he'll be gone, dead, just as he's been dead every one of these forty-one years, these fifteen thousand days, these three hundred and fifty-nine thousand hours. But I also know that if I drove to the beach right now, I'd see the moon casting its road out over the water. That if I knelt and took some of that water in my palm, it would hold the radiance. It would retain the radiance. Droplets like mercury, heavy with light.

A NOTE ON THE AUTHOR

David Leavitt's books include the story collection *Family Dancing* (finalist for the PEN/Faulkner Award and the National Book Critics Circle Award) and the novels *The Lost Language of Cranes*, *The Body of Jonah Boyd*, *The Indian Clerk* (finalist for the PEN/Faulkner Award and shortlisted for the IMPAC Dublin Literary Award) and *The Two Hotel Francforts*. He is also the author of two nonfiction works, *The Man Who Knew Too Much: Alan Turing and the Invention of the Computer* and *Florence, A Delicate Case*. His writing has appeared in the *New Yorker*, the *New York Times*, the *Washington Post*, *Harper's*, *Vogue*, and *The Paris Review*, among other publications. He lives in Gainesville, Florida, where he is professor of English at the University of Florida and edits the literary magazine *Subtropics*.

MORE FROM DAVID LEAVITT

"One of the major voices of contemporary fiction." *—The Guardian*

Family Dancing

"Astonishing . . . funny, eloquent, and wise."
—The New York Times
"Brilliantly written." *—San Francisco Chronicle*

Trade paperback ISBN: 978-1-62040-704-2
eISBN: 978-1-62040-705-9

The Indian Clerk

"Richly imagined . . . Offers the pleasure
of escape into another world."
—The New York Times Book Review
"Ambitious, meaty . . . Refreshingly
original."
—San Francisco Chronicle

Paperback ISBN: 978-1-59691-041-6
eISBN: 978-1-59691-840-5

The Lost Language of Cranes

"A tour de force." *—The New York Times*
"Brilliant, wise . . . It would be hard to
overpraise this book." *—Vogue*

Trade paperback ISBN: 978-1-62040-702-8
eISBN: 978-1-62040-703-5

The Two Hotel Francforts

"Crackling with intrigue and illicit
romance."
—O, the Oprah Magazine
"Moving, ravishing and fiercely ambitious,
this is a novel to treasure." *—The Guardian*

Paperback ISBN: 978-1-59691-043-0
eISBN: 978-1-60819-599-2

Available now wherever books are sold
www.bloomsbury.com